Living in the Weather of the World

Living in the Weather of the World

RICHARD BAUSCH

Alfred A. Knopf
NEW YORK
2017

THIS IS A BORZOI BOOK
PUBLISHED BY ALFRED A. KNOPF

Copyright © 2017 by Richard Bausch

All rights reserved. Published in the United States by Alfred A. Knopf, a division of Penguin Random House LLC, New York, and distributed in Canada by Random House of Canada, a division of Penguin Random House Canada Limited, Toronto.

www.aaknopf.com

Knopf, Borzoi Books, and the colophon are registered trademarks of Penguin Random House LLC.

Several of these stories have appeared, sometimes in different forms, in the following magazines and publications: "The Same People," in Atlantic Monthly; "Walking Distance," "Unknown," "In the Museum of the Americas," "The Hotel Macabre," "Still Here, Still There," and "Sympathy" in Narrative Magazine; "We Belong Together" and "Veterans Night" in Ploughshares; "The Bridge to China" in The Southwest Review; "Map Reading" and "The Lineaments of Gratified Desire" in the Virginia Quarterly Review; "The Knoll" in Listening to Ourselves, an anthology of radio stories edited by Alan Cheuse and Caroline Marshall. "Map Reading" also appeared in Pushcart Prize XL. "Night" appeared in a special anthology edited by Roddy Doyle, called Fighting Words, to increase literacy and benefit young people at risk.

Library of Congress Cataloging-in-Publication Data
Names: Bausch, Richard, [date] author.
Title: Living in the weather of the world / by Richard Bausch.
Description: First Edition. | New York : Alfred A. Knopf, 2017.
Identifiers: LCCN 2016045231 (print) | LCCN 2016052893 (ebook) | ISBN 9780451494825 (hardback) | ISBN 9780451494832 (ebook)
Subjects: | BISAC: FICTION / Literary. | FICTION / Short Stories (single author).
Classification: LCC PS3552.A846 A6 2017 (print) | LCC PS3552.A846 (ebook) | DDC 813/.54—dc23
LC record available at https://lccn.loc.gov/2016045231

Jacket image by 101cats/E+/Getty Images
Jacket design by Janet Hansen

Manufactured in the United States of America
First Edition

For Lisa and Lila
sweet companions

. . . what people visit on each other out of something like love. It's enough for all the world's woe . . . you don't even need hate to have a perfectly miserable time.
—Annie Field

Contents

Living in the Weather of the World

WALKING DISTANCE

Joseph Koren was a young married man who lived in a small, rented house in the High Point Terrace district of Memphis. His wife, Ella, was beautiful and daily exhibited little enigmatic facets that he lay thinking about in bed at night like a kid playing some kind of fantasy game: she was impulsive and quick eyed and fierce, and had mood swings; her temperamental nature and sharp wit fascinated him. He admired her dark skin and the luster of her black hair, her deep-brown eyes, the soft curves at the corner of her mouth, the sound of her voice. Sometimes he would find himself watching her sleep, appreciating the lines of her body and the way her thumb curled into her fist, which rested on the pillow.

He had spent so much time alone growing up, just him and his mother in a small apartment near the university, where she worked until the year he entered the police academy. That year, his mother passed away, like a sort of unspoken expression concerning her feelings about his wanting to join the police force. Because he was shy and clumsy with people, her going seemed like some final declaration, a judgment whose coming had always been expected. When he met Ella, who at the time was a temp in the courthouse offices, it was his nervous shyness and his quiet humor that charmed her. Now he was often filled with a sense of near disbelief at his own good fortune. He felt lucky, and he liked the way the others, his shift mates in the precinct and everyone he knew and worked with, followed her with their gaze, the way they looked at him and envied him this shining girl. Sometimes, when he watched her sleep, she would suddenly open her eyes and look at him as if she did not recognize him. "Don't do that," she would say. "It's creepy."

"I can't help it. I can't believe you're here."

"Well, stop it."

Today, they had a small disagreeable exchange before she got into the shower, and she gave him a sour look as she turned to put the water on. He closed the bathroom door quietly and went to look out the picture window in the living room. Mimosa Avenue shone peacefully there, almost blurry in the sun's brilliance. It looked like one of those big paintings in the Brooks Museum: brightness spilling through newly full trees, soft fresh blossoms everywhere. He was taking two days off before being on for twenty-six, and he was about to embark on his daily morning walk—four miles around the Galloway Golf Club. Citywide celebrations for Memphis in May were gearing up, and police presence would of course have to be increased and maintained. He did not mind being asked to pull the extra days; it was all right. Twenty-six straight days. There would be a nice ten-day break at the end of it all. Still, this morning he wondered if she was irritable because of the extra work. He did like it, and he liked his colleagues, who all knew with whom he spent his nights. And for a man with his strong aesthetic sense, there could be no other city in the world quite so beautiful as Memphis in spring.

Well, she would feel fresh after the shower, and the prettiness of the day would win her back. He felt that he understood her, and it was pleasant to think about the slow brightening of her mood as the morning progressed.

She would be herself again by the time he returned from his walk.

He had put on his floppy sweatshirt with the cutaway sleeves, jeans, and sneakers, and tucked his service revolver in his belt—not secure as regulations called for, but comfortable according to the dictates of habit.

First, though, he would make breakfast.

She came in after her shower and went straight to the refrigerator. Always the same routine in the mornings. Coffee and orange juice. There was something endearing about it. He had made the coffee and poured the orange juice, but this morning she poured milk without saying anything and took her place at the table. He set the bowl of scrambled eggs down, and a plate with two buttered English muffins and four strips of microwaved bacon. He was a cop who could do things in the home, and people had always said he would be a wonderful family man.

She ate half a muffin, half of one strip of bacon, and very little of the eggs. He was hungry, and he took the rest. They didn't say anything, drinking the coffee and watching Comedy Central without quite taking it in. He saw a place in her still-wet hair where it was disarranged in such a way as to show part of her scalp. Her demeanor seemed more than the normal morning grumpiness, and so he poured a second cup of the coffee. She tapped the edge of the table with her fingers.

Finally, he said, "Good coffee?"

Nothing.

"Come on. You can tell me if you don't like it."

"Let's just get through the morning, Joseph," she said. "Okay?"

There had been recent intervals of missed signals between them, but he thought of it as being in the nature of things, part of the ebb and flow of marriage between two strong-willed people. After all, they were still relatively new: a little more than two years. Just now, gazing across the table at that place in her hair, he had the urge to needle her, tease her out of her gloominess. "Well, yeah, we should try and make it through if we can. And hope nobody dies."

"I don't feel like talking," she said. "Let's just leave it there, please."

"Hey. Am I in trouble?" He saw the same sour look she had given him earlier when she turned on the shower water. "Ella?"

She said, "This morning—first thing in the morning—you have to hand me all that crap about the bathroom trash can."

"You're kidding."

"Well, Jesus. It's not like we're old people. You're so—fussy. Christ. You act like you're fifty years old."

"I simply asked—again—that when you're sitting on the toilet and have to blow your nose with the toilet paper, you put the toilet paper into the toilet instead of the trash can. Come on. It's a small bathroom to begin with, and it's no fun to clean—"

"*I'm* the one who cleans it."

"Well, *I'm* the one who cleaned it this morning when I got up and there was dirty toilet paper all over the floor because the trash can was overflowing with it. It's so simple and easy just to drop the thing in the toilet instead of the trash can. Right?"

She began clearing the dishes away with a briskness that annoyed him. Deciding simply to go on with his walk and let things settle a little, he put the coffee cup down, rose, and moved to the door. "Come on. This isn't worth ruining a nice day."

"If you wouldn't *nag* me about it," she said from the kitchen sink. "You're like an old *lady.* My mother's less fussy than you are."

"I'll be back in a little bit." He forced a smile. "*Okay?* I didn't mean to upset you. I fixed you a nice breakfast, right? Even though you didn't want it. But hey, it's spring, right? Life's good. Come on."

"You keep harping on it."

"Well, I'm happy. Life *is* good. We should be celebrating all the time."

"I'm talking about the other thing."

"The toilet paper?"

"Yes. Jesus."

"Well, but you keep *doing* it."

"Don't raise your voice to me."

"I didn't raise my voice," he said. Then, raising his voice, he went on: "THIS IS RAISING MY VOICE."

She opened the dishwasher and put something in it, then

slammed it shut, and there was the muffled sound inside it of glass breaking.

"Whoa," he said. "Come *on*. I'm just kidding you."

"You love me."

"Oh, baby. More all the time."

"You love me so much."

"Yes."

"Beyond normal," she said. "It's—it's idolatry."

He bowed. "My goddess."

"It's not normal. I need you to back *up*."

"Hey. It's such a pretty day."

"Yes, it's such a pretty day."

"Let's not have a single gloomy minute."

"I was *glad* about the twenty-six straight days."

He waited.

"Do you see now? I felt happy about it. Relieved."

"I don't think I—"

"I felt relieved about the time without you here."

"You mean—"

"Look, I—you know I—" She seemed to let down. "God. It's no use."

"I'm sorry."

"No, it's—there's no sense trying anymore. I just can't do it anymore."

"What?"

"I said I can't—you heard me. I can't *do* it anymore. I'm dying."

"You're—*hey*."

"It's not working for me, Joseph. I'm sorry." She sat down and began to cry.

He walked over and sat across from her.

She was wiping her eyes, not looking at him. Perhaps a full minute went by. "There isn't anyone else, either. Okay?"

"*What?*"

"I'm saying—Jesus Christ! Are you hearing me? I can't be here anymore. I have to go. I'm going. I'm leaving."

What came out of him then must have sounded like scoffing. "Over an argument about toilet paper?" He took a breath and steadied himself. *"Hey."*

"Oh, God. Not that. Everything." She sighed. It sounded like relief. "Just—just—everything. I've kept it to myself."

"Kept *what* to yourself."

"This. *This.* I—I think—I think we made a mistake, okay? I'm not happy here."

"Well, you could've fooled *me.* Two years. What the hell."

"Can you just try to understand? It's—I don't feel anything anymore. It started a long time ago."

"Really. Ages, huh. The first month?"

"Stop it."

"All those times you yelled and dug your nails in my back when we were down on the Gulf that week?"

She gasped into one folded hand.

"All the laughs we have, Jesus, Ella."

Silence. Only the sniffling.

"Okay, you're depressed. You've dealt with that before, right? That passes, remember?"

"No. This is *different.*"

"How?" Reaching across the table, he took hold of her wrists. She pulled out of his grasp. *"Stop* it. Please."

He watched her try to get ahold of herself. "My mother—my—my mother offered to buy me a ticket to Chicago to visit. I'm going to take her up on it."

He stood. "So that's just—*that*? Out of the freaking blue? You're leaving me?"

She only stared, sobbing.

He saw his own shaking hand as he reached to push the screen door open. He stepped out and turned to look at her through the screen. "Well, you know what? Turns out I need to get away from *you* to keep from breaking things up in here."

"Just go. Leave me alone. Please."

He strode away, like a kind of falling.

At the corner he stopped and turned to look at the house. They had been so excited about it when they rented it. "Toilet paper," he muttered. "Christ."

But he had to admit to himself, now, that there had been signs.

No, what he had to admit was that this that had just unfolded in his rented kitchen was not as surprising as he would have thought. He had wondered if she might be getting depressed again. The year before they were married she went into "one of her tailspins," as her father put it, and was on Zoloft for a few months. She called the trouble—which according to her father had been chronic through her teen years—her dead time, because, she said, a tremendous apathy would come over her.

Apathy. Christ. Sometimes he wanted to tell her about how it really was for him, as a boy. You're down, he would say to her. You think you're low. I never knew my father. He shot himself with a rifle when I was two. I grew up terrified all the time, and I thought suicide was just the way everybody died.

"Apathy," he muttered. "God*damn* it."

But she hadn't been on any medication since before they were married. And for the past few weeks, as spring arrived, hadn't there been passes when they were lighthearted, and her loveliness and their mutual desire warmed him? Warmed them both? Wasn't that true?

WALKING FAST, as if about to break into a run, he slapped his fist into his own palm and then stopped and took a breath. He started back to the house, but then turned and went on, with a sensation of deep exhaustion. He was short of breath, his whole torso aching. "God," he murmured. "Oh, Christ."

The day shone like benevolence itself, not a cloud in the sky. It wasn't fair.

He was aware of the revolver under the tail of his sweatshirt almost as a kind of pathology. He reached under the sweatshirt and touched it. Then stopped again, and started shaking, looking at the houses along the quiet street. The handsome lawns, the sun and shade, and the leafy trees whose shifting shades of green showed the breezes playing across them.

The walk around the golf course always took him to South Galloway Drive, a street of very large old houses with circular driveways and big wooden doors. There was one house fronted by a low white brick wall, in the wide lawn of which an enormous willow oak stood, a thing that looked like fifteen full-grown trees growing out of one massive trunk. His walk always wound to that house and then he would make his way back over to Walnut Grove and High Point Terrace.

Only yesterday morning, he had sat in the kitchen with her, talking about where they might go for vacation in July. She wanted to go south to the Gulf and New Orleans, and he wanted to go east to Alabama and Guntersville Lake. They had friends in both places, and their disagreement about which to visit was full of teasing and good nature and either place would be fine.

"I don't care if we spend the whole week at the Department of Motor Vehicles, as long as I'm with you," he'd said. And this had pleased her. He was sure of it. And, in that moment, seeing this, he was pleased with himself. Hadn't he hugged her, and hadn't she nestled at his neck?

They'd had a good life, hadn't they?

He was thinking this, in a breath-stealing fury, coming along toward the house with the giant willow oak, when he saw a big man walk out of the sixth fairway of the golf course and trot a little to come into the road a few yards ahead of him.

"Hey," the man said.

Koren nodded at him.

"Out walking, huh."

"Yeah," he answered tonelessly, without slowing his pace.

"You live around here?"

"Yes, I do." He spoke through narrow lips.

"Close by?"

Koren looked past him, still walking. Surely his demeanor expressed his wish to be left alone.

The man stayed a couple of steps ahead of him, maintaining the pace. For a few moments there was just the sound of their shoes on the pavement. A car swung by them, driven by a woman, with two children in the backseat. The car was dirty, and there was a dent on the back fender, the bumper swinging slightly, loose. Koren saw this and marked it; you would have to pull over a person driving a car in that condition.

"Nice morning," the man said, as if to remind Koren of his presence. He was well over six feet tall, easily two hundred seventy pounds, a full head taller than Koren, and very pale, even a little sickly looking, though the waxy flesh around his face was heavy, the grizzled chin going straight down into the neck. He wore a baseball cap with the FedEx logo on it, only the word was FEDUP. He had a striped pullover shirt, dark new-looking jeans, and running shoes. An earring sparkled in his left ear.

"You lived here long?"

"Look, do you want something?" Koren said. "Because I'm not really in the mood for company."

"Just curious, man."

They kept walking.

Finally Koren said, "Okay, you want to go ahead or should I?"

"You got any money on you?"

"Do I have any money on me."

"Well, what it is, you never know when something might happen. We're always within range, sort of, ain't we. Right around the corner from disaster. Right? Because, see, I'm what you might call a bandit." The man lifted his shirt just enough to show the handle of a pistol. "This has kind of a hair trigger, you know, and it can do a lot of damage."

Koren kept on walking. He was thinking about the toilet paper in the trash can in the little bathroom, the glass breaking in the dishwasher.

The big man kept pace with him, evidently waiting for some reaction. "Look at these houses," he said. "These're some rich people's houses right here."

"Better move off, sir."

"You live here."

"I walk here."

"You wanna stop now? Because, well, what if I did a little target practice on you, just for the fun of it."

He halted. "Just go on, okay?"

"I know there's a problem with believing this is happening. But, man, it really is happening. And I *will* shoot you right quick if you don't do exactly what I want you to do, you know."

Koren glared at him. "I'm gonna give you one chance."

"*You'll* give *me*—look, I don't think you understand what this is."

He felt the heat expanding in his limbs.

"Hey," the big man said. "Here's the deal. This is a robbery. We keep walking. We go to your house. Get your bankbook. You get me some money, and I don't shoot you and you never see me again."

"I don't think so. *You* keep walking. I'll wait here until you're out of sight."

"Really."

"Yeah. Really. This hasn't been the best morning for me. You know? And I'm in a rage right now, and the fact is, it's got nothing to do with you. Nothing. So, you know, you mess with me and something really bad might happen."

"Well, what if I just take your wallet and your watch?"

"Why don't you just get the fuck away from me."

The man took the gun out. It was a Luger. He held it lightly in his hand and sighted with it, just past where the other was standing.

"Oh, wow," Koren said. "And I've already had a ridiculous morning. Nice morning like this, arguing over toilet paper."

"What?"

"Yeah. A silly-ass thing like that."

"What the hell're you talking about, man. This ain't *Oprah*."

"Your intent is to rob me, then. Is that right?"

"Let's say that's exactly right. And my intent is also to hurt you if you do anything rash. And if you run, you know, I'll shoot and I'll hit something that'll cripple you. I'm pretty good."

"All right." Koren reached into his back pocket for his wallet. "Here."

"You won't regret it," said the thief, taking it in one hand. "This is actually your lucky day. I'm not gonna hurt you. I've decided to be ben-NEV-u-lent." He smiled, opening the wallet.

Koren brought out his service revolver.

For a second, the other just stared. Then he quickly held up his hands, dropping the wallet and the Luger. "Oh, look—there's no bullets in it—I swear. It's a dummy. I couldn't shoot myself with it."

"You have the right to remain silent," Koren told him. "And anything you say can be used against you in a court of law."

"A cop. Jesus. You're police. Mine's not a real gun, man. I don't own a real gun. The barrel's sealed."

Koren felt something climb to his brain stem from far down his spine. He cocked the revolver, stepped over, and put the barrel of it just at the other's mouth. "Open up."

"This—this is an arrest, right?"

"Open up. Wide."

"Oh, man. *Don't*."

"Nice and wide, this one *is* real, and it also has a hair trigger."

"But you're a—you're a po*lice*man."

"Yeah, I'm a citizen, too, and this morning I'm really *pissed off.* Open up."

"You're not gonna shoot me, though," the thief said, then slowly opened his mouth.

Koren put the barrel of the gun into it. "Now close up tight."

The other's eyes were wide and white and his whole body was shaking. His lips came closed around the barrel.

"What's it taste like?" Koren asked him.

"Pweesgh. Oh, pweesgh don' shoop."

"I was gonna take a peaceful walk on a sunny day, and my wife wants to argue with me and then out of nowhere she makes everything a complete and utter ruin. Ends everything, everything. My whole fucking life, you know? And then you come along."

"Oh, God. Nyo."

"You come at the very exact wrong time."

"Oh." The man sobbed, and shook, and then urinated himself, standing there. The pool spread at his feet. "Oh, God."

Koren looked at his own hand, holding the gun, and the sick-blue color of the other's lips around the barrel. Now he would squeeze the trigger. Now. He saw it all—the blast and the falling and the sudden splatter of bleeding—in the shaking instant that, with an icy shiver along his spine, and with great slow care, he removed the gun barrel from the slack mouth, and stepped back.

The man put both hands over his lips, staring, shaking. He gagged, and then coughed, crying. "You arrest somebody, yeah, but this—this ain't right."

"Yeah. It's wrong. Like pulling a fake gun to rob somebody on a morning walk. Somebody perfectly innocent and not deserving anything bad. Who hasn't done anything wrong. Not one goddamn thing wrong."

"Oh, Christ."

A moment later, Koren said, "Tell me your name."

"Breedlove, sir. I'm really—I'm *really* sorry. I wouldn't've hurt you. I've never hurt anybody."

"Well, Mr. Breedlove, you're under arrest."

"Yes, sir. I deserve it, sir. Under arrest. Right. Sir." The big man looked down, standing in the wet circle his urine had made. "Just please don't shoot me." He sniffled.

Koren indicated the Luger and the wallet. "Hand me that."

The bigger man warily bent down and retrieved them, then handed them over. Koren put the Luger into his belt, pocketed his wallet, and pointed to the low white brick wall on the left side of the road. "Have a seat."

The other walked over and sat down. "I'm a mess." He kept crying softly.

"Yeah, well, so am I." Koren, still holding his revolver, brought his cell phone out of the pouch on his sweatshirt, and then sat down himself.

"You're gonna call a car, right?"

"Yeah."

"Okay." The big man seemed happy about it.

"You know what kind of morning this has been for me?" Koren asked him, and was surprised at how quickly the rest of it came out. "My wife told me this morning, man. She's leaving me. I thought we were happy. I'm falling over, you know? I'm sailing down. Plummeting. I can't believe it."

"Jesus."

"Yeah." He put the service revolver back into the belt of his jeans, with the Luger. Then he put his cell phone away, too. "So, you know, maybe you're just a very lucky man this time."

"If I'd've known. I wouldn't've bothered you, really."

This made them both laugh. There was something nearly panic-stricken about it.

"Jesus," said Breedlove. "I didn't mean that as a joke. Sorry."

Koren glanced at him, a tall slovenly overweight man, sitting slumped on the low wall, hands folded between his knees, head down, staring forlornly at the surface of the road. "What got you into this kind of trouble, anyway?"

After a moment, the other gave a small halfhearted shrug. "Usual, I guess."

"You married?"

"Was."

"Tell me."

"We didn't get along."

"Tell me."

"Nothing much to tell. She took up with somebody she worked with. She had a pretty good job. Trouble is, I don't have any *skills*." He sobbed, sniffled, wiped his nose with his sleeve. "I have no self-pity, though. Never gave it a thought." Again he wiped his nose. And again he sobbed. "Sorry."

"So you don't have a job."

"Naw, I do. Work in a gas station out on Forty."

"So what was this about?"

Breedlove sighed and shrugged. "Extra money, I don't really know. I thought about it a long time."

"And this was really your first."

He actually smiled a little, shaking his head. "Yeah. Stupid, huh."

"Look at that tree," Koren told him. "You ever see anything like that?"

"Big, yeah. Willow oaks grow big."

"Strong, too. Roots'll break up a road."

"I saw lightning hit one, once."

"Think of the massiveness of it. Must be a hundred fifty years old."

"At least."

"When did your wife leave you?"

"Years ago."

"You with somebody now?"

"Not for a while."

"I don't know what I'll do. What do you do, your wife wants to leave you because of an argument over toilet paper."

There was a pause. They were staring out at the golf course, the trees lining the fairway.

"Man." Breedlove emitted a little gasping sigh. He was still shaking. "I've never been so scared. Look at me. Jesus."

"Were you ever happy, you and your wife?"

"Sure, sometimes. At the beginning."

"Mine gets it into her head she's unhappy—"

"Well," said Breedlove. "I gotta admit I wasn't much to live with. Trouble is I have no *skills*."

"Yeah, you said that."

"Sorry." Now there seemed a kind of weighted hesitation.

Koren remembered with a shock that earlier he had put the barrel of his service revolver in the man's mouth and that he had been talking about toilet paper. The fact of it made him laugh again, too loud this time, so that the other stared, wide eyed. "Was something," Koren got out. "Way you tried to talk with that gun barrel in your mouth."

"Oh. Jesus. Never been so scared."

"And here we are—" The laugh wouldn't let him form the words. He wanted to say "talking women and big-assed old trees and toilet paper and happiness," but he only managed the first two words.

Breedlove seemed not to understand him. "Boy," he said, shaking his head. "Yeah. Women." He rubbed his face with his fat hands.

Koren saw the dimples in the backs of them where the knuckles would be. He stood slowly and held out the barrel-sealed Luger. "Here. Go on, man. Go."

"You—really?"

"Yeah."

The other looked at the Luger. "You keep it?"

"What would *I* do with it?"

He took it.

"Just walk on back the way you came and don't ever do anything like this again."

"No, I won't. Yes, sir. You can bet on that one. No kidding. Thank you, so much, sir." He started hesitantly away, moving like someone in great age, mincing, tottering slightly, and then trying to hurry, not looking back.

Koren thought about all the extra days of work to come, and he would arrive home each of those days to the empty little house. He would open the door and walk in, alone. Everyone would know about it, that she had left him, that she was gone for good. And there wasn't even anyone else she was leaving him for. It would be better, really, if there was someone else, or if he had done some one thing, cheated on her or was a drunk or something. Anything. He had come very close to killing Breedlove, just minutes ago. He imagined putting the barrel of the service revolver in his own mouth, and then understood with a fright, in a new way, like blood knowledge, like something from earliest memory, how a man could come to that. He shivered and sat back down, going over everything, thinking unwillingly and with sickening force of his father, while seeing again the way the gun barrel looked with Breedlove's lips around it. The panic in the face, the wide crying eyes. The moment had seemed inevitable, as if it had been planned for him from far off, and he felt it now like destiny, a thing coming near that he would not be able to avoid or escape. He watched Breedlove go on across the sixth fairway, nearly at a run now, the wide darker place showing on the seat of the jeans and down both legs.

He had never felt sorrier for anybody in his life.

THE BRIDGE TO CHINA

for Lisa Blanc

These first weeks of autumn have been hard, both boys gone and the house all to herself. She arrives after each day's work with the sinking realization that no one else is coming home. The place seems nearly cavernous.

This is not unexpected. It's a thing she's dreaded since the older one, Edward, left for the University of Chicago to study business, four years ago. Edward now has a job with an insurance firm in the city. He's always reminded her, sometimes not so unpleasantly, of his father: thorough, decisive, even methodical; very good-looking, but also, at times, a bit humorless. Sometimes casually dishonest. He seldom calls, and never visits, though he lives closer. Well, he's busy. And he was always more his father's boy.

The younger son, Cody, after two years as a clerk at Kroger's, left for Southern California this past August to study literature at Chapman University. He's the star of her heart, and she speaks to him on the telephone or texts with him several times a week, more often than when he lived at home. It's *his* leaving that has given her this forsaken feeling. And it's he who says she ought to join an online dating service.

"Don't be ridiculous," she says quickly, and experiences the sense that she's fending something off. It surprises her. "I'm too busy anyway."

"Eliza," he says. Calling her by name is an aspect of his new adult life far away. "Millions of people use dating sites. And they work."

"You're being silly."

"A girl I took out last week—her dad used one and he's getting married."

"Did you find *her* that way?"

"She's in my Chaucer class."

"Well, maybe I'll take a Chaucer class. But I'm not looking to get married."

"It's just a suggestion," Cody says. "You've been talking about the empty house."

"I was describing the territory, darling. It's like I've got an appointment to show it and the people don't come."

"Oh, God, Mom. See?"

"That's just you being gone. I'll get used to it. It's life, that's all."

"But it doesn't have to be so hard, right?"

"Honey, it is what it is. I get home, I notice the empty rooms, and there's a moment. But I have a glass of wine, and make myself something to eat, and pretty soon I'm enjoying the quiet. I watch a movie or read for a while. And then I go to bed. When you work the hours I do, and at my age, sleep is nice."

"Listen to you. You're not even fifty."

"You could say it that way or you could say I'm *pushing* fifty."

He pauses. Then: "You always worked too hard."

"Thank you."

"I'm not criticizing. I just don't think you have to be alone. You deserve someone cool and funny and gentle."

"It's a very social business, my work. I make friends. I meet people all the time, honey. Very nice people."

"Yeah, but that's showing houses and talking to lenders. There's not much actual socializing with that kind of thing. Right?"

"How long do you think it would take to build a bridge to China?" When both boys were small, this was something she asked them whenever they began their child's questions about lies, absent fathers, air, the end of the world, stars and darkness and the meaning of everything.

"Okay, okay," he says with a soft laugh. "But that's not what I'm talking about."

"Well, let's talk about something else."

"The work always kept you too busy to think of yourself. It was always Edward and me and the work. If you ask me, you deserve some good times now."

"I didn't ask you, baby. And I like my work. That's good times. It is. And I'm good at it."

"Okay." Her young son sighs. "Just sayin'."

A WOMAN OF MEANS, as the phrase goes, still attractive at forty-nine, doing work she does indeed like. But in the following days she thinks about the empty house when she's working. Seeing the gladness of couples for whom she finds dwelling places makes her happy, but there's a melancholy in it, too, now.

"I really miss my boys," she says to one of her colleagues, whose last child left in the summer for a stint in the army. The two of them are sitting in her office, with the picture window facing out onto the traffic of Poplar Avenue, passing cars flashing reflected sun. "You had five—five—grow up and leave. How'd you do it?"

The colleague, whose name is Darnell, makes a motion with her hands, as if she's gently but forcefully pushing someone away from herself. "Like this."

"You're kidding."

"I'm absolutely not kidding. I'd started dating Brad. And I wanted time with him. And they had their own lives and all that, except where they still needed things from me, like doing their laundry and paying their bills and cooking for them. So it was 'I love ya, boys, and now it's time to go out on your own, you know? Bye-bye.'"

They watch a man in a baseball cap crossing the wide avenue. His cap blows off in the wind, and he nearly gets hit stepping forward into the next lane and the flow of traffic to retrieve it. There's the screech of car brakes. Eliza gasps and puts her hand to her mouth. "God, did you see that?"

"He almost bought it."

"It's so hard, thinking of Cody all the way in California."

"I'm sure Cody looks both ways before crossing the street."

"It's so far. He might as well be on the moon."

"It's a plane ride. Come on. You've gotta find somebody nice to go around with. It's time to think of yourself. Really. You should start dating again."

ONE LATE EVENING she goes on a site herself and spends valuable time surfing through the faces, the descriptions of histories, hobbies, accomplishments, and requirements. The posts are often so similar as to seem dull: so many passionate, spiritual, and fun-loving men. But there *are* remarks about favorite pieces or styles of music, and some about books and movies, too. Finally she fills out a profile and joins.

BestMatch.com.

But then weeks go by. Occasionally she checks in and finds several inquiries—gentlemen in their late forties and early fifties whose smiling photographs tend to seem rather discouragingly of that category of person who hasn't aged well. Substantial seeming, round faced, with good teeth and all their hair. Two with beards. But many are clearly a little or a lot overweight. Her own photo is recent, and is a good one. She likes the way her dark hair frames her face.

One man's photo does please her for the fact that he's not exactly smiling. There's just the slightest turn at the edge of his mouth. His hair's thinning. His expression seems faintly doubtful, appears in fact to reflect her own sense of not being quite sold on the idea.

"I'm fifty-two, and a widower," says his profile. "By the time Abraham Lincoln was my age, he was president. I'm an associate professor of English at Rhodes College, and I live in the Cooper-Young district, in a nice house I've owned since 1990. I have three grown daughters, who will all vouch for me. I don't have any pets, though I did own a dog for twelve years. But that was ten years ago now. I have a Ph.D. from Vanderbilt; I play some piano, a little guitar, but mostly I like to listen and I like all kinds of music. Everything from Palestrina to Lady Gaga. I read mostly the writers I teach—so Shakespeare, the Romantics. I like poetry and novels but I read history, too. I like to talk, and be talked to, and especially I like to be told stories. I like that you said you raised two boys alone, and that you sell real estate and that putting people into nice homes delights you. And I very much like your face—there's kindness in it."

She writes him back, that late afternoon, from her office. And by the time she gets home, he has responded with a phone number. How simple. She pours herself a white wine, drops an ice cube into it, and sits down at the kitchen table to call him.

"Hello." No question in it. She likes the nearly gruff baritone sound of the voice.

"Hi. Is this Scott?"

"Yes."

"This is Eliza."

"Yes, you actually called me."

"Wasn't I supposed to?"

"Oh, believe me, I'm happy you did."

There's a pause.

"So what do we do now?" she says. "I've never done this before."

"Neither me." He gives forth a small laugh, and she laughs, too. Then it's quiet again.

"We can talk awhile," he says. "A few times if you like, before we meet."

She's a salesperson, after all. She gets along with people and is not afraid to meet strangers. "Well, let's meet. Don't you think?"

He suggests a restaurant out in Cordova, called Pasta Italia. An excellent quiet little place, with a good wine list and a pasta dish he loves called *rosette al forno.*

"I love Italian," she says. "Well, like everyone else."

He laughs again. It's charming. He'll pick her up in an hour. "Is that—would that be all right?"

"Sure." She gives him the address, and they hang up. After showering and putting her hair up, she spends a little more time than usual deciding what she'll wear. She doesn't want to be too overtly sexy, but she doesn't want the look of her professional life, either. This isn't a walk-through or a showing. She chooses a white blouse, slacks, and sandals.

In the kitchen she drinks down the wine, rinses the glass, then calls Cody. His message plays: "You know what to do."

She doesn't wait for the beep. He calls, less than a minute later. "I was in the shower. Everything all right?"

"Everything's fine. I have a date. I thought you'd like to know."

"Oh good." He clears his throat. "I think I'm coming down with a cold."

She says, "Are you taking care of yourself? I keep thinking of a man I saw who almost got hit on Poplar, going after his baseball cap."

"This your date?"

"No—something I saw from the window at work."

"Well, I never cross the street here. I don't go out, actually. I stay pretty much in the closet. And then there's the ventilated steel box where I sleep."

"Okay," she says. "Sorry. It's my prerogative to worry."

"Well, but *I'm* worried now. How do you know this fellow you've got a date with? He's not off one of those online sites, is he? Because I understand they're full of crazy people and sex offenders."

She doesn't feel like the teasing, so she decides not to tell him about BestMatch.com. "You're so *very* funny, darling. I met him in my Chaucer class."

"Ha."

"You're the one who suggested online dating."

"So this *is* from a dating site."

"I'm thinking about that bridge to China."

"Which site did you use?"

"Have you talked to your brother?"

"Not in a while. You?"

"I'd bet it's been longer since *I* talked to him."

"Well, he's a busy guy."

After a brief pause, he says, "I was just kidding about the crazy people and the sex offenders."

"Wish me luck tonight?"

"I'll call you at midnight," Cody says. "Check up on you."

She laughs. "You do that."

IN THE REST of the hour of waiting she tries to read, and twice she gets up to look at herself and fuss with her hair. He did say he liked her face, and in the online picture her face is framed by her hair. She decides to take it down. She shakes her head, fluffs it, turns her face to one side and then the other.

Sitting in the living room by the window looking out onto the street, she imagines an evening leading to laughter, friendship— and, why not? Romance. The men she's occasionally gone out with over the years were pleasing in their way, but they were all in the business, and their talk finally depleted her. She likes her work, but not to be going on about it all the waking hours of the day. She had one blind date, a year ago now, an acquaintance of Darnell's, a man who turned out to be at least seven inches shorter than she, and who, at one point during a terrible dinner at Paulette's, leaned into her and said, "I want to give you my pleasures. Come home with me."

In a word, no.

It reminded her of the line *Come with me to the Casbah,* and she did not even know where the line came from. She nearly laughed in his face.

· · ·

SHE GETS UP NOW, moves to the stove, reaches into the cabinet above it, and brings out a bottle of Elijah Craig. She pours herself half a shot glass of it and sips it down. Two sips. This whole thing's beginning to feel like a mistake. She paces a little and realizes she's wringing her hands. Ridiculous. Looking at herself in the mirror again, she smiles to check her teeth. Finally she sits at the window in the living room and waits, going through some papers for a closing that's coming up this week.

When he pulls up, she worries about protocol: should she ask him in? He's parked there at the curb and seems to be hesitating about getting out of the car. It comes to her that he's nervous, too. She steps out. It's gotten a little cooler since she came home. The air is fresh and smells of the magnolia in the yard. He stands from the car and gazes at her over the roof.

"Want to come in and have a glass of wine first?"

"I'm sorry," he says. "I made the reservation for six o'clock."

She walks over, and after a half second's hesitation he hurries around to greet her. They actually shake hands. For a few seconds it's like so many passes she experiences greeting prospective buyers all week. He opens the car door, and she gets in, and now it's like a date—it *is* a date—waiting until he walks around to get in behind the wheel. She lifts herself slightly and adjusts her slacks at the knee.

As he settles in, he says, "It's about fifteen minutes from here, but they'll hold it for us." Edging the car forward, he turns to check for oncoming traffic.

"There's almost never any traffic on this road," she says.

"Quiet neighborhood."

They remark on the cooler air, the lovely green of the trees overhanging the road. It's mid-October, but the leaves won't begin turning for another month. One of the beautiful things about Memphis is the long fall, always the most beautiful weather, cool and sunny and breezy. He says that's what he loves about it.

She says, "I like the sense that I'm living in a small town, even though I know it's a big city. There's just something about it."

"Always lived here?"

"I grew up in Knoxville. Moved here when I was in high school, though. How about you?"

"New Orleans until I was nineteen. Then the air force. Then Vanderbilt, then Chicago for three years in my early thirties. I taught at Northwestern."

"My son Edward lives there now. He went to the U of Chicago."

"Great town. But I couldn't wait to get back south."

"Weather?"

"I think it was the people. Not bad people up there, but I missed everyone I knew. And then Northwestern wouldn't give me tenure. That might've had something to do with it." His smile is a little sheepish, even with the faintly sardonic tone.

THE RESTAURANT IS WEDGED into a row of shops. There's a parking spot right in front. They get out and walk up onto the little stoop, and he opens the door for her. Inside, it's cooler. The place itself is quite small. There are wooden beams in the ceiling and tables ranged along opposite walls. An archway in back leads into a hallway and restrooms. In the center of the space, and the first thing you see as you enter, is a half-barrel-sized cheese wheel above which, like the crown of a cap, a dark wooden circular ledge contains small plates, utensils, and napkins.

The hostess is young and long limbed, and Eliza thinks she's seen her before. This comes to her as a topic for conversation: *You meet so many people in my business.* The hostess with the vaguely familiar face seats them at a table next to the curtained front window and places two menus down with the wine list.

He says, "Want to order the wine?"

"You choose," she tells him with what she intends as an encouraging smile.

There are three other couples at tables on the other side, and a family of five in the alcovelike corner, seated around a circular table. He looks over at them. "I never see a young family that I don't start doing math."

"Math."

"Yeah. Imagining how old they are, and how old I was when. It goes so fast." Something catches in his voice, but perhaps she's imagined it.

A waitress comes and puts a basket of fresh-baked bread on the table. She introduces herself as Cindy. She has a pretty overbite smile and seems a bit too cheerful. Scott takes a piece of the bread, looking at the wine list. He says, "I'm thinking Montepulciano d'Abruzzo."

"I like all the red wines," Eliza tells him.

He orders it. Cindy the cute waitress leaves, and they sit there for a time, occupied with the bread.

"It's still warm," he says. "With a crispy crust. Scrumptious."

Eliza nods: "Mmmm."

A little later, he says, "So your boys are grown."

"Yep."

"And you raised them alone."

"Well, for the last fifteen years. My husband lives in Pensacola now. With another wife, his third. He's kept up with the boys, though. I mean they're in touch."

"Are *you* in touch with him?"

"Sometimes. It's cordial enough."

"I don't mean to pry."

"No, it's fine. My youngest, Cody, was only five when the marriage ended. His brother Edward was nine. For a while I think Edward blamed me, because I'm the one who initiated the divorce." She sighs. "It's all evened out, though he does see his father a little more often. I mean, well, they like more of the same things, anyway."

"And you've been too busy to remarry?"

"I don't know. Could be I just haven't met anyone. But I've had the boys to raise. It was pretty busy most of the time—first when they were small, elementary school, all that. Edward had ADD and ADHD, and there was that business, too. And then the baseball practices and the soccer and the drama club. I had some friends I'd see occasionally, and I'd go out and breathe a little bit, get some adult conversation about something other than escrow." She laughs. "I sound unhappy about it. I love my work, in fact."

"You said in the profile—yes—that it delights you to place good people in nice houses."

"Homes," she gently corrects. "I did say that. Right. I'm sorry."

"Oh, no. Don't apologize."

She goes on, really just to fill the silence that threatens. "But it was hard sometimes to carve out any time. I mean it can be pretty demanding work. There's no set hours, and if you want to do it well, it does mean putting in some time, you know."

"I can tell just from hearing you talk that you're very good at it."

"You're sweet to say that. And now tell me more about you."

"Well, you know I'm new to this, too. I've only been alone a year."

Cindy the waitress brings the bottle of wine, and briefly they have this with which to occupy themselves. After he sips and nods, she pours the two glasses and asks if they're ready to order.

"I'm sorry, Cindy," he tells her. "We haven't even looked at the menu."

"That's so romantic," she answers, and marches off.

Eliza, seeing his embarrassment, says, "Tell me about your girls."

He's gazing into the wine. "They're the best people I know. Or am ever likely to know." His eyes well up.

She waits, sipping from her own glass. "Do they live close?"

"One does." He smiles. "Lilly. She lives in the converted garage of a big house in Chickasaw Gardens. Teaches at Christian Brothers. Math."

"She the oldest?"

"No. The youngest. My oldest, Caroline, lives in Saint Louis. Married to a sweet man, a dentist. She's actually studying for a real estate license. I visit them now and then. Holidays. My middle daughter, Tracy, lives in Boston and isn't married, though she's living with a musician. They seem to get along fine. He travels a lot."

Eliza says, "I'm missing my younger one, who just left in August. I mean the house seems too quiet, now. Though—what am I saying. He was always out running around town when he *was* home."

Cindy comes by the table again and pauses.

"One minute more," he says. They look at their menus. "The *rosette al forno* is the best thing here, if you like pasta."

"Okay," Eliza says.

He asks for the small mixed salads to be brought with the entrée. "And for our entrées, we'll have the rosettes."

"I don't blame you." Cindy gives them her lovely overbite smile. She takes the menus and moves off.

"Sweet smile," Eliza says. "And I think I've met the hostess before."

"Tell me more about *you*," he says.

"Well. I sell real estate." She laughs a little shakily, but sits straight and continues. "And I'd be glad to talk with your daughter about it."

He nods. "That might be just the thing."

"I met my husband on a blind date. Which this sort of *is*, isn't it."

"In a way." He smiles.

"I don't know why I mentioned my husband. It's been so long. And I was more than ready for the marriage to end before it did end."

"Was it after your divorce that you got into real estate?"

"I got my license three years before. But I think partly I knew that things were falling apart—so who knows."

"My wife and I were together for twenty-nine years."

She sees that his eyes are welling up again and turns her attention elsewhere, to the ruby darkness of the wine, the cheese wheel, people in the alcove.

"Excuse me," he says, and abruptly leaves the table.

She watches him move to the hallway where the restrooms are, his shoulders hunched, his gait unsteady and actually weaving a little. She takes another sip of the wine and decides that she doesn't really like it much. It's too heavy and leaves an unpleasant taste of something like cigar smoke. Perhaps five minutes pass. When Cindy comes by and offers to fill her glass, she puts the palm of her hand over the lip of it. Cindy nods and moves off. Two couples arrive, and then a party of seven, agents, she realizes, one of whom she knows slightly. A woman with a hurried manner that actually stems from anxiety about forgetfulness. She's always referring to her iPhone. Eliza has quite liked her the few times they've met. The woman doesn't see her, and Scott comes back to the table, holding a handkerchief to his nose. He wipes his face with it and puts it back. "I'm so sorry."

Eliza shrugs. "People have to use the facilities." She means this to reassure him.

"You're sweet."

Cindy brings their entrées. The small salad, and the rosettes, pasta-wrapped prosciutto with Fontina cheese in béchamel sauce. While they eat the salad quietly, more people come in. The agent at the other table sees Eliza and gets up to come over.

"Someone I know," Eliza says, low.

He turns slightly.

And she realizes, to her horror, that she can't remember the woman's name. "Hello," she says, standing, they embrace. Scott stands, too.

"You teach at Rhodes," the woman says to him. "I took a survey of modern lit class from you—God, must be a dozen years ago. Of course you don't remember me."

"I remember," Scott says.

"You gave me a B. And I *was* relieved, let me tell you. But come on. Surely you can't remember a student from that long ago."

He smiles, nodding. "No, I really do."

"I was blond. And a *lot* skinnier."

"Chloe, right?"

Delighted, she takes his hand with both of hers. "Wow. That's amazing." She lets go. "I remember your wife came to class and talked about that woman poet. Oh, what was her name. See? *My* memory's terrible. Something—something about chess? Francesca something? I kept my notes."

"You mean Elizabeth Bishop?"

"Bishop, that's it. Sorry. Chess. God, what a stupe I am. Well, I remember I liked her, and I liked what she had to say, although I don't know anything at all about poetry. Tell her I still think of her."

"So do I," he says, low, bowing his head slightly.

"Oh. Oh, God—I'm so sorry."

"Well, nice to see you," he says to her.

"Yes. Sorry, I really didn't mean to interrupt." She returns to her table and, looking back, waves to Eliza, who lifts her hand, and then lets it drop.

She sits down slowly and sees the stricken expression on his face as he settles into his chair and takes a bite of the pasta.

She takes a little of hers and has another swallow of the wine, concentrating on it. He puts his fork down and begins fumbling with his napkin, folding it and then opening it out and refolding it.

"Your wife taught English, too?" she manages.

"Sometimes. She didn't like teaching. But she did her dissertation on Elizabeth Bishop, and she was trying to turn that into a—a commercially viable—" He stops. "A book for the general public."

Eliza waits.

"But you know—she always—the family—the family always came first. And there was *my* book."

"You were working on a book, too."

"Not really. I liked to think I was. You know. I'd sit and try to write some sentences—but it was more of a pretense, really. I didn't have the talent even if I'd had the patience, which I didn't." He seems now to have mastered himself, and he has more of the wine. Though he shakes his head, clearly going over everything inside. "I'm sorry," he tells her. "I was off somewhere. We used to say, when one of us was daydreaming, 'You're way off in China.'"

"Oh," Eliza says. "That's—when the boys were small and were full of questions and I was tired of them or just plain tired, I'd turn it around by asking them how long it would take to build a bridge there."

"To China."

She nods happily. "It always stopped them. I mean they'd really start trying to think about it. A bridge across the ocean. I'd tell them I just didn't know and I wish they could tell me."

"That's good. A good one."

"Tell me about your book," she says. "I don't think I've ever known anyone who wrote a book."

"It was supposed to be a novel. I told people it was. But she—my wife, Shannon—she always took second place. Always put all of us first. And, you know, she did have talent." On the last word, his voice breaks. He picks up the table napkin and puts it to his mouth. "God, I'm so sorry," he mumbles through the balled-up cloth in his fist. Now he's crying, sitting there with his hands together holding the napkin over his mouth, the tears streaming down his cheeks. "Forgive me." The words are muffled.

"No," Eliza says, quickly. "Of course not. I understand. I do."

"Excuse me." Again he's up and lumbering toward the hallway to the restrooms.

She watches the others talk and laugh and eat and drink, people having a calm pleasurable evening meal in the quiet restaurant. One couple leaves, talking about thunderstorms. She thinks of weather as a subject.

Another several minutes later, he comes back. His eyes are red and still wet. He sits down and wipes his face with his handkerchief, blows his nose, then stuffs the handkerchief in his pants pocket and reaches for his table napkin. "I'm so sorry."

She's taken a bite of the pasta and has to wait a second. "It's all right. Really, I know."

"You think you can go on a little—have a little harmless companionship."

"Of course. But it'll be all right. You'll be all right. You just have to let some more time pass."

"I—well, I lied." He sniffles, wipes his eyes again. He hasn't really touched his meal.

"Your *rosette al forno*'s getting cold," she says.

"It's been almost three years."

"Excuse me?"

"She's been gone two years and seven months."

"Your wife."

"Yes." He sobs twice. The sound comes from him like a kind of barking, and now others are pausing and looking over at them. Chloe, at the other table, simply stares.

Eliza reaches across and touches his wrist. "There, now. Really. You're gonna be fine."

"Can you please forgive me," he sobs. And once more he's up, heading to the restrooms, coughing and crying.

Chloe comes over. "Is there anything I can do?"

"I wish there was," Eliza says. "I wish there was something anybody could do."

"And I brought it up. Brought *her* up."

"We were already talking about her," Eliza says. "Better go back, now."

She waits there with the table napkin folded neatly in her lap, and her wine not quite finished, her pasta mostly uneaten. People leave. Others arrive. Finally he comes back, composed, moving with a kind of careful ponderous slowness. He sits down. "Some date."

"It's fine," she says.

"I'm not hungry anymore. I feel a little sick, actually."

She thinks of Cody and what she'll tell him about this evening. It'll be a story. But then she rejects the thought and reaches over to touch Scott's wrist again. "Have you talked to your daughters about this—this that you're—going through."

"Not really. I've had to show them strength, you know."

"You should tell them about it."

"I'm fifty-two and they want me to check into assisted living or something." He sighs, and sits back. "I do feel better talking to you about it. No fun for you, though."

"Well."

"You know we fought a lot. We were passionate." His voice breaks.

"I think I'd like to take a walk. Let's settle up and go out and get some air."

"That would be nice." His eyes fill again.

"Let me buy the dinner," she says.

"Oh, I wouldn't—wouldn't hear of it."

"Well, do you mind if I wait outside while you take care of it?"

"All the way to China, right?"

"Don't be silly." She rises, drapes her purse over her arm, and moves to the door. "I'll be right out here, okay?"

"I'm really so very sorry," he says. "Forgive me?"

She smiles, waves this off, then steps out. The air's chilly now, fragrant with the vapors from the kitchen. Heavy clouds mass where the sun's fading to orange, with night-blue sky above it all. A storm's coming. She folds her arms at her waist and faces the street, planning how she'll let him know that she should go home. She imagines the plausible reasons for needing to be there, pictures the quiet ride to come. Chloe will probably talk about the whole thing, of course, and it may get back to Darnell and others in her office, and for them it will probably be a funny story. She herself might tell it as a joke on herself. Still, she finds herself feeling sorrowful now, and maybe she'll see if he wants to have coffee or something, after all. Except that this would mean listening to him go on about past love, lost passion, and the haunting absences. She looks out at the highway, the far lowering sun, and catches herself thinking of a bridge all the way to China, and then of this man as someone at the end of a lonely journey across unimaginable distance.

IN THE MUSEUM OF THE AMERICAS

Lately, after working, or trying to work, he visits the Museum of the Americas. He wanders in the South American wing and looks at the figures amid artifacts in the glassed-in cases. Time collapses. Cortez is a few miles away. He has been with those who pushed back the Toltecs, Zapotecs, Mayans. There is no wristwatch on his arm, and he tells time by the use of five tons of stone. In a display case, under glass, are bones, the blade of a knife. He can believe that his people live on floating islands and that they farm corn, beans, peppers, tobacco. The air is clearer. He has a dark young wife. His days are peaceful, and he knows what is expected. He's taller, younger, stronger. Violent. He has no children. He's bronze colored from the sun, and he can see the polished walls of Tenochtitlán in the distance. No one ever heard of a car. The clatter of the world, its weather and mechanical slaughter and devices, is somewhere far off. He doesn't hear the noise of it anymore.

"Do you know where you are now?"

"William P. Howell. Fantasy writer. Divorced. Forty-eight. Wife living with someone else. Pregnant with his child. One afternoon I start over there, planning what I'll say. I don't know Alphonse Blum, a boy running after a ball, afraid of his father who is too strict. An imaginative boy worried about his pancreas, at nine years old. This bright child with the skinny legs and the dark skin. I have no sense of him lying awake at night imagining himself a superhero."

"This is good. Go on."

"William P. Howell. I make up other worlds. Peoples. Conflicts that have to do with saving all humankind, the whole unwitting world. Never hurt a soul."

"Here. Wipe your eyes. Talk about yourself a little. It's all right and it's true."

If he had a son, the son would also be dark. A boy with hair that shines with sunlight, down to his shoulders. He would be so strong, and fast. With the power of the solar winds. Change worlds.

"Go on. You never hurt a soul. Remember, you intended no harm."

In his part of the city, the streets are crowded with others. Each life gathers and glides past him. He thinks of the great dedication of the pyramid temple in Tenochtitlán: the sacrifice of twenty thousand lives.

"When you can speak. You know . . ."

He has the museum. He walks in every day and waits for the faint but bearable condolence of the settling dust. It doesn't matter what else there has been in a day—work, imagining the evil sorcerers, the dark alchemists, the battles with weapons fashioned from light, writing the sentences, going on each day, in the so-called healing process, the kindness of others (priests, friends, professional listeners like this one, the parents of the boy), the weight of his grief, the food he swallows, the blur of seeing all day, the music coming out of the walls where he fails to find the necessary reasons. He craves the museum.

"You had a moment's inattention. A lapse. A man driving home at sundown. It's been months now. And it wasn't your fault. The police report says that he ran out between two cars."

Doctors, counselors, the difficult forgiveness of two young people who can't bring themselves to mean it, friends, women and men whose faces change when he walks in or turns to face them. No one knows quite how to put it away. Nothing in his work will put it away and the work was always designed to put it away, the whole weight of the inevitable and the terrible. The work was always leading to the fantastic victories, the triumph of love and innocence and beauty. He makes the false gestures of the form of expression he cannot bring himself to use now. The hours are filled writing lists, facts, dates, histories. The dead civilizations.

Others have told him what they can tell him. It could happen to anyone. He has friends who watch him now, and worry. He loves them. He can't stand the thought of losing anyone at all. He doesn't drive anymore. But in the Museum of the Americas, among the yellow pieces of temple wall and the shards of pottery and the depictions of Chapultepec, the anguish begins to change at last, begins to shift, like a lengthening of light.

When he was an American on a normal day with half the world hungry and the wars on the far continent, he did not feel the weight of the sky. The tonnage of the present. He can't support it now. He hears the clatter of the bones slamming against metal. He sees the instruments of emergency and procedure. He looks at the whitened faces of the others and sees blood on the little finger of the boy's small dark left hand, and then the door closes on it all. He sees it and he sees it and he sees it and he sees it.

"There's more to say, isn't there?"

"William P. Howell. My God."

"Do you want some time?"

In the Museum of the Americas, there are stories of slaughter fixed and gone in time. The country was taken in blood. It's all there, the guilty centuries.

"Do you want me to leave you alone?"

Please. He'll make his own way out, avoiding eye contact, hurrying along like anyone else, in the brightness, the chaos and terror of the street.

They're half an hour late for lunch with Tina. Cathy's driving. Cathy said she'd leave him if he lied to her about other women again, and now she's leaving. It all came out this morning. He feels sick. She seems calm, determined, cold.

Early spring. The country's crazy with color. Everything blooming, everything lush and fresh, the very air promising renewal and replenishment. The car radio is on low. The only sound. The presidential election has worn into its third year, and the air is full of exaggerated campaign talk, lies, and attacks. Empty promises. Nothing will change. Or else it will.

The restaurant where Tina waits is called Belle. It has a glass front and thirties retro décor. Tina's stylish and statuesque, a vegetarian. She's eating the salad she ordered. A basket of bread and a half carafe of Sancerre are on the table. You can see her in the window of the place. She waves to them and smiles.

Breskoff gets out of the car. All the promise of his twenties and early thirties has played out in a string of compromises. It hurts him that all the people he now works with are on their way elsewhere, believing, with good reason, that better things are ahead. He told Cathy in the beginning that if they had Tina's friendship it could help him get ahead in the agency. Another lie. Tina went to another agency after one little year, but they're all friends and he kept seeing her. They kept seeing her. She has come to their house for Thanksgiving. Several Thanksgivings. He isn't going anywhere in the agency, which sells advertising to radio stations. Advertising. More lies.

Getting out of the car, he feels a sudden terror about this change:

Cathy leaving him, ending things. His gorge rises. He watches her drive down the block. She'll have the locks changed on all the doors of home. He looks at Tina in the window with her puzzled expression.

When he steps through the shadow in the entrance, he sees his own face in the reflection, pale as death. He goes into the men's room and washes his face, gagging at the sink. When he comes out, she waves at him again, still looking puzzled, and troubled, too, now. He walks over to her and sits down. "She knows," he says. "She's leaving me."

Tina stares.

"I guess it was always coming to this."

"Oh, God," she says. "*That's* what's going on."

"This morning," he tells her. "It's why we were late."

"What she must think of me."

"No, it's all me. Believe me."

"There's so much you don't know about women. And I'm not even joking."

"Well, it's out. And over," he says. And now he experiences a surprising sudden lifting inside. It's almost elation. The thing is here at last and will settle in its own way, and they'll go through it together. They're free. It has just come to him, looking at the soft curve of her neck, that they are, in fact, free.

She takes a sip of the wine. Her hand shakes. He says: "I feel like my whole life is a series of broken promises. The whole world." He's very dramatic, controlling the panic. He knows she likes the drama and has always found him attractive in his despair. Despair has been their ethos. But he believes it, too, now, and feels it. "I'm—I was so tired of all the lies."

"All those broken promises," she says. "Whose were they?"

"I'm talking about life. And—and happiness."

"But you made promises, too."

"What're you getting at?"

"I'm just responding to you, sweetie. You said broken promises."

"All right. Mine, too. My whole life—"

She takes a last bite of her salad, and then finishes the wine in her glass. She shakes her head, setting the glass down soundlessly on the table.

"But all that's done with now, and we're free," he says.

She murmurs, "Oh." Then: "God."

"I know," he tells her. "But it was coming to this and we knew that."

"I guess we did."

He pours a little of the wine and drinks it down.

"You're so hurt, my darling. Look at you. You look like death."

"Let me get a real drink." He signals the waiter across the room. The waiter knows them from previous visits. He walks over. Breskoff orders a scotch, double.

She waves away anything else for her and sits there looking at him.

"I'm sorry," he says, playing it. "Really. I'll be fine. This is a good thing. It's what we've wanted for so long. It's freedom."

"You don't sound like you believe it."

"It's not a matter of faith."

She's silent.

"Is it."

Presently the waiter brings the drink. Breskoff takes a long swallow of it. "I guess I thought it would play out a little less—I don't know, less abruptly."

"*Abruptly.* What an odd word that is. I think that is really such a very odd word."

"It's a word."

She pours more wine into her glass and sips it, gazing at him over the lip of the glass.

He leans forward, to click his glass against hers. "To freedom."

She says, "Yes, freedom." They touch glasses and drink.

"I love you," he says.

"You sound like someone bringing death news."

"I love you," he says again.

"Maybe this isn't the time to talk like this. You said it was a little sudden for you. I mean abrupt. Sorry."

"It was upsetting. Yes. The way it all just came tumbling out. But it's done."

She reaches across the table and puts her hand on his. "I feel awful, honey. But I can't stay here."

He says, "What?"

"I can't. I feel ill."

She does not look ill. Her eyes glitter. He says, "Don't you understand what this means? Cathy knows. She's leaving me. It's done. I can come home with you tonight."

"But do *you* hear what *you* just said?"

He looks down at his hands where they cradle the drink.

"She's leaving *you*."

"But it's—it's what we wanted. What *I* wanted anyway."

"No. You're not listening."

"What difference does all that make? We're free now."

"When you got out of that car and started in here, you looked like a man who had just learned he was going to die in the morning. You were scared down to your bones."

He drinks. Then: "Jesus Christ, Tina."

"The look on your face as she drove away."

"Baby," he says. "It was upsetting, sure—"

She interrupts him. "No. You were a man who was realizing something terrible. It was all over you like a—like a light."

The waiter comes to ask what he wants to eat.

"I'm not hungry," Breskoff says.

"Put the whiskey on mine," she says. The waiter leaves with her credit card. The two of them sit there while the others in the place talk and laugh.

"I've taken a job in LA," she says. "I couldn't turn it down."

"What?"

"Don't worry. Bicoastal is possible, right? Lots of people do it."

"Bi—" he begins.

"I really literally couldn't turn it down."

It occurs to him, with exactly the same level of annoyance that might be caused by the erratic lifting and settling on his skin of a housefly, that he has never liked the frequency with which she uses the word *literally*.

"Anyway, I think it's best." She takes the last of the wine.

On the other side of the room, a man sings part of a song to two couples. The two couples join in. They're obviously old friends. Others nearby toast the good spring weather, agreeing that it has been a long, terrible winter. At the entrance to the restrooms, a waitress drops a tray with two glasses on it. A man at the nearby table helps her pick it up.

The waiter brings Tina her check. She signs it.

Breskoff looks out at the street. Many people hurrying by in the bright sun, and cars stopping and then idling forward. The glass on the storefronts across the way glares at him.

She stands, and then leans down and barely brushes his forehead with her cool lips. "Bye, lover. I'll be in touch. I need some time. I think maybe we both need some time."

"Wait," he says. "What?"

"I'll call you," she says. "Really."

"Tina?"

"Promise," she says.

He can't catch his breath, can't speak, can't think. The words die at his lips. He watches her stride out into the sunny street and on, disappearing into the busy press of strangers going to and fro. The sun gleams on the blond crown of her head. This firelike light, this shimmer, is what he'll remember about her through all the years left to him.

NIGHT

At last, he's asleep, one heavy leg over her thigh. He snores and sighs, sounding afraid and small. She lies quiet, nursing a cut on the left side of her mouth that hurts every time she stretches it in the grimace that comes with the other pains, the twisted joint of her elbow, the swollen place on the side of her head above the ear. She strives for absolute stillness, but winces, breathing, from the bruised bones in her side.

She used to spend these wakeful hours planning how to please him. Now she plans escape. When he moves and turns on his side, facing the wall, she gets herself to the farthest edge of the mattress. She dreams of getting away, but she's caught, and this is only a child's daydream of putting the world in the shape of her longing. He stirs, a quick movement at his ankles, and is still. If only she could sleep. It won't come. The little boy in the other room, Mickey, six years old, moans and then cries out. A nightmare. It happens, and then there's stillness, and it happens again. She gets carefully slowly soundlessly out of the bed and moves into the hall, to the doorway of his room. His toys are scattered on the floor, a litter she must negotiate to get to him.

"Mickey."

"What."

"You had a bad dream. Do you want a glass of water? Want me to read you a story?"

"No." His eyes are wide in the dimness.

"It's okay, honey. Daddy's just tired."

"I'm ascared."

"Nothing to be afraid of. I'll sit here until you fall asleep."

"I wish Daddy would go away."

"Shh. Go to sleep."

"Why do daddies hit mommies?"

"It'll be all right, honey. He's just very tired. Try to go to sleep now."

"I can't."

"Sure you can." She bends down to kiss the side of his face, but her side catches and stops her. She takes a breath, then, moving slowly, manages it.

"Mommy, can we go away?"

"Don't be silly. Try to go to sleep."

"I wanna go away." He begins to sniffle.

"Baby, please. Please be quiet."

He's crying now. She pulls him to her, and they rock there on the edge of his bed. She thinks of picking him up and sneaking out to the car. But it's his car, and there's no money and nowhere to go, and nothing to do. Once she called the police and they came and took him away for two hours and then he was back, and with one hand gripping her by the neck he asked if she wanted to press charges. She couldn't get the air to say she wouldn't tell, wouldn't tell, wouldn't tell.

The boy sobs quietly, muffled against the cloth over her sore shoulder.

"Honey, it doesn't happen all the time."

He sniffles and wipes his palm across his nose.

"Does Daddy have to go away soon?"

"Yes. He has to make a trip next week."

The boy rests there in her arms, and in a while she feels him lapsing into a kind of exhausted dazed wakefulness, until at last he begins to drift. She hums a little, patting the back of his head.

Finally, his breathing is regular. She gingerly sets him down, covers him, and rises, making her way soundlessly to the hall and on to the entrance of the bedroom. There's no light; she has to feel her way. Coming to the edge of the bed, she lets herself down with great delicacy. Then she's lying on her side, eyes open, crying without sound, looking at the subtle shifts of light on the wall and ceiling as traffic moves by on the road outside the window.

Perhaps she sleeps. She sees her mother, who's recently gone. It's like a visit. Mother has come to her in the night to tell her about things. She has had this dream repeatedly over the past two months. Her mother comes to see her and they do not talk about marriage. It's always the same. They do not talk about wedding plans. It's all there in the background, eerily, while her mother goes on about people they both used to know. She tries to tell her mother that things aren't always how they seem and it's strange that one of the things she liked most about Nathan was how neat he was: socks lined up in the drawers, shirts pressed and ironed, ties in perfect rows according to color, everything so neat. She thought this was one of his good qualities, not a thing out of place. The very hairs of his head accounted for. Her mother goes on talking, hearing nothing. Mother shushes her even as the words come. She says it: *It's bad now, Mama. You should've looked out for me. You should've listened to me. You shouldn't've shut me out about it. Everything had to be so pleasant and polite and you wouldn't look.* In the dream she tells her mother about all the hours of hiding and cowering and the time she went to the police and they came and took him away and in two hours he was out on bail and home and the night went on and on. She's saying all this out, it seems, but also trying to fall asleep.

And now something changes in the dreaming. She becomes aware of a stir, just inside the bedroom door, and thinks of the boy. But in half sleep she senses that it isn't Mickey at all. A tall shadow is there, an intruder, certain as dying. Without will, still half sleeping, she sees herself rise and offer herself to him. *Take me with you,* she imagines saying. *Take me.*

No sound comes but her breathing and the snoring beside her. She's been asleep for hours. It's getting light out. A shadow moves across the foot of the bed, and her own lack of fear surprises her. *Maybe he'll kill me.*

She knows with a shock that this thought is what her daily hours are made of, and that she has a little boy she must protect and keep. Dreaming, she sits up in the bed. The intruder is quite still. Quiet as a thought. She can smell his fear in the dream. Suddenly his stuttering breath comes toward her. But it's her own breath, her own fear. She and the dream-someone are together in the terror of discovery, and then he turns and is gone and she's awake. The room is empty, tinged with the slightest touch of light from the street. She believes it about the intruder and then does not believe it. He was a thing she saw out of hope that something would happen to change everything. That there has been no intruder in the night seems like the greatest sorrow. There is the rest of the night to do. She lies down in its mantle, and looks at the idea that she might have moved to make someone, the anyone of the dream, kill her. When at last she sleeps again, she doesn't dream at all.

In the morning, a single sparrow beats at the window, over and over—begging entry, wanting in, believing this is safety.

THE KNOLL

Nov. 22, 1963

The two men did not know each other. There had been several meetings where they were both present, and they had spoken once near the coffee machine during a break in the planning. A simple nod and hello. Nobody confided anything then. The planning sessions had gone on and on, through every possible contingency, the session leaders always shifting, different ones each time, from first briefings to field exercises—each one seeming more nervous than the one who preceded him, trying to anticipate everything, reduce it all to a perfectly understood series of steps, and always in possession of further dark information concerning the organization's peril.

His part was simple: dismantle and pack the article of utility—as it was called—collect all discharged shells, and move off. He had practiced with several other men, never the same one twice, and he knew what to expect. The "Utilizer" would utilize, then hand him the article of utility and head for the end of the fence to intercept any curious bystanders with his Secret Service badge and his air of authority. *Dismantle and pack the article of utility, collect all discharged shells, and move off.* Except that now he was standing here in the broken sunlight, under the shade of the live oak tree, with this other, who was easily in his late forties. A World War II veteran, then. They hadn't spoken yet, had only traded silent recognition of each other.

The older man now checked his watch, kneeled, and set his suede case down at the base of the fence under the shrubs there, looking around. There were railroad cars a few feet away, as in the drawings. The sun was too bright at the edges of the shaded places in the yard.

"So," the older man said. "Nice bright day."

No answer seemed necessary.

"I said, 'Nice bright day.'"

"Okay," said the younger man. "Didn't think you required an answer."

"You a college boy?"

"No."

"Sound like a college boy." The older man offered his hand. "Utilizer." So he was going to use his code name.

"Okay. Sanitation."

"You sound like a college boy, Sanitation."

"Didn't go."

"Really." The older man, Utilizer, said. "Sound like a college boy."

Beyond the fence, down the small partly shaded embankment, people were gathering. Along either side of the street they took their places—men and women and babies in strollers. Children ran and played and chased one another in the grass. Secretaries and office people, people with welcome signs and carrying cameras, sat on the curb.

"Were you in the war?" Sanitation asked.

The older man stared at him.

"Hey. Just making conversation."

"Passing time, huh."

"Yeah, okay, sure."

"It passes quick, don't it. Too much talk. You see the paper this morning?"

In the newspaper there had been a picture of the Designated Item inside a red target with words calling for his impeachment.

"I saw it."

"Big talk," Utilizer said.

Sanitation nodded. "Bad use of space, too. Useless."

"Yeah," said the other. "Cheap goddamn running of the mouth."

"Loose lips sink ships, right? Isn't that what they said in your war?"

Utilizer seemed not to have heard.

Presently, Sanitation said, "So *were* you in the war?"

"Was I in the war."

"That's my question."

"All right. Let's say I was in the *wars*."

"Germans or Japs?"

Again, the older man stared.

"Just polite talk," Sanitation said, and smiled.

"Okay. I fought the Japs. The Asians."

"The Pacific."

"Yeah, and Korea, too." There was a pocked, eroded look to Utilizer's cheeks, and his eyes were faintly yellow around the irises. It was Sanitation's guess that he was a drinker.

"I haven't fought in any wars," he told him.

Utilizer nodded. "Yeah, you're a young fella."

"Not that young."

"College kid."

"No."

"Hell, boy. It's all over you."

"Told you I didn't go to college," Sanitation said.

"Could've fooled me."

He now took his own small leather case out of his coat. The other was still kneeling. The grass here was burned by the sun, which came in under the shade, through the spaces between branches. The ground all around them was littered with bright fallen leaves. Utilizer opened his case, took one look around himself, then removed the rifle from it. The barrel was oiled, and it shone in the sunlight. He sighted along the barrel, put it on its stock, and got slowly to his feet. "Damn knees. Okay, let's have the scope."

Sanitation handed it to him, and he attached it to the rifle. "Good. Well, the real reason I thought you were a college boy is you got that college-boy haircut. You got that look, you know. And you do sound like it."

"Don't let the look—or the talk—fool you."

"Hey, I like college boys. College is good for you. Couldn't get my son to see that."

"What's he do."

"You college boys are just full of questions."

"Like I said, man, I didn't go. I guess your son didn't, either. Wondered what he did instead."

"Well, he's not in the battle to save Democracy, I'll tell you that much."

The younger man said nothing.

"He works in a goddamn grocery store when he works at all."

"A grocery store? One of these new chain stores?"

"A chain, yeah—when he works at all. Mostly just hangs around the house and gets in the way."

"You don't get along."

"You writing a book, college boy?"

"Yeah. Sure. History."

"I read somewhere that it's a frightening realization that we live in history," Utilizer said. "But that's nothing. The scariest realization is that we live in nature."

"Now *you* sound like a college type."

"Nah. Actually I heard it somewhere."

"Yeah? Where'd you hear it?"

"Sitting in Santa's lap at the department store."

"Just talk, right?"

"Uh-huh. Conversation is important to you. You been talking to anybody?"

"Nobody but you, man. I've been a sphinx to everybody else."

"Really."

"A stone. A statue. An oil painting."

"You know what I heard?" Utilizer said. "I heard you asked to be excused from this particular task."

"Where'd you hear that? Who've *you* been talking to."

"Man, I'm in the inner circle. I'm up on everything."

"Like to know who told you that."

"I don't remember."

"Somebody in close is a liar, man."

"*You* say." Utilizer looked into him.

"Okay. You know what?" Sanitation said. "You do your job, and I'll do mine."

"You see what trouble you can get into with your mouth. Thought I should remind you."

"You're the one talking now. Right?"

Utilizer smiled. "Guess everything depends on the subject matter, huh."

The younger man had removed the clips from his bag and put one in his belt. Then he stood and gave the other one to Utilizer, who put the clip in, then sighted along the barrel again. His movements were very quick and efficient. "Good," he said. Then: "How about you. You get along with your old man?"

"This okay for subject matter?"

"Sure. Why not?"

They were quiet for a space.

"So, you get along with your old man?"

"Not anymore."

"Guess that's the way these days."

"My old man's dead."

"Oh. Sorry to hear that."

"He was a nice guy, my father."

"Yeah, what'd he do?"

"Ran a grocery store."

Utilizer left a pause.

"It's the truth. Not a chain store, either. Appleton, Wisconsin. Decent man. Good to his family. Worked his ass off and never asked for a thing from anybody. Voted Democratic all his life, too. Man, he believed in the Democratic way. Read everything Lincoln ever said or wrote."

"Lincoln was a Republican, old son."

"My father always said Lincoln'd be a Democrat if he lived now."

"Did he vote for the Designated Item?"

"Died five years ago."

"That's what—'fifty-eight. So, he lived to vote for Stevenson one more time."

"Cut the comedy," Sanitation said.

"I didn't mean it that way. A man's vote is sacred. My old man voted for Roosevelt four separate times and was elected to the city council twice himself."

"What'd *he* do?"

"He did a lot of heavy drinking in the evenings. Also he sold houses. Dealt mostly with foreclosures through the banks. But what he did mostly was the drinking in the evenings."

"My old man's store got closed down by a bank. Couple of years before he died. Nobody appreciates the small stores anymore. It's all changing."

"Well," said Utilizer, "and think of it: if time and circumstances were just right, my good-for-nothing son might've worked for your father. We might've got to know each other."

The younger man said nothing.

"Right?"

"I don't have any qualms about what I'm doing, man."

"I'm talking about time and circumstances," Utilizer told him.

"We're all in the crosshairs," said Sanitation. "Right?"

Utilizer looked at him with his yellow eyes. "Whatever you say." He sighted through the scope again. The crowds along either side of the street were growing. It was past noon. "So your old man died and then what."

"Nothing."

"No college."

"I told you, man. No college."

"But you flunked out of a couple, right?"

Sanitation said nothing.

The other pointed to the side of his own head. "Becoming a good observer—you know?"

"Well, don't believe everything you—observe."

"Oh, I'm a skeptic all the way. And I observe you being a little nervous."

"Just keeping an edge."

"And you had no army or navy? That sort of thing?"

"Strictly stateside, man. Had a camera and took wedding pictures and kids' portraits. I got good with certain kinds of lenses and photographic stuff. But everything seemed like a lie after a while. That's what got me here."

"You decided to be a foot soldier in the fight to preserve Democracy."

"Maybe."

Utilizer smiled. And then the smile went away. "Maybe. But maybe what's really happening is you're looking for famous action."

"I don't know what you mean," said Sanitation.

"We're providing context. Right?"

"I don't get you."

Utilizer smiled still again. "Years from now there'll be theories about it, and everything anybody says about it'll be true."

"You a philosopher?"

"Sure."

"What'll be your version?"

"I'll be elsewhere."

"Where?"

"Not here or there." The smile was still present.

"Okay," Sanitation said.

"A little cryptic, huh." The older man smiled again. There was something not right about the left side of his mouth when his lips pulled back. And the younger man knew suddenly what it was: he had no back teeth on that side.

"Well, keep it cool, college boy."

"You're not making sense."

"I don't get paid to think. Hey. This *is* getting to you a little, huh."

"Right," said the other. "Look at me shake."

"Nerves are usually a healthy thing to have, don't you think? They make you more thorough."

"Yeah, well. I'm fine."

"No need to get worked up, son."

They were quiet. A few yards away, another man stood with a walkie-talkie. He put it to his ear and then spoke into it. Then he looked at the older man and held up five fingers, closed his hand, opened it again, closed it, and opened it.

"Fifteen minutes."

"You think it'll be Go?" Sanitation asked.

"Hard to say." Utilizer sighted through the scope again.

"Actually, I don't think it'll be Go."

"You're a thinker."

"Well, really. Do you?"

"Boy, you think too much, maybe."

"I just want to know if you think it'll really be Go."

"I guess we'll find out, won't we."

"I don't think it actually will."

Behind them the railroad cars clanked and creaked, metal on metal. The cars were being moved a few feet on the tracks, and now they stopped. It was one of those inexplicable shiftings in a railroad yard. The sound startled Sanitation.

"Hey, kid, you getting jumpy, huh. You want something to calm you down?"

Sanitation didn't answer.

"I got a little something'll calm you down."

"I'm calm."

"Yeah, you don't want to call attention to yourself."

"Like I said: stone cold, man."

"Nothing but frozen tundra inside," said Utilizer, with a narrow-eyed look. But he was still smiling. Sanitation saw the place where the teeth were missing on the left side of the mouth. "Nothing but the target and whether or not we're Go."

"Right."

A moment later, Sanitation said, "Do you hope we're Go?"

"I don't have any opinion on the subject."

"What do you think of him, yourself?"

"Who?"

"Come on, man. The Designated Item. Word is he's gonna take us right to communism. Make peace with Cuba."

"No opinion," the older man said. "Except maybe that he's a pretty boy who fucks everything in sight. I heard he doesn't even want to know their names. I've got six daughters, man. But that's nothing to do with it."

"Six daughters."

"Three sets of twins."

"You're bullshitting me."

Utilizer sighted through the scope again. "Of course."

"You don't care one way or the other."

"The chances are better than even that in about thirteen minutes pretty boy will be a dead pretty boy."

"It doesn't bother you who he is? What he's doing?"

Utilizer shook his head. "I figure there's always going to be somebody. Bothers you, though."

"No. But they played that speech about getting along with the Communists."

"I wasn't there that day."

"Virtues of the Russians."

"Bothers you, huh."

"Just curious. Just making conversation."

"I'll tell you what, kid. I think maybe you're in the wrong business."

"What business is that," Sanitation said, with an edge of menace. "Spreading lies?"

"That's all true about the girls, old son."

"I'm talking about me, man. And whoever told you shit about me—that's breaking the rules and I'm going to look for a way to fuck him up, whoever he is." Sanitation heard the small tremor in his own voice and looked away.

"Just making conversation, like you said," Utilizer told him. "Just keeping it light. No need to get shitty."

Sanitation put one hand to the side of his face and wiped the sweat away.

"And what're we doing—we're stopping the Communists and saving Democracy as we know it," Utilizer said. "Right? We're making history."

"Sure."

"But you know what, old son? I don't need bullshit like that to help me focus. This is my job. This is what I do. I don't give a shit about Cuba or the Communists or any of that. Like they always used to say, you know, whatever you choose to do in life, be the best at it. Because it's all a damn competition. I believe that. Strange as that might sound, I believe it. I couldn't get my son to believe it, but I believe it."

Sanitation stared at him and was silent.

"If the kid wanted to be a goddamn ditchdigger, I'd want him to try and be the best one there is, and that's the truth."

"More bullshit," Sanitation said.

"That is correct."

"You don't even have a son."

The other was silent, staring off.

"What do you do when you're not doing—this?" the younger man asked.

"I'm a Studebaker dealer. And I never had any children. That's a rumor, man."

"So it's all lies."

"Could be," Utilizer said. "What do you think."

"I think this is entirely bullshit that you're giving me. And I don't even believe it about the Designated Item skirt chasing. Not with that wife."

"Ah. I heard she's a cold fish."

"Somebody's blowing smoke up your ass, man."

"College boys. Jesus," said Utilizer, stepping up to the fence. "They all want everything handed down to them on a platter."

"I wasn't asking for anything. And I'm no college boy. I told you that already."

"Well, remember *this* about me. I sell Studebakers, anybody asks you."

"You think I'd tell anybody anything?"

"Hey, talk, right? I'm not a gambler. You talk about this, or me, and you die. But I'll tell you what, you could pass me on any street corner in this country and you wouldn't even remember my face, what I was wearing. I look just like everybody else, kid. And what I do, well, it's very, very ordinary and everyday."

They waited quietly. In the distance, they could hear the sound of a band. Then the wind picked up, shook through the top of the tree, and blotted everything else out. Police were stopping traffic on the overpass, nearby. It would be soon now. On the sidewalk next to the street, a man was holding his little girl on his shoulders and bouncing her.

"That just might get in the way of a clear shot," said Sanitation.

"Well," Utilizer said in a flat, dead voice. "Guess I might have to shoot through it."

"God."

"And country, right? God and country. See, I'm just as sharp as any college boy."

"Just fucking cut the college-boy stuff."

"Okay."

A moment later, Utilizer said, "Listen, are you a doubtful boy now? A minute ago you were telling me you had doubts."

"Don't know what you think you heard," said the other.

"I was thinking maybe if you had doubts, I had some, too."

"Doubts about what."

"What if I was thinking that?"

"I said, 'Doubts about what.'"

Utilizer paused a moment. "Don't know," he said. "Whatever you have in mind."

"I don't have any doubts at all. I told you, I don't have any qualms at all."

"Well, that's good. Whatever you say, kid. Remember what I said. I got no opinion about anything."

"Okay, well—that's me, too."

"No, but you've got opinions. You're a kid who thinks about history, I can tell. You're an idealist."

"Just make sure you're ready when the time comes," Sanitation said.

"Hey," said Utilizer. "And isn't this really too bad? We might've been friends."

"You can say that sort of thing," Sanitation said. "But listen— I'm just as focused as you are."

"I was serious, boy. You think I'd joke about a thing like that?"

"If it's Go, I'm ready."

"Nobody said you weren't."

"Nobody better say it."

"That's it. That's the spirit. Stand in there and be tough. But you know, even if it is Go all sorts of other things could happen. I could miss. It's happened. I could miss, see, and muddy up the history so nobody'd ever get it straight. I've heard that he plans to end elections and just stay in office. Suspend the Constitution because of the missile crisis. But there's nothing anybody can do about all that except just being in place and doing the job. That's all there is."

Music had come to them again, flying on the air. It was from a car nearby, on another street. There was activity in the crowd now, cheers beginning at the far end of the street. The two men waited. "And I'll tell you, they better decide quick," the older one said.

At this moment, standing a few yards away, the man who held the walkie-talkie lifted it to his ear, then raised his other hand and held up two fingers. When the younger man saw this, he said, "Go." And a second later, more evenly, he repeated it. "Go."

"You sound like somebody who just saw a ghost."

"Two minutes, man."

Utilizer took one look around and moved closer to the fence, in among the branches of the shrubs growing along the base of it. "Get ready," he said. "This is gonna be over a lot quicker than it got started."

The younger man remembered the training. It was just going to be rote action now. *Dismantle and pack the article of utility, collect all discharged shells, and move off.*

Behind them, the railroad cars had begun rolling again, sending up a hollow metallic clatter. From the other side of the fence you could hear the crowd, the cheering. Everything was louder, and the sun was very bright. The whole, hot light of it. Sounds, colors, odors, were intensified.

"Here we go, sports fans," said Utilizer. "Sic semper fidelis or whatever the hell they say when this happens."

The younger man covered his ears.

And there was a shot, far off. Not here. From somewhere at the other end of the street.

"Jesus Christ," the older man said. "What was that?"

There was another shot.

"What the—who's doing that?" He pressed tighter against the fence. "I'm a son of a—" He was looking at the man with the walkie-talkie, who, Sanitation saw, had ducked down as if fearing that he was being fired upon. Sanitation turned his head and looked at the car coming past, and there was the bright brown hair of the Designated Item, and with the third shot, the head went apart, opened a flap, in blood and spattering, and the man slumped over in the seat, his wife climbing onto the trunk of the car. It was a man and woman and Sanitation saw the pink dress.

Utilizer said, "Jesus Christ. Get out. Don't look back."

Sanitation picked everything up and put it away and started in the opposite direction, toward the train cars. There was commotion all around. He made his way to the parallel street, and down an alley to his car, and got in, with the rifle in its case on the seat at his side. Just as he had been ordered to do. There were sirens. He drove south. Precisely according to plan. He went for miles, keeping consistently to the speed limit. Now and then he looked over at the case with the rifle in it, not even his rifle. Finally, not according to plan, he stopped along the highway and walked up a bank into the brush with it and laid it down. He opened the case and lifted it out, put it back together, and sat on the little rise in the ground with the rifle across his legs. He brought it up to his shoulder and looked through the scope at a bird, high and far. Then he set it on the field itself, nothing but knife grass and weeds and cactus. He fired once, hit a cactus, which blew apart. He fired again on another. And still again. The sound of the shots went off from him, repeating on the distances. When the clip was empty he set the rifle down and stood and went back to the car. He left everything of the disturbances of the last days there in the weeds. Driving north again, he had the radio on, and there were the voices talking about the tragedy, extolling the virtues of the fallen hero, relating stories about the resolute boy destined to be president, as if the narrative required that the boy, even when only a boy, was already complete, carrying the long but insubstantial wish, some fatal determination. The highway stretched on toward the lowering winter sky. Sanitation—whose name was Brian, and who had himself been a lonely and anxious boy, and had left his father's house to get away from lingering judgments and frights, and wanted to be famous and untouchable and to be among the ones who saved Democracy—realized that there wasn't anything to do now, nothing to report, no one to speak to about any of it. It was all meaningless. Random. They had arrested somebody, a madman, someone said, with his own unfathomable reasons that were connected to nothing. It wasn't supposed to be like this. It wasn't supposed to be so awful. The radio droned on in static with its voices lamenting the death of the hero. But now he was only half listening, driving through the increasing darkness, gripping the steering wheel so tight his palms hurt, looking straight ahead, speeding, crying.

SYMPATHY

for Sandra Boles Ballas

Settling back on the sofa, luxuriating in its softness, she spread the warm throw, fresh out of the dryer, over her knees. Perfect for a chilly, overcast fall day. She'd recorded *Bringing Up Baby* on TCM. The boy was off playing basketball. Freddie and his older brother Ben had gone to another of their horror-movie Saturday matinees. Ben's wife was visiting with her mother in Nashville or she would be here, enjoying the laziness of a Saturday afternoon. Well, Faith would say she missed her, watching Cary Grant chase after the little spotted dog while being pursued by the leopard.

But her phone jangled and broke the spell.

At first, she didn't recognize the voice. Janice Keener, the chain-smoking nurse friend with whom she had not spoken in at least a month. "Honey, want me to come get you?"

"Pardon?"

"I'm at the hospital. I just started my shift, but I can come get you."

"Janice?"

"He's in ICU."

"*Who's* in ICU?"

"You don't—Faith, I—Freddie's—Freddie. Freddie's in ICU."

"He's—he went to a movie."

"Honey, he was brought in here five minutes ago—I thought he came from you. I asked where you were. I looked for you but then realized you were probably too upset."

"What's happened?"

"I'm so *sorry*, honey. I waited for you. He was out cold. Some kind of seizure. They were working on him. I thought heart attack right away. He didn't—you weren't with him?"

"Janice, he went to a movie. With his brother Ben."

"Oh, honey—I want you to know I'll be here if you—I mean—I'll—I'm here. I'll be—I'll take time off if I have to. If you need me to come get you."

"A heart attack? Did you say heart attack?"

"They're checking for it, working on him. He was out cold."

"Yes," said Faith. "But he's had low blood sugar before. And passed out."

"Well—he—he was breathing all right. That much I know. That's probably all it is, then. And, honey, I'm here for you no matter what."

She remembered that Janice was prone to catastrophic imaginings and conclusions. "Well, what happened? Did they get into an accident?"

"Nobody said anything. I just saw him—I saw—you know, he was out cold. He could've taken a fall in the—he could've hit his head or something."

"You say he was breathing all right, though?"

"One of the medics said that, yes."

"Then it's probably the low blood sugar. Was his brother with him? You know, Ben?"

"I just saw Freddie. And he was out cold and they whisked him into the corridor and away."

"People pass out for all sorts of reasons, Janice."

"Hypoglycemia, I know."

"I'll be right there," Faith said.

SHE DRESSED QUICKLY, HAPHAZARDLY, hands shaking, twice having to sit on the bed to get her breath. What if it *was* something awful? But Freddie's father and mother were healthy and fine. The old nurse, as Freddie called her, was always prone to panic about things. But there had been something else in her shaking voice, that cigarette-thick voice.

She ran a brush across her hair, grabbed her purse, and drove to the basketball courts. The boy was in a game. She called to him, and everybody stopped playing. He trotted over. Fifteen years old and selfish, like so many boys that age. Freddie was his stepfather, and they had lately not been getting along. She was between them all the time, and this morning, as was often the case, she had sided with Freddie.

"What's going on?" the boy said, looking annoyed.

She drew in the breath to tell him, but then stopped herself. If it was just the hypoglycemia, there was no reason to say anything. She said, "I've got to be out for a while. I didn't want you to come home and find me gone."

"I won't be home for hours."

"Okay."

"What *is* it?"

"It's fine, Louie. Go play your game."

He trotted back to the edge of the court and said something to the others. She couldn't distinguish the words. She saw him shrug. They gave him the basketball and looked past him at her; there was nothing friendly in their faces. He bounced the ball and only glanced back, then tossed it and went on with his game.

Driving down Poplar on the way to the hospital, she found herself considering him as a stranger might: this slack boy with his pimples and his bad attitude and sullen ways, barely getting by in school, seldom bathing, a smelly, lazy, unfriendly little shit sometimes, who spent too many hours playing video games and texting his PlayStation buddies. Casually intolerant of anybody's authority.

Heart attack, Janice had said.

Fifty-one years old. But Freddie took such good care of himself. His work with Ben as a contractor kept him active and in shape, and he also lifted weights. He was obsessive about it. In fact, this morning's argument had started with a remark Louie made concerning the weight lifting, that Freddie might be interesting if he could carry a conversation instead of a barbell.

Not long ago, talking to Janice, who was older, Faith had heard herself say that she loved her son without liking him very much.

"That's common for the early teens," Janice told her.

"You should hear the way he talks to Freddie. And *me*. His own mother."

"Very much part of the normal pattern. Really."

"That doesn't make it any easier."

"Whoever said it was supposed to be easy? It'll all come back. You'll love him to pieces in a year or so, and you'll like him, too. You might even be best buds for a little while. And then he'll leave you again in a different way."

"Yeah, I know all that. But it doesn't help, knowing all that."

This conversation was another reason she had backed away from Janice, who along with her dire expectations about all the world around her was inclined to lecturing about raising children. Janice had brought up three boys, who were far out of state now—one in California and two on the other coast: New York and Boston. They never came to Tennessee anymore.

AT THE ER, she walked through the automatic door into the outer room, which contained a row of gray plastic chairs against the left wall. Three people sat there—a man holding a bloody washrag over his elbow; a boy looking too white, rocking slowly and moaning with something that was hurting him internally; and a woman, probably his mother, who was gripping his knee with one hand and patting his back with the other. At the far end of the room, behind a small window with a metal push-out tray like a ledge at the bottom, stood a young man in a blue uniform.

"Freddie Hayes," Faith said. "I'm Faith Hayes. Is Janice Keener here?"

The man held up a hand and then moved out of sight. A second later, a door opened to the right of where she stood. She walked in and the young man closed it behind her. Here was Janice, rising from a chair against the wall. Beyond her were cubicles. Faith saw part of a gurney, feet under a blanket.

"This way, honey," Janice said, shaking, leading her around to double doors, into a more open space. A wide hallway with rooms along either side. A few feet away, a doctor stood. He started toward them, giving Janice a harried, faintly disapproving look. Another doctor, a thin, droop-faced blond woman, walked over from another doorway. Both were sallow, frowning. Nightmare shapes and colors.

"You're Mrs. Hayes?"

"Yes."

"You called the ambulance?"

Confused, Faith looked at Janice, who shook her head, eyebrows knitted in the middle of her forehead—that look of distress which used to be something to laugh at. She turned back to the doctor and saw his name tag. "No, Dr. Weil, I didn't—I didn't call the ambulance."

Now the blond woman spoke. Her name tag was unreadable—a long Slavic name. "But you were with him." It was not a question.

Faith simply stared, aghast, back at them.

"Mrs. Hayes," the droop-faced woman said. "This attack happened—"

Dr. Weil interrupted. "Uh, look. Mrs. Hayes—we've already done an angioplasty to open the artery, but he's going to require more extensive treatment. There are four arteries that need attention. I'm talking about bypass surgery."

"All right," Faith said.

"Unfortunately, he's developed a fever, so we're going to have to wait a little. We've given him some medicine to reduce the fever. And it also helps with clotting."

"I—" Faith turned to Janice and, in the fog that was descending in her mind, said, "Where's Ben?"

Janice had that eyebrows-knitted expression on her face.

Dr. Weil spoke again: "I'm afraid for now we have to keep him stable and hope things calm down enough to do what needs doing."

"Okay," Faith said through the thinnest column of breathable air. "But he'll be all right? He's had low blood sugar."

"The only thing to do right now is keep him as stable as possible. But if you'll just go back through there now and fill out some paperwork we need to admit him."

"Can I see my husband?"

"Well, very briefly."

He led them to the third door on the left, which was open. Lying on the gurney inside was Freddie, with tubes in his nostrils and something like a mask over his mouth, other tubes leading into that. More tubes from an apparatus in the corner fed into his arm. A machine next to where he lay made a sound like artificial breathing. At the center of that, a small television screen beeped erratically, a miniature comet of electric light trailing across it.

"Oh, God," Faith said, too loud.

Janice helped her out to the waiting room. There wasn't anyone else there now. Something beeped in the walls, and an indecipherable voice spoke over the intercom beyond the room. There was no answer on Ben's phone. Janice guided her through double doors and down a corridor, where she sat at one of four desks and was given paperwork to fill out. Freddie's health insurance. She filled out everything and then went back to the waiting room. Janice was outside smoking a cigarette. She put it out and came back through the sliding door.

"I'm so sorry, honey," she said, sitting next to Faith.

Faith sighed. "Stop saying that. Please." She tried to call Ben's wife. Nothing but message machines. "Where is Ben?"

"Ben wasn't with him, honey. Why don't you try Mallory?"

"I just did. Mallory's in Nashville, though."

They said nothing for a few moments.

"He went off to the movies with Ben. So where is Ben?"

"Did you see them go?"

"No—he went over there. They were going to this stupid alien flick."

"You can't trust them," Janice said suddenly. "I bet mine cheats because his father did."

"What?"

"Well, but I can't just say that. I don't know. He's gone a lot and he's not interested in *me* anymore, that's for sure. And I gave him three wonderful boys."

Faith said, "What're you talking about?"

The other stared, then seemed to gather herself. "Faith. He—he was naked. They brought him in naked. I thought he came from you." There was barely suppressed animation in Janice's voice. Janice was part of the drama now. Janice, who loved gossip.

Faith couldn't speak.

"I'm so sorry. I should've—I thought—"

It seemed now, in the half trance she was in, that she'd understood as the droop-faced woman doctor with the clustered letters on the name tag spoke. Something in the voice: judgment. "Oh, please," she said to Janice now. "Please, please, leave me alone, can't you?"

"I'm just trying to be here for you. Should I go get Louie? I took the day off."

"Just—maybe, yes."

But Janice didn't move. They were quiet for a long time. Others came through the entrance and made their way to the window. One was a man complaining of chest pain.

"I shouldn't've said all that about Jack," Janice said, low. "I was trying to commiserate with you. Jack's never cheated on me once."

Faith looked at the man with the chest pain as he was helped through the door. He was many years older than Freddie. Another patient was a young woman who paced slowly, holding her wrist. Soon the door opened to her as well.

"What're you thinking?" Janice asked.

"Nothing."

"I'd be so mad at him—and—and afraid for him at the same time, I guess."

"You were going to go get Louie."

"Well, you know, I'm—I feel so bad—I kept thinking what it must've been for you—I thought—"

"I *know* what you thought, Janice. I *get* it now, okay? Jesus."

"I'm sorry."

They sat there in the sounds of the hospital. One by one the others went through the door into the treatment area.

"Where do I go to pick Louie up?"

"Overton Park. The basketball courts."

"You'll be all right here? There's no one else you want me to call?"

"No one else close enough."

Faith watched her go bustling out, and thought about all the people Janice knew, all the ones Janice would talk to. Then she was thinking about what she herself would say or do when the time came. She hadn't entertained the slightest suspicion. The man who was her husband—oh, God. And Ben, the brothers, what had they agreed on together concerning her? They were going—weren't they?—to those horror flicks she and Mallory never wanted to see. Serial murderers, zombies, vampires, snakes, ghosts, entities, aliens. Seeing those movies was like going to a football game for them. They teased Mallory and Faith about not being good sports fans. And they talked about the movies with Mallory, too. What did Ben say to Mallory? Was *Mallory* in on it? Mallory, her friend? She couldn't be sure, now, that the whole matinee horror-movie habit hadn't been an elaborate lie.

Anyway, it had been a lie today.

Where was Ben? Why didn't Mallory answer? She tried their house again. Nothing. Then she called Ben's cell, and this time she left a message. "Ben, where *are* you. Freddie's in ICU with a heart attack. Were you part of this *lie* about today's movie?"

• • •

AN HOUR PASSED. Janice came back with Louie, and it was clear that she had told him about his stepfather's condition. Faith put her arms around him to calm him, and then broke down herself. "I didn't say anything before because I thought it was just his hypoglycemia."

"I didn't cause this," he said, low. "Did I?"

"You didn't—this—this sort of thing builds up over time. And it doesn't have to be anything you eat or anything you did."

"He's not gonna die, right?"

"I don't know," Faith said.

"God. I wish it was last week."

She led him to the chairs, but he couldn't sit still, and started pacing back and forth.

She went and sat next to Janice. "I have to call the parents. I can't get Ben or Mallory. Ben should be the one to call."

"Do you think you'll tell them—you know—"

"I'll leave that up to everybody else."

"I haven't said a word."

Another of the reasons she'd let things lapse with Janice was that the woman was so dense. Faith felt the cruelty of the thought, experiencing in the same moment a tremendous need to be *kindly* now. She touched the other's shoulder. "Thanks for being here." The words sounded empty, completely meaningless. Just noise.

"You don't need me talking about all that," Janice went on, looking like she might begin to cry, too. "I'm so stupid."

Louie was sniffling and wiping his nose with the sleeve of his shirt. He had walked all the way to the automatic sliding door, and when it opened he jumped back, startled.

Faith heard herself say, "I don't understand." It was as if she were answering someone.

Presently the entrance doorway slid open again, and a woman entered, carrying a clear plastic bag with clothes in it—you could see the shadow-shape of a shoe and the sleeve of a jacket. She moved uncertainly to the window, concentrating only on that. She looked terrible: pale features, red eyes, blotches on her cheeks. At the window, she leaned on the little bottom ledge of it and, with effort that seemed to deprive her of the strength to stand without support, murmured, "Freddie Hayes. I have his things."

Janice grabbed Faith's elbow.

Faith watched the woman waiting, one hand on the frame of the door, which presently opened. A young nurse took the bag. Everyone in the hospital must know. The nurse closed the door, and the woman turned, slowly. She went to a chair a few feet farther along the wall and sat down, hands folded tightly over her knees.

Faith saw the look on Louie's face.

"Son?" she said.

He took a gasping breath. "What's *she* doing here?"

Before Faith could say anything, Dr. Weil came in. "May I speak to you?"

She signaled for Louie to follow with her into the other room. When Dr. Weil turned, his gaunt face caught the light. She saw a line of scar tissue near his hairline. He glanced at Louie, and then paused.

"This is my son," Faith said to him.

He nodded. "I'm afraid there's some bad news. We've had to rush him into surgery—the fever's gone but he's had a cerebral event. A hematoma."

She took her son's hand, and squeezed.

"We're doing all we can."

"So—this is—are you telling us—"

He seemed almost hangdog. "Well, we just have to wait and hope." Then he leaned toward them, as if about to reveal a secret. "But I think you should prepare yourself."

They watched him move off, past the white room with the gurney in it, the feet under the blanket.

"Jesus God." Her son stared at the exit leading to the waiting room.

"Louie," she said.

He turned.

"You know her?"

He shook his head, but muttered, "Yeah."

"You knew."

He did not respond.

"You can tell me now," Faith went on. "You knew. That was what was between you. You—you caught him or something. Saw him. Tell me."

"He kept saying it was over. I didn't want you to get hurt."

Fifteen years old.

She put her arms around him again. "Oh, my boy. We have to be strong, now."

His face was blank. And again she was aware of the hollowness of what she had said, and felt the need to ask forgiveness.

"Can you—"

But her son broke in. "Mom, I'm scared."

They went back through to the waiting room. Janice was where she had been. The young woman had rested her head against the chair top, eyes closed.

They walked over to Janice. "Can you take Louie home?"

"No," the boy said.

"Please, Son. There's nothing you can do here now. It's only waiting now."

After a hesitation, he turned to Janice. "Can I come to your place?"

"I wouldn't let you go anywhere else," Janice told him.

Faith waited until they had gone, then turned and approached the young woman. The noise in the halls beyond where they were went on, and the young woman made a sound like trying to fight a cough. It took her what seemed a long time to feel Faith's presence; but finally the red eyes opened, and widened.

"I'm Mrs. Hayes."

"Oh."

"Can I sit down?"

The other nodded. She slumped, hands between her knees. Faith saw the pulsing in the side of her neck.

"Tell me your name, please."

"Tara."

"Tara what?"

The other sobbed. "Olberman."

"I'm Faith."

"I know."

"Where did you meet?"

The sobbing continued through her answer: "I was—it was—he put my kitchen—"

"Is his brother involved?"

The other sniffled. "What?"

"His brother. Did his brother know about it."

"I don't know. I think so."

"How long has it—" Faith stopped.

"Is he—is he—"

"Yes. He's in surgery. But I'm to prepare myself." She felt this as aggression, and for an instant she meant it that way. The other's face whitened slightly, more pale than Faith could believe. "How long?" she asked. "How long has it . . ."

"Last fall . . ."

She saw the days and weeks and months since then, Thanksgiving—the trip to Nashville with Ben and Mallory and their two girls, and the tensions between Louie and them, the time relaxing with Mallory, and Mallory's jokes about the boys as such boys, the hours up late, drinking wine and talking. She thought of Christmas, her happy insistence on opening the gifts in the morning, and making love the night before, and the morning in the living room with the paper scattered everywhere and Louie's delight at the iPad Freddie had gotten for him, and the hope that they might finally begin to get along, her own happiness in the moment of lying down to sleep that night, Freddie already snoring lightly, turned to the wall, his big shoulder that she pulled the blanket over,

and she patted it, feeling proprietary, motherly, glad of the chance
to be tender, and New Year's Eve, again with Ben and Mallory, and
how the brothers laughed and teased each other and argued about
the Titans and Roll Tide and Freddie worrying about his health,
his unease about a little cough, "I've had this cough all winter,"
and the gratitude she felt when Mallory chided him for being an
alarmist, "We've all had the cough, Freddie." Those days, and on
into spring, the weekend in Smoky Mountains Park, seeing the
black bear in the distance, standing so still, and Mallory wanting
to run, though she'd always called Ben her baby bear and collected
little porcelain bears, how Freddie had laughed at her for being
such a coward. And the summer evenings, those hours, the idle
talk into the dark, the nights and predawn mornings shaded with
anxiety, always in the back of her mind, the tensions between Freddie and her son, who had turned all his scant, toddler memories of
his real father into perfection, when the fact was that his real father
was a bully who had very little time for him, or for Faith, and who
went away, *auf immer,* he said, to his native Germany and died in a
crash on the Autobahn . . .

All of this Faith saw in a flash of near dizziness, a rush of memory that hurt, and how could it be that during all those times, good
days and weeks and months, her husband's life was elsewhere? And
Ben had known it. Maybe even Mallory knew it.

The room was too bright, the lightbulbs too fluorescent, all the
colors wrong, the walls tightening, dull, off-white, the too-shiny
linoleum floor with its black smears. She felt the light as a form of
burning, and closed her eyes, and then opened them again. Here
everything was. *Now.* This was the world, *now.* The broken place.
For a few moments she sat despairing horribly in the electric light.
Aware of it as electric, as the light of her time, the Memphis night
coming on. The other woman gagged, and then sobbed, and Faith
kept patting the thin shoulders, suddenly feeling something stir in
her, a surging, a rush and release, and she understood that what she
felt now was simple as a breath; it moved in her, searching through

her blood. She turned to the girl, who really seemed like nothing more than a girl, with her stringy hair and her thin white face and her fright, the brown eyes wide and quick, looking at Faith and then at the room. Faith touched the side of the face.

The girl was still crying. "I'm so *sorry.*"

A nurse, not the doctor, came out and walked over. She seemed uncertain which of them to address. But the expression on her face told them what she had to say. "I'm afraid—" she began.

"I think we know," Faith said.

The nurse nodded and managed to say how sorry she was.

Faith took the girl named Tara very gently into her arms. The sobbing went on.

"I didn't *know.*" Tara coughed and caught her breath. "I didn't think he was—sick in any way. I didn't know he was—married."

"Shhh," Faith said.

"Well, I—I—"

"Don't."

"No, I *did* know. I did. But he—he said he was so *unhappy.*"

"There."

"He did. He—didn't want to—to hurt any feelings, you know. And he—"

"Don't try to talk now."

They sat there while two other people, a man and a woman, walked in and went to the window and came to sit a few chairs down. The man was limping badly.

"I'll have to take care of some things here," Faith said. "You should go now, please."

The girl stood quickly. "I can't—stop thinking about it. I'm so terribly sorry."

"Aren't we lucky to have known him," Faith heard herself say.

The other did not seem to understand how to respond. She nodded vaguely and moved toward the sliding entranceway. The door opened upon her approach, and Faith had the thought that it was as though the building itself knew she was on her way out.

VETERANS NIGHT

Just past midnight, when it looked like things might get out of hand, Greer brought out the baseball bat he kept under the bar and, holding it cocked, edged toward the tall red-haired punk with the bad mouth and his two jerk friends. "Time to go home, boys," he said.

"You better think, man," the redhead said.

"*You* think. While you still got something to think *with*."

The redhead and the two men with him backed out slowly. Greer watched them go, then closed the doors and locked everything up. He let his young friends Hines and Trent stay. They drank cognac, slow, for hours. Greer had a small stash of cocaine, too, that he had stolen from his ex-girlfriend, who kept coming around trying to make up. But she was always toasted and dull, he said. And though he wasn't interested in that life anymore, he didn't want her to get in more trouble than was already her lot in life. That was how Greer expressed himself. Phrases like *lot in life* and talking about *fate* and *karma*. He also used a kind of aural italics. "That girl is fucked *up*," he said. "I don't know *what* she thinks *I* can give her."

He drank the cognac with them after the door was shut, and finally he brought out the Florida snow. They offset the cognac they had been drinking with that.

"We'll get sober *artificially*," Greer said.

"Clear our sinus cavities," said Hines, who reached into his coat pocket and stopped. "Damn," he said, low.

"What?" Trent asked.

"Nothing." Hines turned to Greer. "Glad you didn't have to use the bat."

"Man's a true friend," said Trent, lifting his glass.

"Trash like that," Greer said. "Never had to face anything. Spoiled bunch of materialistic *shits*. I'd've *used* the bat, too. I'd've hit a couple home *runs* on their asses. And they knew it, too."

Hines held up his glass. "To all the owners of baseball bats and all the veterans of foreign wars."

"To us and those *like* us," Greer pronounced. He was old enough to be their father, and they liked him and looked up to him. Trent even tried sometimes to ape the way he talked. He had taken to using the word *karma*. Greer smiled whenever he heard him use it.

He let them stay until the predawn. He cleaned the place up around them and wouldn't let them do anything to help. When the coke was exhausted, they each milked one more drink and had a coffee. Greer, laughing about the look on the redheaded punk's face when the baseball bat came into play, got into a coughing fit, and felt woozy. They had to help him into the bathroom. But when he came out, he said he was fine. "Well, time to close," he said.

Hines and Trent wanted to pay for the cognac, or sign for it, but he wouldn't hear of it. He saw them out of the place, into the cold. Several times he'd remarked that he hadn't done cocaine *or* cognac for years, and they were both worried about his bad heart. Especially Hines.

"Quit worrying, Tommy," Greer said. "I'm golden."

"Come on with us," said Hines.

They lived close.

"Yeah," Trent said. "We've got a little whiskey, too."

Greer waved them off. "I got enough whiskey in here to wash a *car*, are you *kidding*? I could fill a *gas* truck with it. Gotta close up. Still some things to do. I'm *fine*. I'll walk home. You guys go ahead."

"We'll walk you," Tommy Hines offered.

"Nah. Go on."

There were only the lamps up and down the long street, both ways, looking less bright in the grayness. They stood for a few moments as if confused about which direction to take. It was very cold, and there was a breeze that made it worse. They stamped and wrapped their arms around themselves, and Hines tried to light a cigarette with a match, but the matches wouldn't stay lit. Trent ended up doing it with his lighter. They shared the cigarette. They called themselves brothers in arms. They had both served in Iraq and had come home to Memphis within a month of each other. Trent had been in the infantry. Hines had been assigned to the mail dispatch outfit in Baghdad. Trent was wounded by ambush, Hines by an insurgent bomb. Now they were no longer under the protection of Uncle, as Trent expressed it. They had been discharged, with what were called healed wounds, and they had lost any idea of what to do with themselves. They had a little payment each month for their service to the country, but it was not enough to live on. Things were as bad as they could be, really, for both of them. No family to speak of, nobody much they felt any attachment to. They had a small apartment together in Midtown. Five hundred dollars a month. Trent had a job taking deliveries for Buster's Wine and Liquor. Hines was between jobs, which was a source of tension. There had been episodes. Heavy drinking, drunk driving, and petty theft. He had spent some time in the city jail. Trent was overprotective, and in fact the ruckus in Greer's was about that, the tall redheaded punk getting specific about someone not making a salary and living off the land. The tall punk had had dealings with Hines before deployment, and he considered Hines a poor risk for loaning money. He was very loud expressing this. He had been looking for Hines. Trent understood Hines's trouble and was sensitive about it. He wouldn't brook criticism of his friend and brother.

He had ahold of the redheaded punk's shirt, and then the two who were with the punk stepped in, pulling Trent back and holding him, and that's when Greer brought out the baseball bat.

Hines and Trent were regulars, and the punk was somebody off the street. That was how Greer expressed it, but they knew he was only trying to preserve his air of hard-bitten toughness.

Greer was a good man.

"One of the best," Hines said now, as if they had been talking about it.

"I think he'd have killed that guy," said Trent.

They walked with the difficulty to which they were fairly accustomed up to the top of the street, and stood there. The ruin of what used to be the hospital where Elvis was pronounced dead lay before them on the other side of Union Avenue. A big pile of rubble.

"Wonder when they'll get that cleaned up," Hines said. "What's it been, a year since they blew it up?"

"Year—yeah."

"Damn, Stevie. Time sure does fly when you're having fun." Hines was experiencing repeated nightmares about getting blown up.

"I was here for it, you know," Stevie Trent said. He had no use of his right arm, the nerves all severed there, the arm held to his side by a strap, and his left ankle joint was all calcified tissue. "You believe this? There were people crying in the crowd. Big crowd, too. Like he just died."

"Elvis," said Hines. "Damn." The explosion he kept dreaming about was of course more memory than dream. It had caused nerve damage. You couldn't see where the wounds were on his body. He walked with a lurch, like someone missing the necessary musculature to gain much momentum, but the real damage was interior. He suffered a deep fear of changing anything or moving from one spot to another. He had to overcome it with every step. Everything unnerved him and he was always expecting the worst.

"Imagine dying on the toilet," Trent said.

"Let's go on home."

"See if Greer comes out."

They waited. They could see the entrance of the bar, and the light still shining in the window. Farther down, some young men were jiving along, shoving one another and picking up debris and throwing it.

"Let's go," said Hines. "This ain't no hour to be out here."

"Worried about Greer."

The sun was about to come spilling over the line of the horizon.

"We can check with him later today," Hines said. "If I don't lay down I'm gonna fall down."

"You ever see him drink like that?"

"I think the trouble got to him more than he was showing."

"Think he would've used that thing?"

"The bat?" Hines said. "Greer? Oh, he'd've used it all right."

Greer was Vietnam. An old guy with a long history and he had seen a lot of things and done things. There was stuff he still felt guilty for. Trent and Hines had played by the rules. They told Greer that was how it was for them. They had an idealistic way of seeing it all and they were not bitter and had served their country. They had volunteered.

Greer told them he loved them, with tears in his eyes.

That was Greer. "Look at you guys," he said. "You're *boys*. You don't have a pot to *piss* in. I was just like you. I was *exactly* like you. Except I didn't get blown up or shot."

"But it was different for you," Hines told him. "You didn't have 9/11. You had riots and burning cities, man. And Johnson and the draft."

"I was *just* like you," Greer said.

Now, standing up at the corner looking down toward the bar, they saw the young men in the street stop and regard them. They were talking to one another, too far away to hear. Five of them.

"Come on," Trent muttered. "Let's get."

The young men started again, looking stealthy, spreading out.

"Hey, boys," Hines called to them. "You don't want to mess with no war heroes."

The tallest one was the one from earlier in the bar. The redheaded one. He wore his pants so far below his waist it looked funny.

"Hey," said Trent. "You all right today?"

"Ain't got no baseball bat."

"You trying to look like a brother," Hines said. "Why do you think you gotta do that."

"I wouldn't talk without a baseball bat."

"Hey," said Hines. "Don't mess with us, okay? We don't need a baseball bat."

"Really."

Trent said, "Come on, boys. No trouble."

"You don't want any part of us," Hines said. "This could be the worst night of your lives, really."

The boys were moving to make a circle around the two of them.

"Got these friends, Hines," the redheaded one said.

"I see that," said Hines. "Nice to have friends. I've got some, too."

"Where's your friend with the baseball bat?" one of the others said. And they all jumped. One of them pulled Trent down and another started kicking at him. The others, including the redhead, simply danced around Hines, hitting him and swiping at him with their caps. "Living way beyond your means," the redheaded one said. "Ain't that what they say? You got a big deficit, right?"

Hines pulled a small black pistol out of his coat pocket. "Here's how come I don't need a bat," he said.

From the ground, Trent said, "I'm fine, Tommy, please."

The others stood very still.

The tall redhead backed away a little. He held his hands out. "Hines. Goddamn. Okay, man. Okay. I just swiped at you with my hat. A baseball cap. No wood, right? Just a cloth cap."

"Tommy," said Trent.

And in the same instant the punks started to run. Hines crouched a little and fired, twice. One of them fell and was still. The tall redhead went down but got up almost immediately and started running again. Hines fired once more, and the redhead tumbled, rolled, cried out, writhing in the street, across from the church grounds there.

"I told you," Hines shouted. "I told you not to mess with us."

"Jesus Christ," Trent gasped, rising.

Down the street, Greer had come out of the bar and was heading toward them. "What the hell," he said, approaching. "Jesus Christ."

They stood there. The street looked deserted. The wind moved the redheaded one's hair. Greer went to him and then to the other. He came back wringing his hands and shivering. "Goddamn."

Trent sobbed. "Tommy, Jesus. Jesus—oh, Jesus, Tommy."

Hines was looking at his own hand holding the pistol. "I didn't fire one shot over there," he said. "Had a big forty-five automatic the whole time. Not one shot. I worked in an office."

"What do we do?" Trent asked.

"We gotta call the police," Greer said. "Jesus Christ, almighty."

"Fuck." Trent drew his arm across his face. "Oh, fuck me. Fuck!"

Hines let his hand fall to his side. "I wasn't even really mad at them."

The other two stared at him. It had been something like a contest. Target practice. See if he could hit them on the run. No feeling in it. "They didn't even respect us enough to rob us," he heard himself say.

"Stop it," Trent said. "What the hell did you bring that goddamn thing with you for?"

"Isn't that the strangest thing," Hines told him. "I didn't know I had it until we walked into the bar."

Cars were pulling over now. Someone got out and began talking on a cell phone. A crowd had begun to gather, and there were sirens. A few moments later, Hines handed a uniformed policeman the pistol. A cop he recognized from night court handcuffed him.

Trent stood nearby, crying. Greer was answering questions about the night.

Hines said, "I'm sorry, Greer. I don't know, man."

Somebody put one hand on the back of his head, pushing down as they made him get into the backseat of a cop car. He sat there, his hands in the cuffs making it impossible to lean back, and looked out at Stevie Trent and Greer, and at the people standing around. Beyond them was the ruin of the hospital where Elvis had died. It could be somewhere in Iraq. Someone had covered the bodies. The lights were pulsing all around and the sun was up, burning through the haze. The door closed on him.

"I wasn't even particularly mad at them," he said. Hines reflected again that he hadn't known he had the pistol with him, and again about the fact that he had never shot at anything in the shattered country where he had served, where he had been good, and had tried, as much as possible under the circumstances, to be helpful and kind.

UNKNOWN

In the middle of the night, his cell phone vibrates on the nightstand. Reaching fast to pick it up, he knocks over the stack of books there. His wife, Olivia, stirs slightly. He presses the phone tight against his abdomen, removing himself from the bed, and puts the books back one at a time. The phone has stopped. He puts his robe on, makes his way to the middle bathroom, and closes the door. The vibration starts again. Past 3:00 a.m. The little window in the phone says UNKNOWN. But he knows who it is. A month ago she bought a cheap drugstore temporary one with a set number of minutes on it. Not traceable so she can call him sometimes.

Just as he had decided that he should end things.

The vibrating stops. He waits. Long minutes pass. His nerves quieten slightly. When a sound comes from beyond the door, his heart jumps. Here he is, a man afraid of any stir in his own sleeping house. He sighs, glances at the door, listens; no one is up. Silence. The phone vibrates once more in his hand. "Christ." He touches the talk button.

"You're up." Her voice, full of fake cheer.

"It's three o'clock in the morning," he murmurs. "For God's sake."

Nothing.

"What in the world are you thinking, calling me at this hour?"

"You're going away from me. I can feel it."

"Oh, Jesus. *Now* you're calling me with this?"

"But you are. Right?"

"Are you out of your mind?"

"Yes," she sobs.

"Oh, God, don't—don't do this."

"If you weren't already gone you'd reassure me."

"You're not thinking rationally."

"Why'd you cancel this afternoon? That's the second straight time."

"This is—this is nuts."

"Well, why'd you do it?"

"Why do you *think*. Be reasonable."

"Can you tell me what you did tonight?"

"I went to bed like everyone else in the civilized world," he says, low. "Look. You can't do this. Olivia's right there asleep. It could've waked her."

"I had to see you tonight."

"Oh, God."

"We had to talk about it."

"I really couldn't make it today. I swear. There was something at the kids' school and Olivia had a dental appointment."

"But you're backing away. I'm not stupid."

"Please don't do this."

"It'll be the same next week. It'll be something else."

"Stop it, Tess."

"Then tell me it's not true."

"It isn't. It isn't true."

"You're such a terrible liar. I don't know how you've managed it."

"I'm upset. It's the middle of the night. Christ. Please."

"Just tell me the truth. You owe me that much."

He sighs.

"That's what I thought. That's what I've been afraid of."

"I just can't risk it anymore. Can you understand that? We both said it was a fling, for fun—God, you can't say you don't remember that. Remember? Fancy-free? Remember that?"

"Things change."

He listens to her sobbing.

"So it's over then," she sputters. "We're oh, over. A train wreck."

"I'll find a way to get some time tomorrow. We'll talk then."

"I knew it."

"Tess."

"I knew it. Oh my God."

"Please don't do this. We never said it was any—"

But she's hung up. He sits on the closed toilet seat. It's as if he's keeping guard. Perhaps ten minutes go by in the one sound of his breathing. He worries that his voice might've carried farther than he thought. He covers his mouth, then stands and opens the toilet and looks down into the water. He'll call her tomorrow and tell her not ever to do this again. And he'll turn the phone off; he should've turned it off in the first place.

Just as he's opening it to do so, it vibrates again. UNKNOWN. He pushes the talk button and says, "It's the middle of the fucking night."

"I'm scared," she says, with an eerie lightness of tone.

"I'm turning the phone off."

"Everybody's turning things on and off. You'll turn your phone off, I'll turn the gas on."

"*What?*"

"I have to go to sleep."

"You—what the hell are you talking about? Stop that."

"It's done now."

"Are you drunk?"

"It's amazing how easy it is in these old places. You can do it with one hand. Smother the pilot, the flame drops away. Turn the gas on, no flame. Blink, blink."

He stands there in the bathroom light that now seems harsh; too bright. It hurts his eyes. The objects on the little shelf, the towel racks with their folded towels and the designs, one with a bright-eyed smiling teddy bear and the other with dotted frolicking cartoon fish. He puts his back to the door, one hand to his forehead.

"I don't care anymore. I mean it. I'll just sleep now."

"Tess, stop it."

"Goodbye."

"Listen to me."

"Goodbye, my love."

The connection is broken. He touches in the number to her house phone. No answer. He tries it again. Then he quickly opens the RECENT window on his own phone and erases the three calls. All along he's sensed some madness in her. He puts the phone in his robe pocket and stands there, out of breath. He turns the knob on the bathroom door and pulls it toward him a sliver, looking into the dim hallway. Nothing stirring. The girls are asleep. He checks on them, Tricia and Cheryl. The quiet in the rooms is awful. Awful. He can't stop shaking. It's cold. In the bedroom, Olivia's snoring faintly. She always sleeps so well. They have teased about her clear conscience. He's moving around the dark room like a burglar, unable to stop gasping. His stomach is roiling.

Goodbye, my love.

The vibrating again. UNKNOWN. He's almost dressed. He makes his way back into the bathroom and shuts the door.

"Jesus," he says.

"I read that you just go to sleep. But I want to smoke a cigarette. I have the gas all over me. D'you think I can go outside and have one cigarette?"

A little knock sounds. He stuffs the phone in his jeans pocket and opens the door a crack. It's Tricia, the older one. Eight. "I have to go to the bathroom."

"I'm finished," he says. "Go right back to bed when you're through." The phone's pulsing in his pocket. He closes the door on the little girl and goes into the kitchen.

"Now one of the kids is up," he says. "Please, Tess. Don't."

"It's not you." She sounds sleepy. "It's me. Not your fault."

"Are you outside?"

"Yes. I didn't explode."

He hears her exhalation. "You've got to stop this. Stop this right now."

"Are you coming over? Don't come over. That would be silly."

"I told you—one of the kids is up now."

"You're lucky. You're not fancy-free."

He waits. There isn't anything at all to say.

"It's for the best," she says. "Don't you think so? I don't want anything anymore. I'm so tired."

"This is what you want between us now?" he says, deciding that she must be faced down. "This? Threats?"

"No, really," she says. "I won't bother you again."

He hears Tricia come out of the bathroom, the flushing toilet. He gets the phone into his pocket just as she steps to the entrance of the kitchen. "Can I have a glass of milk?"

"It's the middle of the night, sweetie. Go on to bed."

She obeys him. He watches her close the door, carefully, so the latch makes no sound. She's always careful that way, his child with her OCD. And that's what the meeting was about at school today. The possibility that the girl has it, with her concern for the slightest details, her concentration on the minutiae all around her, the repetitions and the counting.

When he puts the phone to his ear, Tess is still there.

"Wanted to say goodbye," she murmurs. "But I already did. It's silly. I know it's no use."

He wants to be direct and calm. "You're just saying these things to get at me. And I want you to stop it. You hear? Because it'll drive me away for sure. We'll talk tomorrow."

"That won't change anything," she says.

"Nothing has to change."

The line is dead.

"Tess?"

Silence.

He stands there, fingers tight around the little phone, staring at the clock. The house creaks—this small, tight, closed house. He steps to the door and through into the hall. Everyone asleep. In the master bedroom he begins, very slowly and carefully, to finish dressing.

He'll leave a note. Say he was restless and wanted to drive around. What's open twenty-four hours? What can he say he wanted or required at this hour of the morning? The Walgreens where Tess works as a pharmacist stays open all night. It's the one he and Olivia use, too.

Olivia turns in the bed and sighs, and folds one arm across her face. A familiar posture in sleep for her, as if something's blazing at her, too bright to look at directly.

He buttons his shirt, barely breathing, trying to think of some safe means of extricating himself. Nothing for it. He'll have to make it up as he goes along. What can he need at the all-night drugstore? Something he desires? A craving? But as he steps outside the house, thinking Tricia might hear him, he stops himself. The neighborhood streetlamps make ponds of spilled light down the street, not one window showing light in the other houses. They're all darker shapes in the dark. Everyone asleep. There's a chill in the air. He goes to the end of the front walk and tries her number, turning to face the house.

No answer. He tries it again. And then once more.

Finally he gets into the car and starts it, and sits there behind the wheel, trying to make up what he'll say.

A moment later he turns the car off and says, aloud, "This is ridiculous."

He gets out, moves back up the walk, and sits on the porch. He makes one last attempt with the number.

She answers. Her voice is drugged sounding, slurring. "H'lo?"

"Just quit this," he says. "Cut it the fuck *out*. You know you don't mean it. I can't get out of the house now. I'll find some way to see you tomorrow."

"You rented me a house." She gives forth a brittle despairing laugh, and then sobs. "God, I'm tired."

"Are you drunk?"

"Sleepy," she says. "I bet I'll oversleep." The laugh comes again.

"There's no reason we can't have lunch tomorrow. I promise."

"Like showin' me the house?"

He says nothing.

"R'member?"

"Yes."

"Who'd've thought. In a showin'. That was risky."

"Oh, God," he says.

"A fling in'n open house."

"Don't."

"It was so good, huh."

He breathes.

"Huh."

Something stirs behind him from inside. He closes the phone and puts it quickly in his pocket, just as the door opens on him.

It's Olivia, in her nightgown. "What're you *doing*?"

"Couldn't sleep," he gets out. "Didn't want to wake you." He sees the outline of her body in the thin cloth.

"Is something wrong? I thought I heard voices."

"Just me. I can't sleep."

"Not sitting in a chair on the porch."

"Thought I might take a walk or something. You remember—back when I was in the army and had insomnia, you've heard me tell this—I used to get up and dress to go out, coat and all, and tell myself I was gonna take a walk. I'd do that and then lay down, telling myself it was just for a minute before going out, and that would do it sometimes. For some reason I'd drop off. I *know* you've heard me talk about it, honey. And sometimes I *would* go for a walk—or even—even a drive, and I'd come back and lay down, and that would be that."

"Why do you—why are you telling me this now?"

"I don't know. You wanted to know why I was out here."

"I remember the getting dressed for a walk," she says. "You'd go for drives?"

"I always told it that way, honey. Yeah. I went for drives."

"There's no need to raise your voice."

He hurries to say, "I'm sorry. Didn't know I was."

"So you were going to come back in and lie down like that?"

"Yeah. After a while. I was just enjoying the night air a little."

"But why can't you sleep?"

"Who knows. Maybe too much coffee. I had two cups before I left work."

"Coffee always does that to you."

"I'm nuts to drink it at all." He smiles at her and feels the phone vibrate in his pocket. She's headed back into the house, and the sound the door makes obscures the low buzz. But she pauses, holding the door slightly open, and looks at him.

"Is that your phone?"

It's stopped. "Don't think so. I didn't feel any vibration."

"Why do you have your phone with you?"

"Oh, come on, baby. I always have it with me. I sell real estate."

"Not at twenty after three in the morning."

"Hey, if anybody wants to look at anything or buy anything, any time of the day or night, I'm ready. I might even start calling people—the way business has been."

She gazes at him. "Are you all right?"

"Fine," he says. "Just a little insomnia."

"Can I fix you a cup of warm milk?"

"I'll be all right."

"You and your phone."

"There's nothing unusual about that," he tells her. Then tries a smile. "Just habit, I guess. I never think about it. Just take it with me."

She holds one hand out, palm down, to get him to lower his voice. "You'll wake the whole neighborhood."

"I swear I don't hear myself."

"You *are* worried about something."

"Go on back to bed, sweetie."

"Sure I can't make you something?"

"No, really. I'll be right in."

He sits quite still. It seems that the night sky is already begin-ning to change to the faintest light at the end of the street. Some-where a dog barks and is answered by another. Nothing else stirs. There's only the constant racket of the night bugs. He's sick to his stomach. At length, he goes out to the end of the sidewalk again, and turns to look at the house, his house, like all the other houses, the place of a man with a family.

He calls her landline again. No answer.

Finally, he gets into the car and heads over there, feeling as though he's riding away from his life and his marriage. He begins to cry. Her house is the same small two-bedroom Craftsman he was showing her last year, when everything began. It was their private joke: what he had to do to get her to rent it. "Might as well this as another," she said at the time. "And I won't have to buy furni-ture. Perfect. Fancy-free. And that's the way to go, right? Nobody depending on you, nothing required by anybody. Footloose and fancy-free." She grinned, and looked at him through a falling lock of dark hair. It was an insinuating glance that brought him up short.

On several occasions he has visited her there during her lunch break from the drugstore.

She has access to drugs, doesn't she? Surely she'd use some medication or other before she'd do a thing like gassing herself with the oven. He has a moment of seeing his own train of thought coldly, and the knowledge rakes through him that she might actu-ally do it: gas herself. She's unbalanced enough to do it. The very thought of her repels him now, and he sees this as an element of his own cupidity. It's excruciatingly clear, a given, the mud on the floor, that he has simply utilized her craziness for his own sexual greed. He begins gagging and coughing and has to pull the car over, where he grips the wheel with both hands, as if he were speeding toward a cliff. Slowly he constructs the idea, reaches for it and holds on to it, that she'll go to sleep and call him tomorrow and threaten or not. That all this worry and fright are simply what she wants, and his panic is absurd, something he'll remember with embarrassment.

He turns around and heads back to his own house.

Ridiculous.

Locking the car, which he never ordinarily does, he makes his way inside. The house is quiet. He reaches into his pocket for the cell phone and sees that there are four text messages. Three from Tess, one from Olivia. Tess's are at the emotional level of high school.

Go 2 sleep

I am

U don't care.

They sicken him.

Olivia's is simple: *Where did you go?*

In the bedroom, she's lying with her back to the door, blankets pulled high. She's very still. He undresses, soundlessly as he can, and lets himself down next to her.

"Honey?" she says, but then sighs and is still. He pats her hip. He loves her. He has been a good man all these years, and something about the other, Tess, even from the beginning, something deranged, wild, troubling, drew him away. He understands in the nerves around his heart that this is indeed what excited him, this element of insane will, this recklessness, a carnal extravagance. *Oh God.*

Not love. Hunger. Pure appetite.

"I never go into a place like this without thinking about sex," she said that first time. "Really. A model bedroom, or where the beds are in the department stores, I always think about having sex there." She said this, and then glanced out the window. It came to him that she was looking at the empty street. He had made her laugh in the car, being self-deprecating. She had made the remark about being fancy-free, giving him that look. She turned and grinned again. "Funny. I feel kind of turned on."

"Me, too," he got out.

And they flew at each other. He did not even know her last name.

"I want this again," she said, when it was done and they were hurrying to dress.

"Yes," he said.

"You ever done this before? Just for a fling?"

"I've got two kids. I'm married."

"Poor guy."

"No."

"Just kidding," she said. And kissed him again, moaning softly, deeply.

That was seven months ago—months filled with interest, exhilaration, vibrancy. The thrilling passes in the sultry Memphis afternoons made everything else seem brighter, sharper. He was a more involved father and husband, a more charming and responsive man. He believed it to be true. And it was a lie. A terrible lie. He did not really know much about her. He knew she lived alone and had no responsibilities to anyone, no family, no boyfriends, few people she spent time with. He knew she had lived in New York, that she smoked dope on occasion and liked movies. He knew she went to Brazil once, for six months, with a woman who had been a classmate in pharmacy school. There was little else. And he found it to be a very satisfying element of things. He had no wish to change or question any of it. Until the Saturday evening when Olivia, sitting across the table from him while the girls watched a movie on Netflix, murmured, "Don't you love me anymore?"

"Hey," he managed. Then: "What's this?"

"You're like somebody playing a part. I'm having trouble recognizing you."

"No," he said. "No," standing and coming around the table to pull her to his chest. "What in the world, darling." And in that moment he decided to end it with the other—find a way to extricate himself. Tess, fancy-free Tess, was abruptly and completely something of which he must learn, like a good man, to deprive himself.

Now he shivers and gets out of the bed again. The thought comes to him, a shock, that he should have called the police. How is it that his guilt has prevented him from seeing that he should call the police? Even if it means the end of his marriage. How can he have hesitated?

As he puts his clothes on again, he has a dialogue playing out in his mind with the police and with Olivia, explaining why the phone call came to him in the first place, and why he should have known enough to call for help.

No. There's nothing but to hope that everything of the night has been a cruel lie, told for effect. He'll call her again. As he moves to the doorway of the room, he remembers her saying that she has nothing and wants nothing. Pausing at the door, he listens. Olivia's very still. There's only the little drone of her snore. In the hall, he comes face-to-face with both daughters. Tricia holds Cheryl's hand.

"Cheryl wet the bed."

"Oh, well—can you help her, honey."

Cheryl stands there, four years old, thumb in mouth, looking sleepy and sad, staring.

"Okay," Tricia says with the air of a tired adult, turning the smaller child toward the bathroom. His little ones, his darlings, and he can't think, can't find the next thing to say or do, the immensity of what may have already happened out in the night gathering upon his heart. It *has* happened. He feels the certainty of it, trying to breathe in, and because he can't do anything else and because this is what he must cling to now with all his strength, he goes to where they are in the bathroom and helps Tricia with her sister, helps with the washing, the clean nightie, his hands shaking, and then the kisses and the lifting of the little girl to take her back to bed, tucking both of them in under the fleece blanket with the big yellow flowers on it. "Good night, sweethearts," he manages.

Olivia wakes. Dawn is coming.

The terrible morning. So much time has passed. While she's in the bathroom brushing her teeth, he steps into the living room, turns on his phone, and taps in the number. He gets it wrong, twice. That sirenlike dystonic sound. After a pause, gasping, he touches the numbers slowly, more carefully, and waits. It rings and rings.

MAP READING

They were to meet at the Empire Hotel lounge on West Sixty-Third Street and Broadway, across from Lincoln Center. She told Brayton she would be wearing a blue woolen hat shaped like a ball, and a lighter-blue topcoat. "They have a great wine list," she said. Then, through a small nervous laugh: "I'll be early and get us a table *away* from the piano." A pause, and then the laugh again. "Believe me, it's best to be away from the piano." She sounded pleasant over the telephone. A soft rich alto voice. She was now twenty-two. Jacques Brayton, né Drew Brayton, was fifty-one. He had never had a conversation with her in his life. Kate. Katie, his half sister.

Her letter, last month, said that she was living in New York now and had made the adult decision to get in touch with him. She had included an address and a phone number. He sent her a postcard: *Welcome to the big city. I don't get into town much, but we should get together.* He hoped she would leave it at that. But she had called him. Their sister, Alice, had given her the number. "I was kind of worried that you wouldn't pick up."

"Don't be silly," he told her. He knew Alice would've given the number with the air of someone expecting nothing less from him.

That was Alice.

He took the train into the city and spent the night and most of the day in the apartment of a friend on East Eighty-Sixth Street. The friend had left for work early in the morning. Brayton, a high-school teacher, occupied himself with grading papers and reading *The Great Gatsby,* yet again, to teach. At four o'clock he went out into the rainy street to look for a cab. The rain was cold. There was surprisingly little traffic. He began to walk, hurrying toward Park Avenue. An easterly wind started up. His umbrella shielded only his head, and by the time a cab stopped for him, his front was soaked.

"West Sixty-Third," he said, shivering. "And Broadway." It occurred to him that this was life in the world: getting yourself drenched even with an umbrella. He had always been inclined to gloomy reflections. Friends noticed this. With several of them he had formed a casual club that never met, called the Doom Brothers Club.

He sat in the cab and tried to shake the icy rainwater from his coat. The cab was not moving. Horns blew. The rain rushed from the dirty sky, and the windshield wipers made a nerve-racking screech every time they swept across.

He used the newspaper he'd been carrying to absorb some of the water. He was shivering. The cabbie, without being asked, turned the heat up. Brayton looked at the back of his head. Dark hair. Dark, deeply lined neck. A beetle-browed round little man of fifty or sixty. "I'm soaked."

The cabbie was silent, shoulders hunched at the wheel. You could hear a Middle Eastern sounding song on the radio, though it was tuned so low you wouldn't be able to distinguish words even if you knew the language. Brayton looked out at the people hurrying along in the windswept rainy street and murmured the name, "Katie." She had called herself Katie. "Hi, this is Katie," she'd said over the telephone. "Thank you for answering."

HE HAD SEEN HER only once, when she was three years old, in Memphis. He had traveled there alone expressly to meet his father's new wife and child. His father got a room for him at the Peabody Hotel and they met down in the big lobby that afternoon, shortly after Brayton arrived from the airport.

"How's your sister and brother-in-law, there, Drew," the old man said.

"Oh, they seem fine."

"Haven't heard a thing from her yet, you know."

The divorce was done, and though their mother had met someone else—a real estate man named Eddie—and seemed happy, this was a sundered family, and Alice wanted nothing to do with the old man or his new wife. Alice and her husband were devout Catholics, and in fact this devoutness was a matter Brayton himself had been at pains to overlook: Alice had problems with Brayton, too. She wanted him to repent. She believed that if he repented and sought help, and got married to a nice girl, it would bring him happiness. She did not like him using the name Jacques, and like her father she continued using his birth name. He told himself the annoyance was minor. He had always been fortunate enough to see happiness as one of the forms of emotional weather. It would always be shifting. He had learned this without words when he was very small and beginning to know that something about him was different. His sister was too simple for the world itself, he had told her once, and she answered, "Unless ye be like little children, ye shall not enter." She actually used the word *ye*. She actually meant that he would not enter.

Nothing for it.

And that afternoon in Memphis, sitting in the lobby of the Peabody Hotel, seeing the cute little girl with soft blue eyes and black, black hair, he felt his own nearness to this member of the broken family as a shock. He could not quite take in her existence. He discovered an odd reluctance to look at her. The greatest likelihood was that there would never be any close relationship between them.

His father's young wife appeared tired and worried. When she wasn't dealing with the baby, she kept wringing her hands in her lap.

Here he himself was, doing his own kind of judging.

They sat around a low table, and aside from a gentle awkwardness nothing seemed particularly out of order.

His father said, "You think she looks a little like her older sister?"

"Can't see it."

"Alice remembers growing up in my house like it was paradise. And she resents—no, she hates—that I broke it up."

Brayton said nothing.

"Well. Anyway."

As five o'clock neared, the old man decided they should stay and watch the famous Peabody Ducks make their anticlimactic waddle along the red carpet from the fountain to the elevator that would take them up to their penthouse home. They all waited and had more drinks while the crowd gathered. The young wife, Delia, wanted to know how he liked teaching, what sort of students he had. She had done some elementary-school teaching, she told him, but that was different. "High school must be so much more demanding."

"Well," he told her, "these days none of them read, and neither do their parents."

"Not like us," said the old man. He had spent his working life as a contractor, building houses. He read history.

"You always had something to read."

"I wasn't being sarcastic."

"I read to him sometimes now," Delia said. "His eyes hurt him."

"Have you had them examined?" Brayton asked him.

"Dry eyes," said the old man. "But you like reading to me, don't you, dear."

"Sure." She was mostly concerned with the little girl now. Katie wanted to get into the fountain with the ducks.

The old man had already had something to drink earlier, and while they waited for the ducks he had three whiskeys on ice. He always drank more than you thought he should, and seldom showed any effects from it. Brayton looked at the high ceiling, and at the gathering crowd. Finally the fanfare played, and then the march, and the famous ducks were prodded along into the elevator going up. The doors closed. Much of the crowd dispersed. And the three-year-old girl pulled down into herself, wanting the birds to come back. It was a long afternoon and evening, Delia trying to manage a cranky child and an increasingly gregarious husband. Brayton, watching her, thought of fine crystal: the kind that broke when sound waves got too high. By the time they walked across the street to Automatic Slim's for dinner, the old man had made friends with several of the barmaids and waiters. At the restaurant, nobody had much appetite. The old man ordered a bottle of Sancerre and drank most of it alone.

"We don't go out much," Delia said, wrestling with the girl.

"Must be hard to find the time."

"We stay home and enjoy this one, mostly." She kissed the top of the child's head.

"You don't need a TV with a kid this age," said the old man. "All the entertainment you need. It's a comedy show just watching them move around. Used to get the same kick watching you, Drew. And your sister."

The child climbed into her mother's lap and whined low about something.

"Past the kid's bedtime." The old man got up and made his unsteady way to the restroom.

"He doesn't usually drink *this* much," said his wife. "I think he wants to celebrate your being here."

"I've never seen him drunk, but I've seen him drink more than this. I wouldn't worry." Brayton smiled at her. "He's from another age, really."

"Oh." She looked down. "I wasn't—I didn't mean to say anything."

"It's fine," he told her. "I didn't either. Really, it's fine."

She gave him a strange, evaluative look.

"What is it?"

"Do you see your coming here as a peace trip?"

He realized that his father's young, anxious wife had also drunk more than was usual for her. "Not necessarily," he said. "I think we're okay. He's—he's got his ideas, you know. I mean—I guess we've had the usual troubles. But it's Alice I think who bothers his sense of peace."

"He was surprised—but very happy you wanted to come." She seemed about to cry. She held the child and nuzzled the little fat neck.

The old man strolled back to the table and pulled out his wallet. "We should get."

"I've already paid," Brayton said.

"Well—if you're sure."

He watched them get themselves into the car, with Delia behind the wheel. They drove off toward Union Avenue, and he waved, without being able to see whether or not they waved back.

In the lobby bar, he met another young man who was looking. They had some drinks together and then went upstairs. The man, Peter, smiled gently when Brayton told him about teaching high school. He said he was a med student at the university. Epidemiology.

"Of course," Brayton said.

"Not what you think," said Peter. "My interest is influenza."

He left before light, and Brayton slept a little more and took a Xanax when he woke. His father called. "We'll have breakfast at the Peabody—pretty good buffet up in the penthouse. We'll meet you there in half an hour."

"I've got a flight at three-thirty."

"Plenty of time."

No use arguing with the old man.

The Peabody penthouse had five long tables, each one laden with dozens of foods to choose from. The city looked gray out the windows. Pale with what he said was a little hangover, drinking black coffee and a Bloody Mary, the old man asked Brayton about girlfriends.

"Actually, there are always several candidates," Brayton answered, not wanting to quarrel over anything, and hoping he sounded casual enough.

Delia looked at him with interest. He wondered what his father had said to her. She was not quite three years older than Brayton himself.

Finally, after a shallow hour of calling him Drew, and avoiding the subject of why Drew was not apparently interested in some one woman, the old man drove his wife and daughter away, Delia making the little girl wave from her child's seat in back.

HE'D KEPT THAT IMAGE for a time. The little sister's uplifted hand in the window of the car. The very heart of possibility. And as the years went by he thought of her now and then, imagining her growing into a teenager, growing up in that house with Brayton Sr., with his heavy judgments and his temper, and Delia, who had seemed so fragile and worried. But he could never see Katie as anything but that little girl. Alice's children, two little boys and a girl, were not much older than she. How strange to think that the little girl straining to put her hands in the water of the fountain in the lobby of the Peabody was another sister. And grown now.

Alice lived in Brooklyn. And because he used to bring the children stuffed toys and performed little magic tricks—disappearing coins and multiplying veils—he was a favorite uncle. He loved them and had learned to disregard Alice's load of sorrow at his life, just as she and her husband had brought themselves to the point of being glad to have him in their home.

Many times when he was with that little family he felt good. In a way it was like throwing something back at the darkness all around. As there were pockets of the burning Middle East that were still locked in the eighth century, so also many places, most places, in his own country were still mired in 1955. He had said this as a joke at their dinner table one night, and she got up and went into the other room, holding a napkin to her face. Her husband, Leonard, a kindly diminutive man with slender delicate white hands, shook his head and concentrated on his steak. He worked as a salesman of hospital supplies.

"I thought it was funny," Brayton said. "She knows I'm joking with her."

"She's been moody," said Leonard. "Means so much to her. We keep praying for you."

"I'm fine," Jacques Brayton said. "Really. More than fine. Couldn't be better."

"She worries."

"Tell her not to worry."

THEIR FATHER AND KATIE'S MOTHER, as far as he knew, were both alive and well in Memphis. He knew from her letter that Katie had finished her degree at Boston University and had been in New York for more than a year. He and his father hadn't spoken in a long time—not even to argue anymore. Everything between them had drifted to silence. But she was a grown somebody, blood kin, and he was curious and nervous, too. Actually quite nervous. This struck him as having unexpectedly to do with his father. He could not explain it to himself otherwise.

He used to meet a man named Clovis at the Empire Hotel lounge, and sometimes Clovis would already have a room. Brayton's life had been spent going from one to another of these kinds of affairs— his own version of serial monogamy: everything carefully arranged and brokered for safety. He was all right with it. While you did not have a choice about your sexuality, there were many choices about how you lived the life given to you. He liked living alone. He went out when he wanted to and he kept his private affairs to himself. It had been several months since the last. The high school at which he taught English was in Clifton, New Jersey. There was a woman in Clifton he saw platonically. They went to movies together, or to dinner, or just out for drinks in the late afternoons after meetings. They seldom spoke about their personal lives.

AT THE HOTEL RESTAURANT, he found a band playing loud while a woman stood on the piano stool wearing a skirt whose hem came only to the top of her thighs. She bent over to slam the keys, exposing her whole backside in black frill-bordered panties. Her playing was fast, loud, highly skilled, and aggressive. Brayton understood that it was not really about the playing, but about the standing on the piano bench in that way, wiggling to the boogie-woogie. He stood in the entrance and looked for the ball-shaped blue woolen hat, and there it was, in the far corner, near the windows looking out on Sixty-Third Street. He went to the table and she stood, tall, slender, with a face that replicated her mother's. He could not convince himself it wasn't Delia.

"Hi," she said.

"Hello."

There was a moment of deciding whether or not to embrace. "I'm afraid I got soaked," he told her, and she helped him off with his coat. Finally, he took the step, and she put her arms out.

"Mom told me to look for a tall man with grass-green eyes."

They sat across from each other. "*I* could just have looked for your *mom*."

"People say that." The piano player's antic singing was filling the place, so they had to shout to be heard.

"You see why I wanted to sit away from the piano."

"She's good."

Katie smiled and took off the hat.

"It's hard to believe you're here," he said.

"I have a vague memory of you, you know. Those Peabody Ducks."

"You wanted to get right in that water with them."

The waiter came. He had a faintly sour expression—someone just awakened from a nap. Brayton asked if red wine would be all right, and she smiled. He ordered a bottle of Bordeaux, and an appetizer of steamed calamari for himself. She asked for a shrimp cocktail. He looked at her hands, the bones of her wrists. She was very thin.

"So, how are your parents?" he asked.

She looked at him. "The same. They never change."

"Does Dad know you're seeing me?"

Her smile was quick, and then it was gone. "We don't talk that often."

"I haven't spoken with him in forever. I don't know how long."

"We haven't been much of a family, have we?"

"I'm pretty certain that's been his choice, wouldn't you say?"

"Well, people make allowances, don't they?"

"You'd say that about him?"

"I don't know. He likes things smooth."

"Pardon?"

"I meant he never talks about what he feels. Never anything about himself. The world is going to hell—you know. Nothing about him*self*."

"Tell me about *your*self."

She hesitated. The waiter brought the wine and then had some trouble opening it. Brayton said, "You want me to do that for you, son?"

But the waiter got it open, thanked him anyway, and poured the taste. The wine was soft and tannic. "Good," Brayton said, nodding.

The waiter poured it, set the bottle down on the table, and walked away. Brayton lifted his glass and shouted against the music, "To families everywhere."

"I'll drink to that." There was something barely controlled in her voice, a tension that gave it the faintest tremor. Probably it was having to talk so loud to be heard.

Again, he said, "Tell me about yourself."

"Not much to tell. I grew up an—an only child. Graduated from Boston. I have a job in public relations at Harper."

The music stopped, and the singer was talking about taking a break.

"You're in publishing?" Brayton asked, happy about the quiet.

"Well, no. Marketing, really."

"But in publishing."

"Lowest of the low rungs on the ladder, you know. I'm just starting."

"Well, but that's great. Do you think you might want to get into the editorial side of it?"

"I took a publishing course in Vancouver last summer. So, sure, maybe. I don't know if I'm smart enough."

"How did you do in the course?"

"It was fun. I did well."

"Then there you are," he said.

"And you teach English, I think?"

He regarded her, taking in the kindly smile.

"Mom said she was pretty sure you teach English."

"I've been at the same school since before you were born. In New Jersey. Clifton."

"I have a friend from New Jersey. She's an older woman. Mom's age. But nice. I met her in Vancouver, if you can believe that."

"Small, small world," he said. But he thought about how immense it was, how a man could have a sister he has seen only once before in his whole life.

They were quiet, sipping the wine. He poured more for them.

"So you're working in publishing, and living in New York."

"I went and saw Alice in Brooklyn."

He waited.

"I wanted to meet her. So I just went over there. And she let me in. She was pretty nice. I met her husband, Leonard. I liked him. I liked them both."

"I don't see much of them since their children moved out."

"Alice was kind of stiff. Well, awkward. Nice, though. I think it was just awkward for her."

"It's ridiculous, you know. After all this time. She's like the Taliban."

"Well." She poured more of the wine for herself and offered it to him. He took the bottle and poured.

"Katie, you're her sister, for God's sake."

She gave him a strained look, then gazed out the window.

"Nothing against Alice," he said. "Nor any other Christians anywhere, elsewhere."

"You both hate him."

"The old man? *Hate*'s too strong a word. I wish him well."

"And Alice?"

"Alice grieves for his soul. Alice is still angry at him. Alice can hold on to anger. Believe me, you've never seen anything like it. She's like a character in a gothic southern novel. And me, well, to be absolutely truthful, I never think about him. He—we never could agree on some things. A lot of things. Important things about which he ought to know better by now. Let's just put it that way."

"Alice grieves for his soul. And is angry."

"Well, Alice and Leonard are of a particular *kind* of Christianity. Jesus Christ as the celestial cop. She grieves for my soul, too."

"I know."

"It's a burden we bear in silence."

"She showed me pictures of Dad when he was younger, with your mother. Your mother was very pretty. Alice cried showing it all to me."

Brayton kept silent.

Katie stared into her wine. "She's just this lonely old Brooklyn lady with a big mole on her neck who wears a scarf to church and shops with a metal wagon."

"Well," he felt compelled to say, "don't give her any political power."

The other shook her head and drank.

"You'd think the divorce just happened."

She said, "I saw the wagon off the back stoop when I went out there to smoke a cigarette. Leonard was so sweet to me, but I had the feeling he spends most of his time watching sports and waiting for her to bring him drinks and food. I had dinner with them. There's a crucifix in every room of the house."

"Oh, it's definitely a Catholic house."

"They seem happy enough together."

"Habit."

"Does that invalidate it?"

"Not at all. That's absolutely the truth of it. Habit or no, it's still a form of domestic bliss."

"You sound bitter."

"Maybe I am, a little. Since that form of happy also allows for some pretty terrible habits of thought."

"Do you still go to Mass?"

He shook his head, smiling at her. "Not since I left home for college."

"Alice and Leonard said grace. We held hands and it was like we were a family."

"You didn't have that growing up."

"Not once." She laughed that soft laugh he remembered from her voice on the phone.

"No," he said. "The old man's never been much for that. The source of his many problems lies elsewhere."

"I used to wish I had whatever it was that made him and Delia so calm. Did you ever wish you had that?"

"No."

"Well, your mother was a pretty woman."

"She still is. And as I said, she's happy, too. At seventy-three, with her second husband. And of course Alice didn't like him at first. Mother was living in sin."

"The phrase is funny isn't it. *Living in sin.* Isn't everyone living in sin?"

"Everyone's living in whatever weather there is where they are." He smiled. And then caught himself wondering how much she knew about him.

"It's such a loaded phrase. *Living in sin.*" She took a long slow sip of her wine. "It always struck me as something religious women said about other women. Almost exclusively."

He said, "Someone should do a linguistic study."

"And you never were like that—that they were living in sin—about him and my mother."

"Never. Of course not."

"And I guess Alice is all right with it now."

"Well, Mom got a dispensation on some technicality, making her marriage to Dad invalid in the *Church*. Which made bastards out of Alice and me. But it saved the whole thing for Alice, and she could accept the old boy—Eddie's his name—still without really liking him much. She's a bit judgmental by nature. Which, of course, she got from Dad. Eddie's all right, really. And he treats Mom like a queen."

"Funny," Kate said. "This is the strangest place."

"Here?" He looked down and then back at her.

"Earth." She grinned.

"And we walk up and down on it?"

She nodded, gazing off. Then: "I didn't know where to go."

"Excuse me?"

"Nothing. Tell me about your life, brother of mine."

The wine was evidently going to her head. She took more of it.

He glanced over for the waiter. "How long does it take to put steamed calamari and a shrimp cocktail together?"

And as if what he had said called her forth, the singer walked up in her brief black skirt and fishnet stockings. He saw the black bow tie at her neck, the puffed white sleeves of her blouse. "Too early?" she said to Katie.

"This is Lanelle," Katie said.

Brayton offered his hand.

"Too early," said Lanelle, sitting down.

He stared.

The waiter came over and gestured. She nodded. He went off. She turned to Brayton and grinned. "They know what I like here between sets."

"You sing and play wonderfully," he said, and tried not to have it sound as empty as it did sound. He couldn't take his eyes from her face. There was something slack in it, a kind of indolent watchfulness. He added, "I mean that. I'm very impressed."

"Lanelle's my roommate," said Katie. "That's why I wanted to meet here."

He glanced at her, then regarded Lanelle again. "You in publishing, too?"

She laughed. "Not so's you'd notice. But it's a pleasure to meet Katie's brother, Drew. Long-lost brother, I should say. I think it's great."

"Jacques," Katie said. "Remember Alice said it's Jacques."

"Oh, forgot—sorry."

"It's been Jacques for about twenty-five years," Brayton said.

"I changed my name, too. Only I won't tell you what it was."

"Edna," Katie said, with a little nudge of the other woman's shoulder. "Maybe we'll all go get something in Chinatown after your last set." She sounded younger, hopeful, and faintly pleading.

"Sounds like fun." Lanelle gave Brayton an appraising look. "You like Chinese?"

"Very much."

"We *love* Chinese." She touched Katie's wrist. "Don't we."

"I think I've got MSG in my blood," Brayton's sister said. The other had taken her hand.

He leaned slightly toward her. "Am I to understand something here?"

"Funny," Katie said, without the slightest inflection.

"Are you—are you on speaking terms with Dad?"

She moved her index finger around the lip of her glass, staring at it. "Like you are, sure."

"Well, I'll be damned," he said.

Lanelle touched his wrist. "It's true, though, isn't it? You see it on the news now. People talking the wave of the future, and famous people coming out and marriages in some states and you start thinking it really is changing. But there's always the individual cases. Right?"

He nodded, and drank the wine.

She went on: "People like us still have to map read."

"Excuse me. Map read?"

She looked at Katie. "I'm ten years older than your sister here."

"You don't look it."

She gave him a sweet smile, charming and perfectly vacant. "Well. Thanks for the compliment. But really—come on. Haven't you been reading the maps all these years? From your own kind of closet?"

The waiter brought her a whiskey, neat, with a little cup of espresso. She drank the whiskey in a gulp, then sipped the espresso.

"We live together as husband and wife," Lanelle said. "Her family—and mine, too—don't really know what to do with it."

"So you—you read the maps."

"We navigate the waters, yeah. But we're out there in the sunny blue."

"I see."

"For love."

"Yes," Brayton said.

Lanelle repeated it. "For love."

He said, "I'm with you."

She finished her espresso, set the cup down, then stood and walked off. He saw her stop at another table and lean over to speak to the woman there.

"You teach English," Katie said to him. "What grade?"

"Twelfth."

"Do the people you work with know?"

He watched Lanelle go on out of sight beyond the bar. "I'm sorry?"

"Do they know about you."

After a brief pause, he said, "Some of them, of course. Friends."

"Crazy, isn't it."

"It's the territory," he said. "You know. Our schizoid country."

"You should do something where you don't have to worry."

"I'm fine, really."

"You're my brother," she said, and raised her glass. "Here's to my one brother. And I didn't know this about you until a couple of years ago." She smiled, but there were tears lining the lower lids of her eyes.

"You all right?"

"Isn't it strange to have better treatment from people—just people—than you ever got from your own family?"

"You mean the parents," he said.

She did not answer. She was pouring more of the wine.

"I think I know what you mean," he said. "You mean all of us."

"We should get another bottle."

"You mean me."

"I wish I'd known about you, and if you'd called now and then, just to be in touch, if we'd been in touch, I think I might've. Because what if you were there when I figured it out? I mean things might not've been so hard for me."

He nodded helplessly. "Right. That's absolutely right. I'm sorry."

"I went through a lot of hell, as a kid. An awful lot of—just—you know, hell." She had turned to the waiter, one hand up. The hand shook slightly, the smallest tremor, while she made a little waving motion. It went all the way to the bottom of his heart.

"God, Katie," he said. "I'm so sorry."

But the music had started up again, and it was clear that she hadn't heard him. She was watching Lanelle move through the room, languid and sultry, mic in hand, singing "Angel Eyes."

THE LINEAMENTS OF GRATIFIED DESIRE

What is it men in women do require?
The lineaments of gratified desire.
What is it women do in men require?
The lineaments of gratified desire.

—WILLIAM BLAKE

I

The woman David Shumaker had thought of as his own, his darling Sonya, was in Los Angeles for a period of weeks, helping her mother through knee replacement surgery and physical therapy. Almost two thousand miles away. At the beginning, he had thought he might go crazy without her. In the tossing nights, he suffered the fear that she would meet and fall in love with another man. He told himself it was just the distance, and his own long-standing insecurity about himself and women.

Now here he was, the one who had met someone else.

He told his father, because his father had introduced him to Sonya. The old man stared, frowning. "I thought you—" He stopped. "This is a joke, right?"

She had been the professor's undergraduate assistant in the math department at Memphis.

"It's no joke, Dad."

His father was quiet for a time. Then: "What's the deal here, Son?"

"I guess I should call and tell her."

"You're really serious."

"I'll get her on the phone and just—spill it, I guess." He had not quite voiced to himself the hope that the other would offer to make the call, given the old student-teacher friendship.

"This new someone else—what's her name?"

"Alexa. Alexa Jamison."

"How long have you known her?"

His first impulse was to lie. But there was no use. "A week," he said.

"A *week*?"

"Yes, sir."

"One *week*? Seven *days*?"

"Well, almost a week. Six days, actually, counting today."

"Jesus Christ, David."

"I know."

The old man tilted his head slightly to one side, as if he had just noticed something about his son's face. But he said nothing. They were in his study, sun and leaf shade in the window. It looked like the light of an ordinary day.

The young man's mother came through the house calling for her husband. "Wilfred? Are you still here? You were going to get milk—" She had come to the door and, seeing her son, walked over to give him a hug. "What a nice surprise."

"Surprise is right," said Professor Shumaker.

"Okay." She folded her arms. "I'm waiting. You sold the painting."

"No."

"I don't think he's ready to talk about it."

"Really." Her tone was light, nearly playful.

"This is serious, Lena."

Shumaker said, "I can't marry Sonya. I'm in love with someone else."

For what seemed a long time, no one spoke.

His mother said, "I've got some work to do. You two talk about it and let me know." She turned and went out, closing the door quietly.

"That's my lady," said the professor. "Through thick and thin she's out the door."

The young man said nothing.

"Little joke."

"Dad, if you saw this woman—"

"If I *saw* her."

"She's the model for my painting. It's a nude."

"A *nude*."

"You knew I was painting her."

"I think I'd've remembered if you said it was a nude."

"It's a commission."

"Nude."

"It happens all the time, Dad."

"No kidding," said the professor with a look.

"It doesn't really have to do with the fact that it's a nude. This— this whole thing just—took hold of me. I'm completely gone on her, and if you saw her, you'd see why."

"What the hell're you *talking* about, boy? If I *saw* her. You mean if I saw her nude?"

"No. Jesus. I know it sounds worse than I mean it."

"It can't sound worse than it *is*."

After a pause, the young man said, "I'll call Sonya and tell her."

"Just like that."

"I won't lie to her."

"Don't lie to *yourself*. That's ego talking, you won't lie to her— that means you want to tell her over the phone. There's been marriage plans, for Christ's sake."

"You're saying I should tell her face-to-face, then."

"What do *you* think?"

"God, I feel awful."

"This thing with—you're sure it's serious? I mean the first time you see her in your life, she takes her clothes off."

"That isn't how it happened. There was—I talked with her. We had coffee."

"And *then* she took her clothes off."

"Dad. Cut it out. No. Look—it's a sitting. A sitting. The model just sits there—"

"I know what a *sitting* is, Son."

The young man waited.

"You were so serious about Sonya. She's been like one of the family. She *is* one of the family."

He looked down. "I swear I never felt anything as strong as this."

The professor seemed to be waiting for him to explain further. Then: "Why're you telling *me*—us—about it anyway?"

"I guess I wanted your advice. I wouldn't have accepted the commission if I thought—I—I wish I hadn't accepted it. But I did, and Alexa's walked into my life, and I'm completely gone."

"And she feels the same way about you."

"It's crazy, I know."

"Well, there's not much to say, then."

Another silence.

"Is there." It wasn't a question.

"Guess not."

"You guess not."

"Dad."

"That poor girl's been like part of the family."

"I feel terrible."

"Well, just don't break it off over the damn telephone. That'd be cowardly."

"It's like I'm cheating on a wife."

"No," Wilfred Shumaker said, simply. "You cheated on your fiancée. And your mother was on the phone with *her* mother just this morning."

11

When he thought about it, he could see that this thing with Alexa Jamison was a betrayal of the *idea* of what Sonya and he had been. The romance of that. Such a sweet beginning and a following inertia. The two families, everybody coming together as part of the story.

It happened this way:

Near the end of the spring semester, he and his father went to a Memphis in May party on the roof of the Madison Hotel. Wilfred introduced Sonya to him as his star pupil. Sonya extended a soft hand, and the young man shook it, and they walked to the table where the wine and the drinks were and waited in line, talking. They liked each other instantly. She had decided that she wanted to teach, and he joked about being in graduate school and still having to be driven around by his father. The ratty old, rusted car he'd been driving since high school was on its last legs, he told her, and so each afternoon after his one graduate class ended he had to hang out in the upstairs terrace of the student center waiting for a ride home with the professor, whose senior seminar in calculus went until five-thirty.

"Of course you *know* how few guys would admit this sort of thing," she said with a perfectly uncomplicated smile. Her straightforwardness was surprising and charming.

"Well," he managed to say, "no sense lying about it."

"Oh, but there *is*. I've lost all respect for your manliness. You don't have a cool car."

"I have a cool bicycle. But it's in my father's garage and I haven't been on it for years."

She bit the edge of her thumbnail and smiled. "I'd get that tattooed on your chest," she said, smiling again.

Later, with his father, being driven to his small efficiency apartment in the Cooper-Young district, he asked about her.

"Well, I don't know all that much. She's got a real talent for mathematical thought and theory, and her parents live out in LA. That's about it."

"I like her," Shumaker said.

The next night, as he stood in the terrace window of the student center and watched people move through the thin mist sweeping across the plaza below, she materialized out of the dimness, smiling up at him, quite lovely, a warm memory in the making. He rushed out to meet her.

"I came here on an impulse," she said. "Hoping I'd see you." Her straightforwardness again.

"I swear you were on my mind," he told her. "And then you stepped out of the mist."

It was true. He had actually been hoping she would appear.

"How poetic." She leaned in and kissed his cheek. "So here we are."

He texted his father to go on home without him.

They went down to the river in her little cluttered car, his knees against the dash because the passenger seat would not slide back. She found a parking space on Riverside Drive, and they walked along the trolley tracks for a block or so. Then he paid for a coach and horses to take them up to the Madison. The whole way up the long hill he kept looking at the side of her face while she talked. She went on in a stream of funny self-deprecation about growing up in Southern California, off Wilshire Boulevard in the City of Angels: the cool nights after blistering afternoons, the smog, the happy hours on the beach, her often troubled high-school days, and how silly that had all been for meaning so much to her at the time. Then there was her piano-playing father, an attorney for Hollywood types, and her actress mother, who had left the business to raise her. And there was Los Angeles itself. Sirens every night. A whole other class of people living up in the hills, in the big houses and the wildly extravagant villas.

Before the coach got up to Main Street, he took her into his arms and kissed her. Magic. They went over to Beale Street and danced at the Rum Boogie Café, and then strolled up to B.B. King's Blues Club for barbecue and beer. It was a lovely long night of easy conversation about their respective circumstances, like old friends catching up with each other. Both were twenty-two and had finished with their undergraduate degrees, his in art and hers in mathematics. They were both unemployed in their respective fields and were making do, as she put it. Along with taking the one art class he was a greeter and server at his uncle Terry's restaurant, and she worked the ticket booth at the Malco Paradiso. He was living in the small efficiency apartment, a converted garage, really, with one window in the closet-sized bathroom and another in the only door, and she lived in a two-bedroom backyard rental house in Chickasaw Gardens, which she had shared with a gay clarinetist named Forest, who left after the first month for India, he said, to avoid the drag of nine-to-five. She'd decided to see if she could make the rent alone and was proudly surprised that she could. And no nine-to-five, either. Six to eleven at night. She laughed softly, saying this, and he said he liked the sound of the laugh. He spoke of the peculiar fact that the way you laughed could absolutely determine how well you did in company, and he faked a goofy mule-sounding bray, just to hear her laugh again. Later, when even the crowd on Beale Street had thinned out, they strolled back down to the river. The light on the water shone, and he had an idea that this would be something about which they would reminisce, telling how they came together. The night shimmered.

That was a year and four months ago.

Once in those first days, they sat together in her car parked at the edge of the river, sipping Chianti and eating figs with walnuts and little wedges of cheese, making up stories about the people who walked by—giving them whole lives and histories and complications, putting sorrows and joys around them like invisible capes as they strolled past. He made sketches of them and showed them to her, and they talked about the series of river scenes he might paint and call the whole exhibit *Mississippi*. Yes, he would do that.

Two weeks later, he bought a ring with a salary advance from Uncle Terry, who sometimes played guitar and sang at the farmers' market on Saturday mornings. He took her to see him play, and then the two of them rode the trolley down to the river and around to Main Street. On the patio of the Blue Fin Café, he dropped the ring into her glass of white wine, as he had seen it done in the movies. She wept when she saw it and, standing to kiss him, knocked the glass over and wept some more.

The following night, they went to his father's house, and Uncle Terry was there, too, and they had a big dinner that Lena had prepared. Sonya's parents spoke to everyone on the telephone. Everyone sang happy birthday to David Shumaker, who was turning twenty-three at the end of the month. The day he bought the ring, he had taken sketches to the dealers on Main Street, and three different galleries showed interest. They would be married as soon as he had his first show, and by that time they might both be teaching. If the exhibit did well, they could do it sooner. It was just a matter of producing enough work, and he was spending long hours each day drawing and doing preliminary sketches of the scenes.

They spent every available moment together through the spring and summer. They confided about secret feelings concerning others, old and new fears, affections, hopes, disappointments. They made love on the ratty old divan in his apartment and spent whole afternoons playing in the sunlight through the one window in the door and planning how life would be after they were married.

In the interim they would earn certification to teach. They might end up teaching in the same school. He would win prizes for his series of paintings called *Mississippi*. They would fly off together into the limitless blue distances. They fantasized that, just as her once-roommate had flown off to avoid the nine-to-five drag, they too would fly away, after Shumaker made big money on the paintings. She with her talent for math would handle the finances, would be his business manager in their travels through India, the far-off exotic ends of the earth. Talking about all this, he made her laugh by pronouncing the country's name in what he called high British: *IN-dyaa*.

IN EARLY SEPTEMBER, after she flew to LA and there were only phone calls between them, it became difficult finding time to talk with her, and, seeking reassurance, he teased about taking a plane out there to surprise her.

"Don't talk like that," she said. "I don't like that."

"I was joking."

"Don't joke. I don't feel like jokes right now."

"Come on," he said. "*You?* Wouldn't you like to see me?"

"My mother's driving me batty. I'm sorry. It's awful to say, but I'd like to see anyone but her these days. And my father's not far behind."

The parents and their troubles.

Each call became a session of complaining about them. Both were in their fifties, and they wanted her to come home for good. They had never dreamed that sending her to the University of Memphis would mean that she would decide to live there. They hated Memphis. Each night at dinner, her father found subtle ways to disparage the place, while her mother grieved sullenly over some perceived slight or other coming from the other two. "Being an only child sucks," she told Shumaker. "I'm between them, and they go back and forth—they can't stand to be in the same room, and then they *can* stand it—you know? All of a sudden they won't take a step without each other. They're the heroes of their own movie about love. There's no middle ground. I'm the middle ground."

In the evenings after the tensions of dinner, her father would sit at the piano in the parlor and pound away on a Chopin nocturne as if it were something requiring that kind of force. And her mother would sit with a TV tray of various snacks and candies at her elbow, her leg supported by a big leather hassock, watching old movies on TCM—those chatty films of the thirties and forties—apparently oblivious to the thundering of the piano. Their daughter was quite adept at describing all this at length. Shumaker listened, and tried to keep track. He thought it was the distance that was making her seem so sour.

"Come home," he said. "Now."

"I can't now. *God!* Quit torturing me. Please."

He did not say, as he wanted to, *Come on, babe. Where's my funny darling?*

He enrolled in classes to earn certification and was looking to find work teaching. There was nothing but substitute jobs. But he went on taking the courses and working for his uncle. He lacked much opportunity to work on his sketches and paintings, and his heart wasn't in it with Sonya so far away, in other weather and time.

All this was before he began work on the portrait. Before he met Alexa Jamison.

III

The commission came from her boyfriend, who wanted it as a birthday gift for himself. She was twenty-five, and the boyfriend was eighty-three. He had made a fortune in local real estate and he managed all the concerts, plays, movie openings, and other events at the Orpheum Theatre. His name was Buddy Lessing. He knew everyone, and according to all the stories about him, he was tight as a drumhead. But evidently he was also cool. He had once smoked dope with Bob Dylan's band. And last summer, within the compass of a single day, he walked on the high catwalk of the Duomo in Florence with a group of tourists, and then later helped thwart a bomb plot in the Frankfurt Airport by noticing a man leaving a bag next to a newspaper kiosk. He led a wild life. People liked him. Women liked him. At least initially. He had been married seven times. One day he ambled into Terry's restaurant with three young men and saw a couple of the young man's paintings hanging along the back wall. One was of Lena Shumaker in tender sunset hues, sitting at the edge of the river with the bridge to Arkansas in the background. The other was of Hemingway in his forties, leaning on a table, thick arms slightly spread, looking off to the right.

"Who did those? They're very good."

"I did," said Shumaker. "That's my mother."

"Very nice."

"And that's Ernest Hemingway."

"No *shit*, son."

"Right."

"I met the guy, you know. When I was a young man. In Cuba. Before Castro. I was a good newspaperman. Once. Back in the early Jurassic period. But I met him. Shook hands with him. Big barrel-chested fella with a limp handshake. But then maybe he was a little sauced."

"Wow." Shumaker had made the painting from a picture in a magazine article.

The man brought a billfold from his suit pocket and took out a photograph. "Think you can do me a painting of this girl?"

"Probably. Sure."

"Beautiful, huh."

"Yes."

"Her name is Alexa. Would you say that's a sexy name?"

"I would, yeah."

"Alexa Jamison. So there's whiskey in it, too."

"Sir?"

"Jameson Irish whiskey, son."

"Oh."

"You think I'm cracked, don't you."

"No, sir."

"I'll pay you a hundred bucks."

"Can't do it for that, sir."

"Kidding. Three hundred."

"No, sir."

"I'll give you seven hundred more."

Shumaker looked at him.

"No doubt you've heard I'm a money squeezer."

"No, sir."

Mr. Lessing seemed suddenly tired of the talk. He sighed. "Fifteen hundred. Not a penny more."

"Yes, sir."

"Yes sir, no sir. Somebody worked on *you* growing up. I don't know that I like the result."

The young man said nothing.

"Your parents still with us?"

He nodded.

"What do they do?"

"My father's in the mathematics department at Memphis. My mother teaches English at Rhodes."

Lessing grinned. "Pedigree."

"Yes, sir."

"Well, so we have a deal. One thing. I want a nude. Think you can do that? Think you can do it without wanting to put your hands on her? She's gonna be my wife."

The young man saw the blotches in the other's skin, the sacks under the watery gray eyes. He said, "It's a professional circumstance, sir. I've done them before." In fact, he had done one, his junior year at Memphis, and the model was someone he knew from other classes, a friend, with ample Renaissance roundnesses from shoulders to hips, and there were nine other students in the room.

"So it would be routine for you."

Shumaker looked at the picture. "Yes."

"Somebody beautiful as this?"

"Well."

"Trick question, kid. There's nobody beautiful as this."

"Yes, sir."

"Right?"

Shumaker told him what he wanted to hear, and indeed the woman in the picture was beautiful.

THE EFFICIENCY APARTMENT had the one window in the door, and when Sonya came to visit him one morning he had made the joke that he saw the painting he could make of her framed there. He had been planning to do so, had made her stand in the window while he imagined it. He had even sketched her for it. And now he was going to do this other, Alexa Jamison, and it would be a nude.

The photograph did not do her justice.

She was astonishing. Shumaker felt that he understood the word *beauty* itself in a new way when he first saw her framed in the window, midmorning light on her blond hair like filamental fragments of the sun itself.

Young as she was, it turned out that she had been previously married and had a child who lived with her mother down in New Orleans. She told Shumaker this in that first meeting. She also claimed that she loved Buddy Lessing. "The most fascinating man," she said. "He told me that of all his wives, except the first one, I'm the best."

"Damn," Shumaker said.

"Well, he's honest. And I like that."

"But—God. He ranks them?"

"I'm the next best. We don't talk about the others."

They went to Otherlands Coffee Bar, and she asked him about

himself. It became something like a job interview. She had a contract Lessing had made up, that he wanted Shumaker to sign. The
contract stipulated that the painting be finished by October 20.
One month. He asked if it could be changed to read "on or about"
that date, and she made the change. "I'll get him to go along."
He saw the smooth skin of her hands, the bitten nails, which only
added to the attractiveness, as if that plain little facet held her to
the earth. He had never seen skin so flawless. Looking into her
soft eyes, he was already thinking of combinations of color. Ocean
water with turquoise depths.

"So," she said. "Tomorrow?"

"Okay."

"What time?"

"Morning? I have classes. And a job that takes up the late afternoons and evenings."

"Morning it is," she said.

Watching her drive away from the café, he thought of Sonya. He
called her number, even though it wasn't yet seven o'clock in LA.
He got her message machine. "Missing you," he said. "I know it's
early."

The following morning, before light, he was up and readying
himself. He had three stretched and primed canvases the size of
windows, and he put one on the easel and set out the paints he
would use and the other tools, the pencils and putty knives and
brushes. He arranged everything supposing she would stand for
the portrait. But when she arrived, smelling of flowers and bath
salts, and immediately got out of her jeans and white blouse, she
went to the unmade divan, and stretched out on her side.

"Um," he said. "Is that—"

She sat up, leaned on one hand, and rested the other on her
upper thigh, legs crossed demurely at the knees. "This is probably
better. You don't want me sitting at that table, do you?"

He was acutely aware of the little triangle of blond hair below
her navel. "No."

"This okay with you, then?" she asked.

"It's good, sure."

"I'm comfortable this way. I might fall asleep lying down."

"No, that's a perfect pose."

Embarrassed, trembling a little, he took up a pencil and, as he did with every portrait, began lightly sketching.

Through that first hour, he was carefully detached, gazing at the several structures of her perfect body as themselves alone, separate forms, as if he were looking at a statue. But then something began to take hold of him, and he stopped work and asked if she would like something cold to drink. The afternoon was terribly hot. Even the air-conditioning was futile against the humidity. The glass of orange juice he poured for her sweated, and she lounged back on the divan, with her top pulled haphazardly over her, and talked about how she never dreamed she could love someone so much older. He thought he heard something faintly sardonic in her tone.

"You're tall and broad shouldered." She sipped the orange juice. "My little boy's father's like you."

"Where's *he?*"

She shrugged. "Gone off." Her shoulders made him think about shoulders as a feature. He had the thought that what he felt now was of the province of fantasy and cliché.

"He ever see his son?"

"Doesn't know about him. Wouldn't care if he did."

"I would," Shumaker said.

"Well, you're different."

"Sounds like *he's* different. I don't know anybody who wouldn't want to see his own son."

"Okay. *He's* different."

"So where's he gone off to?"

Again, she shrugged. "Somewhere out west, I guess. Pacific Northwest, last I heard. He grew a big white beard and looks like Jerry Garcia now. Last time I saw him anyway." Her lips curled slightly at the corners. He thought of kissing them. It wasn't an urge to kiss *her*, but a sense of the luscious ripe softness of the mouth.

He said, "My mother used to say that about me being broad shouldered. Like it's a good thing."

"Oh, it's a *very* good thing."

"I never could see myself as being any different than other guys, though." Suddenly, without premeditation, his whole mind was fixed on saying the right things to make her come to him.

She looked straight at him. "I think you're very attractive. I like your eyes."

"Nothing like how beautiful yours are."

"Your irises don't touch the bottom lids. I don't think I've ever seen that before."

"They don't—I never noticed that." He felt stupid.

"Buddy says he's sure I'll probably take up with other men after we're married."

"He does." The tremulousness of his own voice surprised and embarrassed him. Breathing had become a question of getting the air out of his chest. It seemed to be gathering just under his neck.

"I think he means to tempt me, really. See how far I'll go."

Shumaker waited.

"Wanna see how far I'll go?"

I V

What followed was unlike anything he had ever experienced or dreamed. When at last it was over and they lay breathing and sighing, he said, "You can't marry Lessing. My God."

She smiled, turned, and offered herself for a kiss.

And he was aware of kissing *her* now, not just those lips. He grasped her by the shoulders. "I mean it," he said again. "You can't marry Lessing."

"Don't be absurd." She giggled, almost inaudibly.

He let go and simply lay there for a moment. "But—God. Don't do it."

"He's very nice, you know." But she was starting again, kissing his chest.

"Say you won't," he said.

"Okay," she murmured, and licked down his abdomen.

HE SAW HER four more times that week. The painting, the use of the oils, began as a blur. Twice he started over. At the end of each sitting, there would be another session on the divan, turns and refinements that would give him fever dreams in the night. She told him of her loves, the travels she had done, how it was that she took up with Lessing. None of it made any difference. None of it quite sank in. The sound of her voice quelled all the agitations of his mind.

"You're actually gonna marry Lessing?"

She shrugged. "I've been putting him off awhile now."

"I have to make some headway with this painting."

"We'll play around, and he travels a lot."

"But you don't understand. I'm in love."

She leaned into him, pressing her lips to the side of his neck. Then: "I feel exactly the same. Isn't it amazing."

SONYA CALLED EARLY the next week to say that her parents wanted to come with her when she returned from LA.

For an instant, he could not speak.

"They think the whole family should get together. They've decided to try and make the best of me living in Memphis."

"So they're—"

"They think they're coming with me. Yes."

"I—well, I don't think they should spend the money."

"I don't care about the money. *I'd* rather they stay home."

"You can't get them to stay home?" He almost told her everything.

"I'm going to pitch a fit and see if I can make them put it off."

"That's probably best."

After a beat, she said, "Do you miss me?"

"Don't be silly."

"You sound funny."

He listened for whatever else she might make of things.

"You haven't met someone else, have you?" she asked, clearly teasing.

"Have *you*?" He hoped she had.

"I love you," she said.

Nearly choking on the very air, he said, "Me, too. You."

He drove downtown, to Automatic Slim's, and sat outside on the sidewalk. Two couples were there who knew each other. Normal people having a good time, leading calm, uncomplicated lives. He drank a whiskey, then walked up to the top of Union, and looked out at the river and the bridge to Arkansas.

HE COULD NOT SLEEP, think, eat, *be* with anybody else. He spent hours with the painting after she'd gone, sometimes just sitting, staring at her face, the face he had painted. He knew almost nothing about her. She had a child in New Orleans. She was from there, but lived for a long time in Little Rock. Her father died before she was old enough to remember him. There were no brothers or sisters. She had lived with her mother in Little Rock, and they'd had a falling-out over her relationship with her mother's boyfriend. She said the word *boyfriend* and then smirked. "*Boyfriend* sounds so juvenile. I use *beau*. The first part of the word *beauty*, right? Just add the *t* and *y*."

"You had a relationship with your mother's boyfriend?"

"Beau."

"Okay, beau."

She looked at her bitten nails, and her eyelids came down slightly over those eyes. "A brief one."

"How did you meet Lessing?"

"Let's not talk anymore."

"Please," he said.

"I met him one afternoon. I was walking along Beale Street, looking in the clubs. Broad daylight, and there he was sitting outside the King's Palace Café, smoking a big cigar. First thing he said to me was 'You're exquisite.' Just like that. I said, 'Thanks.' And he said, 'Young lady, I have a lot of money and I'd like to show you a good time.' It was so frank and appealing, you know? And I had no money left, I was out of a job. Actually I was thinking of panhandling."

"What was your job before?"

She considered, but she was still thinking about Lessing. "We're a lot alike, actually. I do have fun with him. He's eighty-three and for him it's all one big game. That's how he thinks of it. A great fun exciting game, and he even calls it that. Everything's just gaming. From one thing to the next. He does what he wants and he sees who he wants and spends what he wants."

"He's eighty-three," Shumaker said. "It's grotesque that you're with him."

"Don't talk like that. Why do you want to ruin everything like that." She seemed about to cry. "People shouldn't say mean things like that. You don't know what you're talking about."

"You're not with him just for the money."

"Maybe I was at first." Her tone now was defiant.

"Look, I'm sorry," Shumaker said. "Please forgive me."

"Here you are with this beautiful gift, young and strong and pretty, and you have to talk like that about a man you don't know."

"Forgive me. Please." He put his arms around her. "Please, I'm in love with you. I'm just jealous. It's just jealousy talking."

They were quiet, then, for a very long while. She fell asleep in his arms. He lay there watching the light move to the other side of the window in the door. His arm hurt. But he kept still, and at last she woke up, yawning, and again he asked for her forgiveness.

HE STARTED GETTING THINGS WRONG at the restaurant. He couldn't make eye contact the way he used to. He led people to unset tables, forgot menus, got orders wrong, and one night he spilled hot coffee in a man's lap. The thick folded napkin there saved the man from being badly burned. His uncle had spoken to his father, and so of course his uncle knew about Alexa.

"You can't keep messing up like this."

"I know." They were in the men's room. Shumaker's hands shook pulling a paper towel from the dispenser. "I'll do better."

"Why don't you bring the girl here?"

His mind was blank.

"You ashamed of us or something? Why hasn't she been to meet your parents, for that matter."

"I'm—I'm painting her. That's the only time I see her."

"You don't ask her out for a date? This girl you're ass over elbows in love with?"

"It's complicated."

"Well, you're a grown man and all that. Your business, but this place is *my* business, and if you keep messing up, I'm going to have to find somebody else."

"Yes, sir."

"Don't 'sir' me, for Christ's sake. I'm your uncle."

"Yes, s—yes."

The next afternoon, at the appointed time, after they had set up and he had tried again with the painting and found that his hands shook too badly to make much progress at all, he went to the divan and sat next to her.

"Well?" she said. "What do you want to do now, lover?" She leaned toward him.

"Come out with me. I want you to meet the family. We could have dinner at my parents' house."

Kissing the side of his face, she said, "I'm occupied in the evenings. You know that."

"You can't get away for one evening?"

Now she stopped, and shook her head. "He's been good to me."

"But you said we could see each other and—"

"I *know* what I said. Oh, baby. Let's not talk about it now." She put her hands in his hair.

V

The next morning, his mother came to the apartment. He was sitting at the table, staring across at the unfinished painting, when he heard the gravel pop in the little driveway outside. Glancing out the window in the door, he saw her car pulling in. He stood as if caught, and knocked the chair over. "Christ." The rasping in his own voice surprised him. He looked at the mess of the place—clothes strewn on the bed and chairs, the scraps of aborted sketches and versions in a welter of brushes and tubes of paint on the one table, and the several finished and unfinished canvases leaning against the wall. Then he was looking for signs of what had transpired on the divan. He covered the painting, righted the chair, and opened the door before his mother could ring the bell.

"So," she said. "Talk to me."

"I'm sorry. I don't know what to say."

"I've been on the phone with Sonya's mother. She's picked me for her new friend, and that carries a price, I'm afraid. I don't mean to sound petty."

He stepped out and closed the door. "Did you tell her?"

She glanced beyond him. "That's *your* job. But I'm thinking I won't pick up anymore when the woman calls. I mean she's talking about all of us getting together. Well, they *would*, wouldn't they, under the circumstances. That's what anyone would expect. It's actually very nice and it fills me with guilt and foreboding and dread. 'So full of artless jealousy is guilt, it spills itself in fearing to be spilt.'" She looked at him. It was a little game they had played since he was in high school: she would toss him quotes from Shakespeare, and he would try to guess the character and the play.

"*Hamlet,*" he said. "Gertrude."

She smiled. "Good." Then, after a brief pause: "You *are* going to take care of this, right?"

He could only nod.

"Come on," she said. "Let's go eat breakfast."

"I've been concentrating so hard on the painting," he told her. "I forget to eat."

"Can I see what you've got so far?"

"Not a chance."

"All right." She stared for a few seconds. Then: "Shall we go?"

A wind was getting up from the west, a thunderstorm approaching. He let her drive him to Brother Juniper's. There was a line. They stood under the porch roof with others and waited. "So when will we have the chance to meet her?"

"It's only been a couple weeks."

The rain started, and over the roofs of the buildings down the street lightning forked and flashed. The rain came down in big drops, then just ceased, and there was only the wind.

"Well. Are we going to meet her? Your hands are shaking."

He folded his arms.

"I don't think I like what this is doing to you."

"I'm fine. I'm working on a painting. You know how dopey I get when I'm painting."

The line in front of them moved. "We want you to bring her to dinner."

"All right."

"Tonight?"

"I'll ask. I'm having trouble with the painting."

"You're looking at the real thing."

"Excuse me?"

"You're in love."

Hearing his mother say the words made him feel suddenly as though there were something profoundly false about it all. He was not prepared for the sensation. When they finally sat down, he had lost his appetite. He ordered coffee and tried to keep his hands still while she ate a Spanish omelet and a bowl of blueberries with yogurt.

"Being in love takes away the appetite," she said, "or else increases it." She smiled. She was a very appealing lady with a rich contralto voice and a charming aphoristic way of speaking. Her students admired her. "Do you know what I think love is really about?"

"Mom."

"Well, I *am* older than you are and I get to make these kinds of pronouncements. Especially to my son, who apparently has no idea."

"I know what I feel," he said.

"Of course you do. And you felt the same thing for Sonya."

"No. I *thought* I did."

"Yes." His mother smiled tolerantly. "Of course. Romeo forgets Rosaline in the first instant he sees Juliet. But they're *children*, you know. Juliet's not yet fourteen."

"I know the play," he said.

"Do you know when I knew I was in love with your father? We were horseback riding and he fell. He looked so silly, and he was embarrassed and tried to hide how bad he'd hurt his hip. That walk, with him struggling so hard to keep from limping. And the hip was badly bruised, you know. I never thought I'd have any interest in him at all. I mean with a name like Wilfred. But there he was trying to hide how much it hurt, and my heart just went crack."

The young man knew something of the story—a version of it: she had always said that it's in our weaknesses and vulnerability that we are most lovable. He said, "I don't know where or how, or anything. I just know I'm gone on her."

"Well, you have to bring her over. And you have to tell Sonya. *In person.*"

"I know. Wilfred already said."

"And don't be a smart ass."

He was silent.

"I assume this new girl has parents we'll have to meet and get to know?"

"No. They're gone." It was simpler just to leave it at that. No part of the history, even what little he knew of it, would please or reassure his mother.

"I've always thought of you as my levelheaded son," she said. "So I'm gonna trust that you know what you're doing."

Smiling at her, he was full of the sense of deceit, and hoped it did not show in his face.

She wiped her mouth with her napkin. Then: "Well, let us know. We'll welcome her."

"Yes, ma'am."

Her eyes narrowed in a way he recognized. "Ma'am?" she said. "What am I, a schoolteacher lady?" Then she made a show of seeming to arrive at a realization, raising her hand, index finger pointing up. "Oh, right. I guess I am, huh."

"Sorry," he told her.

"I think it's a safe bet that you're gonna need that *very* word a *lot* in the days to come."

He nodded, and forced a smile.

V I

Reality seemed to be collapsing. Something had been unleashed in him. As the days went on, he began to see every woman sexually, and he could not keep from imagining them naked in bed. The details of lovemaking, the physiology of it, the fact that they opened their legs in that way, those images kept rushing through him like some sort of pornographic new knowledge. He kept seeing the images, kept seeing *her*. He spent an hour working on the painting and dreaming of her on the morning of Sonya's arrival, and he was late to the airport. He decided to say there had been a backup, an accident on 240. This was a tremendously hot day for fall. Late October and burning. Not a cloud in the sky. There really was a lot of traffic on 240, so it wouldn't be entirely dishonest to say that he had been held up.

And here he was, already thinking about *seeming* honest. He had wanted to be a man like his father, someone of steady quiet integrity. A married man with a family. It went through him like the knowledge of mortality that he had thought of Sonya as the mother of his future children.

Her plane had landed, but was not at the gate. Relieved, he went to Maggie O'Shea's and had a beer. Then he walked over to where she would come out. He waited for what seemed a long time after the plane was shown to be at the gate. And finally here she came. She had put makeup on, and smiled shyly, an uncharacteristically fretful smile.

She put two bags down and stretched out her arms, and he accepted her embrace, breathing the fresh flower scent of her hair. She wore earrings he had given her. Leaning back, arms still around him, she murmured, "Well, aren't you going to kiss me?"

He did so. She moved against him and held tight and opened her mouth. It was a long, terribly uncomfortable kiss. Finally she let him go and he picked up the bags.

"Let me have that one," she said.

"It's heavy."

"It's my purse, you goof."

"It's new."

"There's two more bags coming. I bought some things."

A baritone male voice announced that there were only two places where smoking was allowed in the airport. He heard the name Maggie O'Shea's again.

"Okay," she said. "What's the matter?"

He stopped. There wasn't enough air or light.

"You smell like alcohol, David."

"I had a beer."

"Okay." She waited. "Well?"

"I don't know how to say this."

"You better tell me." Her eyes flashed. "You're scaring me."

"All right. I'm just going to say it out. Okay? I can't—I can't—I—I can't marry you. I'm in love."

"Someone got you pregnant, and so you—" Before she finished the sentence, her eyes widened, and the color began leaving her face.

"I'm so sorry," he said.

"You're *sorry*."

"I fell in love."

"You're not *kidding*."

"No." He felt stronger now, looking into the narrowing dark eyes, the face twisting slightly, all the attractiveness he had seen leeching out in a furious glare.

"You came here to tell me this? You picked me up, just to tell me this?"

"Dad thought I should tell you in person."

"Your father."

Shumaker simply stared.

"And—so we're done, then? You're gonna take me to my place and say goodbye forever."

"We can still be friends," he got out.

In the next instant, it seemed, he was on his back and a man was holding his face between rough, long-fingered hands. "You're all right," the man said. "Help's coming."

"Pardon me?"

"Don't move. You took a fall."

"I've got to pick up Sonya."

"Just stay still."

A void followed. Nothingness, and then he opened his eyes to see people gliding past him. He realized vaguely—as if he were in the middle of trying to parse a dream—that he was being carried out of the airport on a stretcher. A nervous-looking little bald man who was walking along next to the men carrying him spoke: "I saw it all. They were talking and suddenly she hit him with her bag, and he went over. He hit his head pretty hard on the floor."

"Yes, sir. We've got him."

There was another span of absence, of nowhere, not even being cognizant of sleep. He found himself sitting on a hard surface, not much wider than an ironing board, being put carefully down on his back, and riding into a confining off-white tube. And soon he was lying in a bed, and a tall black man with thick dark eyebrows and mustache was standing over him. Shumaker thought of disguises and masks.

"You've had a serious concussion."

"I was supposed to pick up Sonya."

"You have no fracture, but you're going to have to be very still for a while, and rest."

"Fracture?"

"Someone said the young woman hit you with her handbag, and you fell and hit the back of your head."

"But I'm supposed to—Sonya."

"We were told the young woman took a cab home."

"My parents should—I don't understand. I'm supposed to be at my apartment at five."

The doctor looked at his watch. Then: "What day is it?"

Shumaker told him.

"When is your birthday?"

He told him that, too. "Look, I'm all right."

"Not dizzy?"

He tried to sit up, then lay back down. "A little dizzy."

"Let's just wait a couple hours, see how you are. Concussion's nothing to fool with."

"She hit me with her bag?"

"Fellow said you were talking, and she looked to be getting agitated, and suddenly she just up and swung the bag."

"I don't remember any of it. I don't remember seeing her."

"They said she waited for her bags and took them and went on out of the place while people were working over you. You were out cold, apparently."

"I went there to meet her."

"That's the way it is with concussions. You know, you never see the punch that knocks you out. And believe me, you were *out* when they brought you in here."

Suddenly, he was crying. The tall man stood there patiently, one hand on his chest, and waited. But Shumaker couldn't gain control of himself. He broke forth finally, "If I could see someone. My mother or father."

"They should be here soon. There's a police officer here who wants to ask you a couple things. You up to it?"

"I guess."

The police officer, who had been at the airport, walked over with a little notebook and a pencil and asked for his full name and his address. Shumaker gave them to him.

"I'm assuming you knew the young woman?"

"Yes."

"Can you say what happened?"

"I broke up with—I broke our engagement. And I guess she hit me."

The officer wrote something down, and seemed to cough.

"I was gonna do it over the phone, but my father said I should do it in person."

He nodded, and turned and coughed again, and in the next moment Shumaker realized he was laughing. The officer cleared his throat, ran his forearm across his mouth, and took a breath. "Guess you'll want to say something to your father."

"No, sir."

Once more, the cough, the head turning away. Then: "Uh—agh. Well. Do you want to press charges? What she did qualifies as assault and battery."

Shumaker looked at him.

"Well?"

"No, sir."

"You're sure."

"I don't want to see her again."

"I guess not."

"I'd like to forget about it, please."

"I understand," the officer said, folding the notebook. "Well, I guess that's it, then."

"Yes, sir."

It seemed that in a blink he was gone. Replaced by the tall doctor, looming over him, all concentration.

"Did I pass out again?"

"You went to sleep. An hour. See if you can sleep a little more."

"Do my parents know what happened?"

"I believe the young woman may have called your mother. She's—your mother—she's on her way here. They're on their way here."

"The young woman?"

The doctor smiled. "No. Your parents."

"Did I have a CAT scan?"

"That's right. And there's no bleeding."

"I'm tremendously sleepy." He sobbed. "Is this normal?"

"It's all to be expected."

HE SLEPT. NO DREAMS, NOTHING. Only a form of nonbeing that he recognized as the same sort of absence of sensation that had come down on him in the airport. When he woke, he saw his mother sitting in the chair by his bed. His father stood gazing out the window at the darkness.

"How long have I been here?" Shumaker asked her.

"A little over three hours."

His father walked over. "You think you can sit up now?"

"Think so."

"Don't go too fast," said his mother.

He turned on his side and came to a sitting position. There was a little dizziness, but it wore off as he straightened. His mother stood before him and looked into his eyes.

"I have to get in touch with Alexa," he told her.

"You can call her from home."

"I was supposed to meet her at my place. I couldn't get through to her."

"We know why you can't call her, Son." His father came and pulled gently on his arm above the elbow, helping him stand.

The doctor spoke from the door. "Take it slow. No lifting and no straining for at least a week. And you should probably see your family doctor next week. Just to be cautious about it."

"I will," Shumaker said, feeling his father's attention, like being nine years old again.

"You want to talk about it?" the professor asked.

"No."

"You want to tell me what's going on?" demanded his mother of them both, looking from one to the other.

"The new girlfriend belongs to someone else."

"How'd you—?" Shumaker began.

"Mr. Lessing walked into the restaurant looking for you. Told Terry you're doing a portrait of his lady friend."

"Oh."

"Yeah." Wilfred Shumaker turned to his wife. "Lena, give us a second, will you?"

She stared for a moment, then went out.

"Okay, Son. This is just—I'm really worried."

"Dad, she's the most amazing person."

"Really. Okay, why is that? Really. Tell me how you know that. Have you seen her with other people? Is there some public record of service to humankind? What exactly do you know about her, Son?"

"I know I'm in love with her."

"And she's supposed to marry a very powerful man in this city."

"Lessing? He's eighty-three."

His father's voice rose. "Don't be naïve."

For a moment, neither of them spoke.

"You're in here with a concussion. Terry says your work has suffered. You don't come see us—"

"The painting . . ."

"I don't *care* about the painting, okay? I care about you with a concussion and about what else might happen when this Lessing guy gets wind of what's going on. And this—this Alexa, what's *she* doing? How can you go along like this cheating with her and knowing what she's doing when she goes back to *him*? Does that look right to you? How does that *feel*?"

"I just know I have to be with her, Dad."

"Well, where *is* she?"

There wasn't anything to say.

"You have to *be* with her. Does she feel the same way about you? Where is she? Son, you just got clocked by one girl because of this other one, and where *is* she? *Who* is she? Are you in touch with her? *Can* you be in touch with her? You can't bring her over to the house, because this is an *affair*. And you know there's nothing at all romantic about this kind of thing—it's sordid and low and vulgar, and it means lying and stealing around dark corners and worrying all the time about getting caught. Is that the kind of life you want? And for what? For a woman with a good body and sex?"

"Stop it," Shumaker said.

"Well, really, Son. You know what? When I was first married to your mother, I formed a friendship with this other woman, someone in the math department. We were at a conference together, and I got to liking being around her and listening to her talk and watching her move." The professor looked over his shoulder at the doorway, then turned and lowered his voice. "So I said something about her, about how she was sexy, to Terry. You know? Brothers talking. And Terry had already been through his divorce with Megan—well, you never knew Megan. But you know what he said to me? He interrupted me as I was talking, right? Two guys in their twenties, and he shook his head at me and said, 'Buddy, even if she can plug that thing into the wall socket and make it spin. Don't do it.'"

"Jesus," said Shumaker, low.

"It's a rough way to talk, I know. But the point was well taken."

"I don't want to marry Sonya anymore, Dad."

His father raised his voice again. "I'm not *talking* about Sonya. Don't be stupid. This isn't about her. It's not even about this—Alexa person. It's about *you*. What kind of man you want to be. What kind of man I'm afraid you're gonna turn yourself into."

Again, they were both silent.

"Well, it *is* finally your business," said the professor. And then he leaned in close. "But maybe just for me, just as a very small favor for me, okay? Could you maybe take some time—just a while, a little probationary period, say—where you try, for me, and maybe for your mother as well, to stop thinking with your dick." He stared, nodded very slightly, then turned, walked to the door, and looked back. "Come on. We'll take you home."

"My car's at the airport."

"You can't drive." His tone was pure exasperation. He went on with sardonic patience: "We got your car. Your mother drove it back to our place and I followed her. That's why we didn't get here right away. You're not going to your apartment. You have to stay down for a few days. No exertions, no lifting, no driving or drinking. Just rest. You have to come with us."

Shumaker followed his father down the long corridor, where his mother waited, looking sorrowful and embarrassed, too. In the car, they didn't speak. The radio was on low, two men talking about the National Football League.

At the house, his father reached into his jacket pocket, brought out a small cellophane bag, and handed it to him. His cell phone and wallet were inside.

"Personal effects?" Shumaker asked.

His mother gasped. "That is not slightly funny."

"I don't think he meant it to be funny," said his father.

"I'm sorry for all of this," Shumaker told them. He went up to his room and sat on the bed. His parents had stayed downstairs and were talking in low tones; it sounded like an argument. He touched Alexa's number. No answer. There was one message, from the night before—Sonya. "Just getting ready to come home. I can't wait to see you. I love you."

He lay back and listened to it again, and then tried once more to call Alexa. Nothing. Not even a way to leave a message. Just the ringing, while he listened and waited.

HE TRIED THE NUMBER over and over in the next four days. His mother brought food upstairs to the room and attempted to talk to him. His father came in once, but mostly kept to his downstairs study.

"I don't understand why I have to stay here," Shumaker said to his mother.

"You've had a concussion. There's no mystery about it at all. You have to stay down. In case you haven't noticed, you're still unsteady on your feet."

It was true. Getting up in the middle of the night to use the bathroom—the pain medication they had given him had a diuretic effect—he had to keep one hand on the wall and make his way slowly. The world spun. There were headaches. He lay in bed with the cell phone to his ear listening to the ringing of Alexa's. It went on and on. He thought of calling Buddy Lessing. He could use the painting as pretext. But he lacked the nerve. Once he fell asleep with the little phone at his ear, and the faint ringing on the other end, and woke up to find it silent and dead under his arm.

VII

At the end of the long week he got into his rust-eroded car and drove to his apartment and the pile of work, of attempts to depict her in various sketches, and the abortive smearing of oil, as he thought of it, of the painting itself. His mother followed him and watched him go inside. He waved from the door, called to her that he would be at the restaurant that evening.

After he closed the door, he stood for a moment looking at the room: his mother had been busy here. The dishes were put away. The sink was clean. She had spread a comforter on the divan and arranged the chairs around the one table. The recliner on which he had stacked work and clothes was clear, the clothes were hanging in the closet, and the work was neatly arranged on the top shelf of the cinder-block-and-plank bookcase. He moved to the divan and sat crying. There was nothing but junk in his mailbox. He looked into his little refrigerator and found one beer and a Styrofoam container of rice and beans from the Rum Boogie Café. He threw this away and drank the beer. He had a powerful thirst. After the beer, he gulped three tall glasses of water from the tap. Then he walked out into the sun and stood gazing up the short gravel drive to the road, thinking of Alexa. Where was she? He walked down the street to the 7-Eleven and the public phone. But it was broken. There was no handset.

At last he drove to the Orpheum and parked across the street. Tourists had already begun gathering at the head of Beale Street, and police stood at the barricade, smoking and talking. It wasn't even noon yet and the heat was oppressive, humidity rising from the river. There wasn't anyone at the Orpheum. The doors were locked, the big lobby empty and dark. Tonight was classic-movie night: *Desk Set.*

Back at the apartment, he tried to focus on the painting, and three hours passed with the quickness of work time: he looked up and realized that he had spent it toiling with unsteady fingers over one element of the color in the hair framing the face—that face— meticulously putting daubs of tawny shade on one side of a curl, a thin streak of white and gold on the other. He wanted to get it right, the way the sun blazed there. It was as if he were manipulating the light itself from the end of his brush. He stepped back and looked at what he had, the flawless body in that indolent pose. His heart leaped. He threw the brush he was holding against the door—and saw a man standing there, staring in at him through the window. His heart leaped again, and a sound rose from the back of his throat.

The other knocked on the glass, and that also startled him. He reached to open the door, gasping low. "Yes?"

"David Shumaker, right?"

"Yes."

The man wore a sweat-stained Memphis Redbirds baseball cap and a white short-sleeved shirt with big sweat circles under the arms. His unshaven face was squarish, wide jawed, with deep-socketed dull brown eyes and a thin nose that stood out of the center of it like a blade. "I've been coming here every day for a week," he said. "Mr. Lessing wants to know what the progress is on his painting."

"It's not finished."

He reached into his pants pocket and brought out an iPhone. "I'm supposed to take a picture of it."

"It's not ready for that," Shumaker told him quickly. "Please. And my—the—the model hasn't been anyplace where I could find her."

"Nobody could find *you,* man."

"I had an injury. I was in the hospital. I'm back now. And I want to finish the painting."

The man looked past him into the apartment, at the painting. "Looks done to me, man."

"It's not finished," Shumaker said.

"Okay." The other shrugged. "I'll tell him."

"But I need the model." Perhaps this was said a bit too forcefully.

The man's eyes narrowed. "I'll pass it on, buddy."

"Tell her I've been trying to call her," said Shumaker, adding quickly, "I mean could you please tell her for me?"

"Hey, *I'm* not in touch with her, man. I'll tell Mr. Lessing."

"But she's got to know I couldn't call her because I was in the hospital with an injury."

"Got it," the man said, walking away.

"Tell her I'm here," said Shumaker.

HE CAME TO REALIZE, during the course of the long afternoon, that the painting was actually quite good, and that his sense of the smeary nature of it was false, was a kind of holding on. It was a precise and achingly realistic rendering of her physical splendor. There was nothing left to do, short of starting over from some other angle, with another canvas.

And she was nowhere.

She did not come to him or answer her phone through the afternoon and into the evening. He went to the restaurant and took his uncle's questioning about being assaulted in full view of everyone by a young woman in an airport. Others teased him, talking about the fury of a woman scorned. And how even after attacking the offending former fiancé, Sonya had possessed the presence of mind to wait for her luggage before leaving the airport. A couple of the waitstaff knew her, of course, and they were obviously being careful not to speak of what she was doing with herself now, and he did not ask. He performed his job with a kind of blind diligence, always expecting Buddy Lessing to show up, or Alexa. But the night passed, and on his way home he stopped and used a credit card to buy a bottle of straight rye whiskey. When he got to the apartment, he opened the bottle and poured a tumbler full, planning to drink himself into a stupor. It was something he might show Alexa, something that might cause her to take pity on him. But before he had drunk half of what he'd poured, it made him feel sick, and then, as if something in the very air were seeking to instruct him, he developed a toothache. It lasted the night. He ended up rubbing the whiskey on his gums to numb them.

Early that next morning as he started out of the place, sleepless and still feeling the toothache, there she was, coming down the gravel path from the road. He waited in the open door, expecting her to step into his arms. She smiled and edged past him, actually stepped aside when he reached for her. Moving to the divan, she sat down and gazed impassively at the painting on its easel. It was the unemotional stare of someone looking at herself in a mirror. Then she glanced at the room. "You cleaned the place."

"My mother."

"Nice."

"I kept trying to call you," he said. "I've been desperate. I got hurt. I thought you were gone for good. Jesus. I got hurt. I had a fall."

"But you're all right."

"No, I'm not all right." He picked up the bottle of whiskey on the table and placed his paint-stained finger on the line that showed it was almost half gone. "You see this? I drank this down to there. Why didn't you answer me? Why didn't you call me back?" He put the bottle down hard. "You can't imagine what I've—" She had spoken as he began, and he caught himself. "What?"

"We were in Spain."

"Spain."

Smiling that alluring soft-lipped smile, she went on, in a faintly incredulous tone, as if there could be nothing more reasonable than deciding on a whim to fly across the Atlantic. "I *said* we were in *Spain*."

He could not speak.

"Buddy decided he wanted to see Barcelona. And Madrid. And drink Spanish wine."

Silence.

"You know how he is. He's got all the money in the world and he's like a spoiled little boy who can't be controlled."

"I love you," Shumaker told her. "I'm *in* love with you."

"You just love misbehaving with me. Like I love it. I do. And I do misbehave sometimes, you know, just to misbehave. I have fun. And I've just been to Spain."

He took a step toward her. "I love *you*. My God, Alexa."

"You don't *know* me."

"What's changed?" He could barely get the words out.

"Well, we finally got married. On a cruise up the Spanish coast. Buddy and me. The captain married us."

"Oh, God. You—oh, Jesus—"

"It's all right, baby, nothing else has changed. Well, almost nothing else."

"You—" He moved to the recliner and sat down, like a collapse. The painting was across from him, exactly to her left. It was as if she were posing for a photograph of herself with the painting—she had even taken something of the same pose, the legs crossed, the long, lovely torso very straight, so that the breasts stood out.

"Oh, God," he breathed.

"I told you I was engaged. What'd you think that meant?"

"Why didn't you call me back? All those calls."

"I left my phone in Memphis. Isn't that silly? And I couldn't make up an excuse to call you from Spain, on my honeymoon." She sighed; it was more of a little laugh. "Just wouldn't look good. But you know what? It turns out it would've been okay." She looked at the painting. The gesture made it clear that now she was going to change the subject. With an air of someone who feels relief after long effort, she said, "Ah, so it's done now. And what a perfect likeness."

"Please leave," he managed to say.

"No, but I mean it really *is* okay." She pulled the skirt she wore up over her knees. "Come here, lover."

After another series of inexpressibly dazzling passes on the divan, she sat up and stretched, as if just waking from a nap. Gazing at her long spine, he realized finally that it wasn't the things she did during sex so much as the extraordinary flawlessness of all her features, of every turn of flesh and hair, and the slender hands, the eyes, the unreal fineness of her form and her willingness to use herself for delights. She looked over her shoulder at him.

"Oh, Christ," he said. "I don't care. He's an old, old man. I don't care. I'll wait for something to happen."

"Stop it. Stop that."

"No, I mean it. And we can go on like this. I'll find a way to make it last. I'll fuck this painting up—I'll splash black paint on it or burn it, so I have to start over."

She laughed.

He lay there watching this. The laugh went on. "No," she got out finally. "Don't do that. I'm telling you. Really, it's all right."

"I don't get it."

"Well, see—thing is, he knows all about it."

"He—*what*? He knows about *this*?"

"It came out when we were in Madrid. And he—well, he wants to watch us. He—he says he wants to sit and watch us do it."

"He *knows* about us."

She merely gazed back, a stare as blank as that of a carved-stone face. "Seventy-three calls from you on my phone. No explaining that anyway, right?"

A sudden rush of fright gripped him. "You're serious."

"So even if it didn't come out when we were in Spain."

"Jesus Christ."

Neither of them spoke for a few seconds.

"And?" Shumaker demanded.

"And what? He wants to watch us."

"Jesus. The answer's no, right?"

"Well, I guess. If you say so."

He was unable to utter a word.

"But I don't know. I mean I think it might be kind of kinky."

"*Kinky,*" he said. "Kind of? *Kind* of kinky?"

"Darling. It's all—being alive. New things. I'm not settling down for any one man, and he's all right with that. He's very cool."

"I know, but—no. No, we love each other."

"Well." Her cell phone buzzed in her purse on the floor. She took it out and looked at the little window. "It's him."

"Don't answer it."

She smiled with a coy tilt of her head, brushed the lustrous strands of hair from the side of her face, and held the phone to her ear. "Hi."

Shumaker put his slacks on and went to the door and out. There didn't seem to be any strength in his legs. The sun blazed through the pine boughs and leaves of the trees; the smell of crepe myrtle was so heavy that his gorge rose. He wanted to go back to before he ever knew her, wanted out of this urging of his body when she was near. He saw in a moment of sickening clarity that spiritually she repelled him. There was nothing he liked about her. And he wanted her so much that here he was, now, standing in the heat and thickness of the summer afternoon, entertaining the idea of going through with it—giving Buddy Lessing what he desired—as long as he, Shumaker, could go on being with her.

"God," he said aloud. Then again, under his breath. "Oh, *God.*"

She came out, dressed, her purse over her shoulder. "I have to go."

"Yeah."

"Do you want me to come back?"

He shook his head. But as she started to where she had parked, he said, "Yes."

She stopped and turned. "The painting's really fine."

"Yeah," he said. "Beautiful."

"I'll tell Buddy."

"No—look. It's not finished. I've still got some work to do on it."

"I sure can't see *what*."

They were standing perhaps ten feet apart. "Well, you'll just have to trust me. I know what I'm doing. It needs a few more touches."

"Is that an excuse for *us*?"

"No," he said flatly, certain that she wouldn't believe him, and feeling sick again, but now not for what this was but for the prospect of not seeing her again. Before she started on, he said, "You're just—it's just—gaming with you, isn't it."

"Gaming?"

He waited.

"Funny thing to say. That's Buddy's word. Anyway I loved every minute of being with you. You're very nice, you know. A tender lover."

"You, too," he told her. It was automatic, though it came from the pit of his stomach.

"So, I guess we'll want to think about more work on the painting." She winked.

"No, I finished it." He nearly choked on the words.

"Well, just—let me know." She turned and strolled toward her car, the purse draped over her shoulder.

VIII

That evening at the restaurant he went through the long minutes smiling and nodding, and seeming himself, and was surprised that he could manage it.

When he got back to the apartment he sat staring at the painting—his work. He could not go to sleep, could not concentrate. He watched TV and drank some of the whiskey, and then had coffee, looking at the painting from every angle. He felt no sense of her as being *like* a drug. She *was* the drug, the addicting difficulty itself. He could not unthink, unsee, unremember everything that had passed between them. It all played across his mind like a mural in hell.

He stared at the painting, the depiction, and thought about how she was the fullest delineation of his most secret yearning heart. He couldn't sleep.

At dawn, he called the number. No answer. He took a long walk, down to Otherlands, and sat watching happy people talking and laughing and eating. The day was already too warm. He ordered a black coffee and granola, but finished neither. Twice more he tried to call. Nothing. Back at the apartment, he brought out another primed canvas and started to paint. He had no idea of anything but was simply making strokes with the brush in the array of colors. An exercise in manipulating the shades of light and shapes of color, and very quickly it ended, ran out, like a strand of thought. He put it aside. And got another frame and started something else. There was the hoped-for show to think about.

He spent the day working, sketches, arrangements of lines and light—he had always preferred portraits, and occasionally scenes, busy and bright and full of mottled sun and shade as Renoir's *Luncheon of the Boating Party*. But these were simply different gradations of form and tint, abstract and pointless, too. All that day he kept trying to call her, and all that day he got nothing but the steady rattle on the other end.

He called in sick at the restaurant.

On Monday the restaurant was closed, and he spent the whole day painting, eating little, drinking small half shots from the bottle of whiskey. He wasn't tasting it. It was merely to calm himself, get his hands steady. Now and then he gazed at Alexa in her square of canvas, that exquisite shape, the lush pelagic color of the eyes, the voluptuousness of the mouth, the immaculate lines of the neck and shoulders and breasts, the little blond triangle, the perfect skin.

Tuesday morning the man in the Memphis Redbirds cap came to collect the painting. He held out a check for a thousand dollars.

"It's supposed to be fifteen hundred," Shumaker said. "And it's still not finished."

"Right. This is for the painting in its unfinished state."

"I can't let it go for that."

"Mr. Lessing thought you might feel that way. I'm authorized to give you another hundred. But I'm leaving here this morning with the painting." The look in the deep-socketed eyes, under the bill of the cap, was determined and unfriendly, and calmly fierce.

Shumaker stepped back from the door and let him enter. There wasn't anything else to do. It would be useless to get beat up for it. They walked over together and stood looking at the painting. "Jesus. What do you call it?"

"I don't have any name for it. *Her* name."

"She sure is a looker."

Shumaker was silent.

"You got something to put it in?"

"Yes."

When it was safely crated and put away in the backseat of the car, the man tipped the cap and said, "Do you want that other hundred?"

Shumaker took it. "Will you see Mr. Lessing's wife today?"

The other smiled. "They're off somewhere overseas again. They left yesterday."

"Oh."

He watched the man drive away, then went back into the apartment and drank some more of the whiskey. His heart hurt—a slow, pulsing, heavy stone in the middle of his chest. He couldn't breathe out fully. There was the rest of the day to do, and he lacked the strength to draw air into his lungs. He thought of dying. Every motion took an effort.

At last, he drove to his parents' house and went in. No one was home. *He* was home. He walked from room to room, and for a time he sat in front of the television. He even slept a little. He had an unpleasant dream, not quite at the level of nightmare: some form of string or cord that he had swallowed somehow and could not remove from his mouth, and in the dream he kept pulling on it and watching it pile up at his feet. Awakening from this, he stood and looked around himself and felt vaguely sick. He was moving groggily through the foyer on his way out, when his father arrived from an afternoon meeting. "What brings you here?"

"I don't know. Just felt like it."

"Where's your girl."

"She's not a girl, Dad."

"You know what I meant. Don't be so damn particular."

"She's gone. Sonya's gone, too. They're both gone."

"You all right?"

"I guess."

The professor watched him for a few moments. "Did you finish the painting?"

"It's—there's some things I wanted to do with it. But a guy came and took it away."

"Well. Good."

They were silent, neither of them moving.

"Like to've seen it."

"It's a good painting," Shumaker said. "Anyway."

"Maybe old man Lessing'll want to show it off somewhere."

There was a pause.

"I'm sure it *is* good, Son."

"They're married now, Dad. They got married overseas."

"No kidding."

"The captain of a ship they were on."

After a brief pause, the professor said, "Jesus Christ."

They were still standing in the hall when Lena arrived. She had two bags of groceries. "Well," she said. "You two. Want to lend me a hand here?"

They took the bags from her and went into the kitchen. There was a half-eaten apple on the counter and some slices of mango on the cutting board, where she had been preparing something. "Are you staying?" she said, taking the groceries out of the bag and putting them away—milk, bread, mixed greens, broccoli. The paper bags rattled. The refrigerator door made its little sucking sound when she opened it. Everything was itself. It all made him eerily dizzy. He thought of the concussion.

"You all right?" his father asked again.

The young man nodded absently. "Gotta go to work at the restaurant."

"You don't look all right," Lena said. "Somebody let me in on it, please."

"Both girls—uh, both *women* are apparently gone."

"Well, I know the one is. I saw a piece in the *Appeal* this morning about Buddy Lessing being in the Loire Valley for the summer with his new wife."

"I've gotta go," Shumaker said.

"Stay for dinner," said his mother.

He walked over and kissed her cheek, then patted his father's shoulder, and made his way out. He drove to the restaurant and spent his work time concentrating on being polite and thorough, doing what was required, being good. He even thought of it that way. It was as if there were something he had to mollify, something in the surrounding air. At the end of the night he drove to the apartment and let himself in. There wasn't much to eat. He made a peanut-butter sandwich and sat eating it without much pleasure, drinking more of the whiskey. Half a cocktail glass of it this time. He looked at all the paintings he had begun and abandoned. It was difficult to imagine where he might go, or how it would be if he got past this empty feeling. Finally he tried to sleep, and couldn't. The hours of the night stretched before him like a vast expanse across which he had to pass, inch by inch, nothing changing, the light not coming, the clock hands still as painted ones.

When he noticed the sunlight pouring in through the window in the door, he realized that he must have drifted a little.

And there, in the window of the door, was Sonya.

I X

He nearly ducked away. She just stood there looking at him through the glass. Finally he moved to the door and opened it.

"Hi," she said.

He stepped out and closed the door behind him, thinking—before he remembered that the painting was no longer there—that he must not let her see it. He could not return her gaze. "How've you been?" he asked, and was appalled at the absurdity of the question.

"How do you *think* I've been?"

"Sorry." This seemed absurd, too.

"You look bad. Is it the—the injury?"

"Didn't sleep too well. Not the injury—no."

She appeared to gather herself, took a breath. "Well, I'm here because my mother insists I do it before I go home."

"You're—" Suddenly he didn't want to lose her, and he almost blurted it out. He saw the intricate foliate green of her irises, the clear sparkle of them in the early morning light, and his whole mind seemed to falter. Everything was roiling inside him, and she stood there not seeing it. "Back to LA?"

"You've guessed it," she said, with a fleeting smile.

In the long silence that followed, a bird repeated a two-note song three times: *pee-wit, pee-wit, pee-wit.* When abruptly she moved toward him, he started to recoil, and there was a pause, a moment of shared embarrassment, of being unpleasantly reminded of the reason for such a reaction. She kissed his cheek lightly and stood back. "I'm—I'm really sorry for hitting you—for hurting—injuring you. I apologize—there."

"No need," he got out, and then wanted to say more. Except that he had no breath.

"But—well, you never should've waited to tell me like that."

"No, I know." He wanted to tell her again that it had been his father's insistence. He thought of Memphis in May.

"That hurt me—very badly."

"God, I'm so sorry. I know."

"Well, of course that wasn't the real hurt."

"I'm sorry for all of it. Everything. I can't tell you."

"The real hurt was that you—that we—"

"I understand. I know." The words were rushed and full of a tone of avoidance now. Hearing himself, he wanted to reach over and take her hand. "I didn't mean—I—I never—"

Her expression grew dreamy. "I was so happy coming back—so happy." Her eyes welled up. "Do you remember when I came out of the mist—" She sniffled, wiped her eyes with the backs of her hands. "Well, that's pointless."

"And we—we sat in the car and put those stories on the people going by—"

"Yes," she said. "Oh, I know. Yes."

"Please," he began. "I wish none of this—I wish it hadn't—"

"Oh," she said. "Well, you know, me too. Anyway, I'm sorry I hit you." Abruptly she strode toward the car.

"I didn't mean *us*," he called after her.

She stopped and turned. "That's good to know."

"I wish things were different."

She gazed at him for a long, silent few moments. And he had a kind of premonitory rush of knowing that no matter where he would travel or whom he would come to know in his life, or what he would come to do, he would always carry the regret for this. He thought of the painting and wished it destroyed. He had gotten so much of everything wrong.

"Sonya," he said. "I'm stupid. I was so stupid. I—I can't figure it out. I don't know what happened to me."

She nodded, sighing, as if agreeing to something quite simple concerning them both. "You got hit over the head."

Crying silently, watching her go, he gathered his breath and called, "Come back? Please?"

Again she stopped and faced him. "Can't," she sobbed, her lips trembling, tears streaming down her face. "Just—can't. It's all—all gone now. Our marvelous love." She went to the car, hurrying a little, as if fearing that her strength would not carry her far enough. Getting in, with a little struggle, and without looking back at him, she pulled the door shut and started the engine, which chugged and seemed about to stall, but then caught, and roared. She put both hands on the wheel, a tight grip, and drove out of his life forever.

THE SAME PEOPLE

Near twilight of a day in June. The veranda of a resort hotel on the Inishowen Peninsula overlooking Lough Foyle in County Donegal. Though it's well past nine o'clock in the evening, plenty of sunlight still bathes the tops of the far, low hills on the other side of the expanse of mostly calm water. From the wide veranda, with its tables set for dinner, you can see breezes blowing across the water's surface. Two people, a man and a woman in their late seventies, move with a slow, wobbly, careful gait, as if the ground beneath them were shifting, across to a small, square table along the railing. She uses a cane, and he holds one of her arms. She wears a dark blue dress and thick-soled black shoes, and he has a white sport coat on, and tan slacks. The coat seems too loose fitting for him, and the cuffs of the slacks bunch in folds on the tops of his brown loafers. When she's seated and he has taken his place across from her—moving slowly enough for one to see that he, too, even without a cane, is very shaky on his feet—they look out at the lake, hills, and sky. They seem, for the moment, content.

Near them a young couple sits with a toddler, who sings to himself and runs from one side of the patio to the other. The young couple sip cold beer. The woman calls to the toddler, a boy with bright red hair and fat little stubby doll-like arms and legs. "Come here. Come *here.* Stay away from the railing."

The boy becomes noisier, and the elderly couple watch him. He's not listening to his mother, who keeps telling him not to climb on the railing. He's in no danger of falling through, but his mother is clearly nervous about it anyway. She gets up and hurries over to him, lifts him, and carries him, his fat legs kicking, back to their table.

"Energetic young fellow," the old man says to her.

"Yes," she says. "Sometimes I don't know what to do."

"Such pretty red hair," the old woman tells her.

"My hair used to be that color," the old man says.

The waiter comes to their table, puts menus down, and asks if they would like something to drink. "Can we see the wine list?" the old man asks.

"Yes, of course. Sorry."

The waiter walks off. The man reaches into his jacket pocket and brings out a small camera. He holds it up, adjusts the focus, and takes a picture of his wife. He puts it down in his lap and says, "Smile? Please?" His tone is that of a person asking two polite questions for which he expects no answer.

She gives a happy smile, but her eyes show no mirth.

He looks through the lens again, pauses, and snaps the picture. Then he puts the camera back into his coat pocket.

The toddler walks to their table and stands staring.

"Hello," the old man says to him.

"I'm James," the child says. "I don't like it here."

"But it's such a pretty place. Why don't you like it?"

"You have brown shoes."

"Yes, I do. Very good—you know your colors."

"I don't like brown."

"I don't either."

"Then why're you wearing brown?"

"James," the boy's mother says. "Come here. Stop bothering those nice people."

"You have a stick," the boy says to the old woman.

"Yes. It's called a cane."

"Are you very bad?"

"Well, I don't know—do you think so?"

"You have a stick."

The boy's parents rise from their table, holding their beers, and move to the railing, the boy's mother calling to him. "James. Come *here.*"

He waits for a little while, then reaches over and runs his fingers down the shaft of the cane, as if wanting to challenge the adults with his bravery, and his refusal to listen to his mother.

"James!" his mother says. And with a little yell, he turns and runs to her.

"Never cease to be amazed at the frank gaze of a child," the old man says to the boy's mother.

She seems not to know quite how to take the remark. She smiles politely and nods. The little boy runs off in the other direction, and she puts her glass of beer down and follows.

"James," the boy's father says without conviction, swallowing his own beer and leaning on the railing.

The old man brings the camera out and takes another picture and then puts it back.

"Would you say I look to be at peace with things?" his wife asks.

"Please," he says.

"I wish we'd had children," she says, low.

He doesn't answer right away. His gaze is direct. He seems to be considering. But then he simply stares off. "The light stays so long in these northern latitudes."

"I wish it especially now," she says.

They're quiet again, watching the gulls sail and dip above the minutely rippling surface of the water below.

The waiter brings the wine list and waits for a moment. The old man takes a while reading over the choices, and so the waiter moves away, over to the young couple, who are finished with their beers. The woman has lifted the little boy and carries him toward the entrance to the dining room. The man settles with the waiter and waves politely at the old couple as he turns to follow his wife and son.

"Americans?" the old man asks the waiter.

"Yes, sir," the waiter tells him. "From New York, they said."

"They seem like nice people."

The waiter makes a sound of polite agreement that isn't quite a word. He stands there while the old man goes down the list of wines. In the next instant the woman coughs, deep. She fishes a handkerchief out of her purse and holds it tight to her mouth. The waiter sees blood there, and moves off. She wipes her lips, folds the handkerchief tightly, and puts it back in her purse. "Is it all right?" she says to her husband.

He leans forward to look closely at her. "It's fine."

She sits back and folds her arms, as if against a sudden chill. "I may need my shawl."

"You want me to go get it?"

"Not yet. No. It's fine."

He watches the waiter come back.

"Is everything all right, sir?"

"Yes, we'll have a bottle of this Chablis."

"Right."

When the waiter's gone, the old man fetches forth the camera again and holds it up. She gazes out at the lake and the hills in the distance, the lowering white clouds there, tinged with sun. He snaps still another picture.

"You and your archival urge," she says.

He puts the camera back.

"A trait of yours that I always felt was a kind of failing."

"Then it's a common one."

"Not living in the moment. Yes, that's true."

"You've never looked more beautiful to me," he says.

She resists another cough, holds it in with her closed fist, then relaxes again. "I wish I had been religious."

"You've been spiritual."

"Yes, I know," she says. Then, in a kind of recitation: "The religious person is afraid of going to hell. The spiritual person has already been there."

"I used to think I knew so much. Don't chide me with it."

They both smile, not looking at each other. "That little boy. I didn't find him at all cute."

"No," he says.

"What do you suppose he meant, asking if I'm bad?"

"Something about the cane, maybe?"

"You have to admit that I've never had any sentimentality about boys and little girls and babies."

The waiter brings the wine, opens it, and pours a little, and the old man lifts the glass to his nose and breathes. "Very good," he says. The waiter pours, taking his time. The wine is soft gold, the sun showing in it, sparkling in facets. "Nothing like the color of a good white Burgundy," the old man says. The waiter acknowledges this without real interest, sets the bottle wrapped in a little towel in a metal cooler on the table between them, and walks away. He's a tall Irish boy with a buzz cut who takes pride in his physique. His black shirt is cut to fit him taperingly, and his sleeves are folded back to show the thickness of his forearms.

"You always had such a capacity for *appreciating* things," she says.

He sips the wine, turns the glass a little, looking at it, then sips again. It's as if he's performing for her. "It's quite delicious."

"Is it better than it would be if you were going to have it again tomorrow? And the day after that?"

"I can't really tell. And we weren't going to speak of this tonight."

"Isn't everything supposed to be enhanced by this circumstance?"

"Dear."

"That little boy, with his straight-on way of looking at us. Do you suppose he could tell something?"

"No. And stop it."

"I don't remember when I began to know about it myself," she says. "*That's* strange, given that my mother—well. But I was very small, not much past three, when she went."

"I was older, when it came to me, I guess. Though I always—" He stops, takes a swallow of the wine, and gazes out at the lake and the sky.

"I know," she says. "I'll quit."

"We'll talk about whatever you want to talk about. But we did agree not to mention it."

"I used to say I never wanted to live forever."

"No. I know," he says. "I remember. Please."

She smiles, without quite looking at him. "But I *am* bad, aren't I? Such a strange thing for a little boy to say." She takes more of the wine, but lifting a glass is obviously difficult for her. Her hand shakes. Again they're quiet. He reaches for the camera, holds it up, and snaps yet another picture, then puts it away again.

"Do you really think the pictures will mean anything to anybody?"

"How can you say that? Of course they will. And they'll show everyone that we were completely together in this, and at peace with it."

"I'm not at peace with it, though. You are. You are supremely, depressingly at peace with it."

"Do you want to call it off?"

"I'm being bad," she says. "I have a stick."

He sips the wine. She takes some, too. They're quiet for several moments. They hear the gulls cry, sailing low over the wind-rippled water. The breeze blows through her hair, and she raises the collar of her dress.

"Should I get your shawl?" he asks.

She appears not to have heard him. "Did you see that article about how, in some billions of years, however many years, Venus might collide with the earth?"

"No."

"It was in the paper. With an artist's depiction."

"Billions of years."

"That seems somehow more daunting as a concept than simply to say *eternity*."

"I used to think of all the paintings, statues, and books," he says. "I remember hating to think of them ever going away, even in billions of years."

"You wanted to live forever."

He's quiet a moment. Then: "No, my darling. I didn't say that. But we all do. In some way we all certainly do, or did. Isn't that true?"

"I'm chiding you again."

They drink more wine and watch the light begin to fade beyond the hills. The dark shades of green are growing still darker across the way, and parts of the shoreline opposite them have receded into shadow, pools of blackness at the edge of black water.

"Do you think you might've been happier if we'd had children?" she asks.

"I've been so happy with you." His eyes brim, and he wipes them with the fingers of his left hand. It's a motion a little like brushing away an insect. In his right hand he holds his glass of wine, and he does not put it down. He drinks what is left in the glass, then picks up the bottle and pours more for himself. He offers the bottle to her.

"Only a little," she says, holding out her glass.

He pours it and sets the bottle down.

"I believe we—that is, people—people wouldn't know love, if it weren't for—for, you know, the fact of the end being there—" She waves the thought away and has another small drink of the wine.

"The worst people I've ever known," he tells her, "had no sense of it at all."

"That little boy, grown, without having gained the knowledge."

"Yes."

"Is that what makes us gentle, do you suppose?"

"You and me?"

"All right."

"I would like to think we were always gentle people," he says. His voice breaks. "Teaching is a good way to lead a life."

"Our all-important work."

"That's right. Our work. Right."

"Poor man. I'm giving you a bad time."

"No," he says.

"I think I'm trying to talk you out of it again."

"Can we not do this?"

Once more they're silent, staring out at the serrations in the water.

She says, "I'm surprised at the need to keep from saying ultimate kinds of things. You know, 'the fall of a sparrow' and all that."

"'The fall of a sparrow,' yes. But the sparrow is brought down. Someone shoots it."

"Oh, right."

"It's true."

"In its way. I seem to want to recount all our stages of unlikeliness as a couple. Well, some people said. I thought sometimes we would both go on to other people. Both of us. Remember the time I threw all your clothes out in the front yard? And that neighbor—my goodness, I can't recall his name. He took a picture."

"It was so long ago," says the old man. "We were different people. Just babies."

"But what was his name?"

"I remember that it was the same name as a British historical figure—not a king."

"Not Disraeli. Montgomery?"

"Chamberlain, wasn't it?"

"No," she says. "Further back than that. I'm sure."

"I remember it began with a C. It wasn't Chamberlain?"

"God," she says. "I want that name back like my life, just now."

He reaches across the table and takes her hand. "What does it matter. Anyway, I'm sure it was Chamberlain."

"No, it *wasn't*. And if only you weren't always so sure of everything."

His voice is barely audible. "I'm just trying to help."

"We always did what you wanted to do. I've always let you have your way."

"I think we always tried to do that for each other, darling."

"What about Mimsy Stratton?"

"Now, why are you bringing *that* up? Now of all times. My God—Mimsy *Stratton*."

"You know I still try to picture you with her. Even now, this morning, when you woke up to my coughing, and you were so solicitous and sweet and tired, and we were decided and sure about everything. I thought of it as a possibility anyway, like daydreaming a future."

"You know very well I could never have had a future with someone like Mimsy Stratton."

"You were obsessed with her."

"I could never have had a future with someone like Mimsy Stratton. And it was almost thirty years ago, and we were different people."

The waiter comes back out and walks over to them. He pours more wine in both glasses. Not much is left in the bottle. "More wine?" he says.

"I think I would like a cold draft of something," the old man says.

"Yes," his wife says. "A Moretti. Do you have Moretti?"

"Yes, ma'am."

"Two of them, in iced glasses."

The two people watch him go, and then turn to face each other. They hold up their glasses, touch them, and drink. He pours the last little bit into his glass and swallows that, too.

"Do you think you would have remarried?" she asks quietly, without looking at him.

"Darling. We've been over it and over it. I won't be here without you. We've done this. We've decided. Please."

She sets down the glass, then folds her hands around the bottom of the stem, looking down at it. "I used to believe I could live forever if I was allowed to."

"I don't feel the wine," he says. "I usually feel white wine faster than this. I drank most of this bottle."

"I wish we'd had the one child," she says, suddenly. "That's what I wish."

"If you will please, please, not do this."

"I do have that as a regret, dear. And it's deep. And long standing, too. I'm sorry. I'm sorry to bring it up. But I did what you wanted then, and I'm doing what you want now, and it's always been about doing what you want, including not bringing up certain people."

"We can talk about anything you want, then. Let's talk about it. Mimsy Stratton moved north and married someone from India, who died in New York on 9/11 of a septic duodenal ulcer. One of the non–Twin Towers deaths recorded on that particular day. She had a big family with him and got terribly fat. She was never anyone but a person I worked with and respected and liked. And she couldn't understand what you thought you saw about her, and we were not even friends anymore when she moved away. And we would never have known any of this about her if you hadn't kept up with her, and that was what *you* wanted. I haven't thought about her in ages."

"We were so passionate all the time," she says. "Weren't we?"

The waiter brings the beer on a little silver tray. The glasses are dull white with the ice coating, and the foam at the top of them is creamy looking. He puts the tray down and walks away. The old man sips the beer, then wipes the foam from his mouth. "This tastes perfectly wonderful," he says. "You should try it."

"Not just yet," she murmurs. "I wonder why any of this means anything to me *now*. You wouldn't think it would matter. But just this minute it does. I have to say, it does." She watches him sip the beer. The light has almost gone from the sky, and the water below them is becoming pure darkness, on into the purplish haze obscuring the other side of the lake. "Oh, my dear. I'm so frightened. I've never been as frightened as I am right now."

He gets up and moves around the table to her side. She puts her arms around his waist and holds on. "Are we terrible, selfish people?"

"I won't hear it," he tells her. "Now, I mean it. Stop this."

"If I weren't so frightened of the pain."

"Here," he says, wiping her face gently, leaning over her.

"It's a sin. We'll look bad."

"No."

"I'm terrified," she murmurs. "I want there to be something."

"My love," he says. "We'll just take the pills and go to sleep together. We'll just be going to sleep like we have all these years."

"I've wanted to be strong for you."

"You have, my darling girl. You always have."

She cries a little, and sniffles, and holds the handkerchief to her face. Some others come out from the hotel dining room. Three couples, evidently having a good time with whiskey. They're talking loudly about the virtues of different malt scotches. Someone in the bar has prepared a flight, as it's called, of the different kinds. Two of the men are chasing theirs with Guinness. Claiming that the whiskey makes the nutty flavor of the Guinness even stronger.

"Why aren't you afraid?" she asks him. "You don't seem the slightest bit afraid."

He lets her hold on a moment longer, then reaches down and pats her shoulder and kisses the side of her face.

"I'm better," she tells him. "Please. Sit down now."

He does so. For a while they watch the others, who stand at the railing and talk and laugh and make jokes about something that has transpired in the town. One of the men was in an altercation with the local constable about a broken taillight on a rental car.

"Nothing I have done or read has prepared me for this," the old woman says. "Yet I've been thinking about it my whole life. Isn't that remarkable?"

Her husband nods. He's holding his glass of beer but not drinking from it.

"Premorbidity—can you imagine him using such a word? I'm to have very little premorbidity. My entire life has been that, hasn't it?"

"No," he tells her. "Mine has. You were always *in* your life up to the hilt. You never gave it a thought. I was the one who was thinking about it all the time and worrying myself sick over nothing. My stupid hypochondria."

"You talked about it," she says. "I kept it to myself."

"You were the brave, centered one, always."

"I'd have had children," she says flatly. "Or I'd have had the one."

He puts the beer glass down and covers his face with his hands. It's a motion of great weariness more than anything, rubbing his eyes, while the people nearby get louder and more raucous, sampling their whiskeys and seeming far past the ability to distinguish the subtleties of the enterprise. Their laughter rises into the night. He looks up at the stars beginning to sparkle at the top of the sky, the last daylight gone, and the moon rising. The light from inside the hotel is all the light there is now.

"Really, why aren't you afraid at all—even a little?"

"I thought we had both made peace with it," he says.

"No, I have made no peace with it. That's your idea of it."

He says nothing.

"Another kind of sickness," she mutters. "Also long standing."

"I don't understand you."

"What will happen to the pictures?" she asks.

"It's a record of us now. For Flo and the rest of them."

"You were always coming to this," she says. "It has nothing to do with my sister."

He sniffles, turning from the noise, and from her, too. But then he straightens and faces her and slowly nods. "I know."

"I always hated it."

"Yes," he says.

"Your damn dying. Always your dying."

"Please, darling."

"I wish we'd had our girl."

"I'm sorry," he says. "We don't know that it was a girl."

"A girl," she says.

He takes a long swallow of the beer and then sets the glass down with a suddenness. "Cromwell."

She looks at him. "That was it, yes. Cromwell." Her tone is devoid of inflection.

"Cromwell," says her husband.

She breathes, coughs, sighs, and then sits straighter, as if adjusting to a cramp in her lower back. "I want to go wherever there is to go as *me*," she says. "Myself. I never would've believed it. And I want to carry my sorrows with me and all my regrets and frustrations and every single minute of every single day. Forever. If I can think of it, why can't I have it?"

"Darling," he says.

"I wish you weren't so happy about it."

"No," he says. "You have no idea."

"I do. I know. I can't help it."

He gulps the beer down. She has a sip of hers. He brings the camera out again and can't quite get it to focus. The noise is increasing from the others on the veranda, and someone drops a glass that rolls and does not break. The whole gathering marvels at this, as if it were some kind of miracle. One of them, a heavy, shaggy blond man, comes over and offers to take the old couple's picture. The old man hands him the camera, stands, shakily, and moves his chair around to sit next to his wife. The heavy man says, "Smile," and they smile, and he snaps the picture.

"Thank you," says the old man, putting the camera back in his coat pocket. He pulls his chair around and faces her again across the table.

His wife watches him run his hands over his face. "I'll never forgive you," she says, low.

The others in the darkness begin laughing at a remark one of them has made about a girlfriend's propensity for spilling things and breaking glasses. "She knocked a scrim over once. Shattered a whole cabinet of fine crystal. We were eating at some rich lady's house in Rome."

"I'd like to go to Rome," one of the others, a young woman, says. "That's one of the places I want to see before I'm through."

"You could spend a year there and not come close to seeing it all."

The old gentleman leans across the little table and takes his wife's hand. "Do you want to go up now?"

"No, let's stay here. Just a little longer. Please?"

He squeezes her hand and turns to look for the waiter. High overhead, a jet is crossing the sky, and someone remarks that it looks like a shooting star.

K enneth Broley, Julia's former father-in-law, spent a summer
running the semi-submarine tour here, before he went into
the army in 1966. "Magical place, Catalina," he'd said to her toward
the end of his life. "I had such good times there." His voice soft-
ened with the pleasure of remembering. In fact, at times it seemed
that the family's memories of the island's charms stemmed from
the kind old man's nostalgia alone—though they had spent several
vacations here when Will was a boy. They all talked about going
back someday—except of course for Kenneth's wife, Eunice, with
that prim throat-clearing way of talking, sitting ramrod straight
in her black rocker, her small white hands with the polished red
talons resting in her lap. "An *awful* lot of tourists, of course. But if
you don't mind them, I suppose it's nice."

Suppose.

In that disinclined reluctantly acknowledging tone, and of
course *nice* was one of her staple words, used most often either
as a demand or with irony. Nice. *Be nice. That's not nice. I suppose
he's nice enough. That would be nice, I guess.* Mrs. Broley leeched
strength from anyone who came near her, starting with her husband, and including two daughters, two sons, and their respective
wives and children.

But that's all gone, isn't it? *They're* all gone. The family never
returned to Catalina while she was with Will, and her divorce from
Will was a decade ago, within a year of Kenneth Broley's death.
That poor man rented a room at a cheap motel not two miles from
his house, and in his carefully packed briefcase he had a plastic bag,
a pint of vodka, and a bottle of sleeping pills. He sat on the sofa in

front of the television, took the pills, drank most of the vodka, and then pulled the bag over his head. The following morning, he was found by the motel cleaning crew, lying on his side, legs folded up to accommodate the shortness of the sofa. He left no note, though Julia, who grieved for him as if he were her own father, believed he had been driven to it by his wife. Of course she never spoke of it.

Will and his brother and sisters and that horrible old lady are still back in Memphis as far as she knows. Julia's with Blake now, and she's only thinking about these others because she and Blake are here on this delayed honeymoon.

And earlier today, at straight-up noon, that honeymoon was effectively ruined, one day in.

Blake's older sister, Charlotte, has called to say she'll be arriving on the last boat. She's sorry for interrupting their little holiday (her words), she knows they've been planning it for some time and it's overdue, but there's nowhere else to turn. She requires the company of her younger brother, and she hopes Julia won't mind. She flew into John Wayne from Ann Arbor this morning. Her marriage is coming apart. Again. In her life with the husband, Brian, she severed so many ties (it's been more than twelve years since she published her short novel, *Mozart's Ghost*). He's a minister in some Baptist sect, and she will tell you she gave up everything for him, this distinguished-looking handsome middle-aged man. How could she have mistaken his definiteness and decisive manner as being charming instead of what they really are: priggishness and bigotry. She can't stand the pompous bastard another minute. Blake, hanging up the phone, quoted this last in a flat tone, a man reciting something disheartening. "She actually called him that." He looked down at the floor. "Disaster for us, of course."

Julia agreed, nearly at the top of her voice, standing in the doorway of the honeymoon suite, the pretty room, site of the wrecked good time because Charlotte was making a statement. One of her journeys away, the third separation. Charlotte and the severe husband, according to Charlotte, have always had a physical hunger for each other. Charlotte keeps going back. "Why's it have to be this time that she *doesn't* go back?" Julia wept. "Why can't she do it one more stupid time? Why can't she? Why can't she ruin someone *else's* honeymoon?"

"Listen to yourself," Blake said. "You're not making any sense."

"I don't *have* to make sense. This was supposed to be a honeymoon."

"Please," he told her. "We'll just go on another one. Before fall."

"You know we won't have the money. I want my honeymoon. I have a right to it, and I want it. I want my honeymoon."

"Stop it. You sound ten years old. You realize you actually stamped your foot just now?"

She stamped it again, glaring. "I wish we'd never tried to do this. This is worse than if we hadn't done it at *all*."

"Julia, for God's sake please get ahold of yourself. What the hell."

THAT WAS NOON.

Now, waiting on the pier in the long shadows of five o'clock, after hours of only practical communications about the time and the necessary actions to procure another room so late, he says, "I promise we're going to have this honeymoon before the summer's over. You'll see."

"I needed this time, Blake. *We* needed this time."

"We'll make it work. We'll go into debt if we have to. We'll have our honeymoon."

"I'm beginning to wish we hadn't come *here*."

"It's wonderful here. It's perfect," he says.

"My former father-in-law—I told you. The semi-sub. This was their vacation place when Will was a boy."

"Yes, yes. But I like it. We can make it ours, can't we? I mean it's made for us. It's just right for us."

As though to accentuate his words, a freshet of sea air touches her face, like a caress. Across the way, beyond the forest of boat masts and the water, stands the spherical island museum with its graceful columns, the tree-dotted stony hill rising steeply to its left, toward the clear sky. Along that side, lined by palms, you can see the boardwalk and the row of shops, restaurants, and hotels of Avalon. Lover's Cove. Close by, they hear the sound of a motorcycle or outboard. It ceases, then starts up again, and finally sputters out.

"Weather's so nice," he ventures.

She gives forth a small, rueful laugh.

"What?"

"I was thinking about those people—my former parents-in-law. The Broleys. Sad Kenneth and his horrible wife. Prim, proper, poisonous, lethal Eunice."

"Never had the pleasure." His tone is thinly sardonic.

"Eunice's special word was *nice.* She could cut through stone with it, way she used it."

"Nice?"

"That's the word."

"Pretty innocuous if you ask me. People use it without even thinking."

"She used it thinking."

"It's just a word."

"The way a knife is just a knife. Believe me. The woman was pure negation. She wore the poor man out. God, I wanted him to stand up to her. He was the only one in that family who was truly kind. And she ordered him around like a servant she didn't respect or like very much. 'Yes, dear. Yes, dear.' And everything, literally, really, everything was negative. I think she—well, never mind."

"He killed himself, right?"

She nods. "Let's talk about something else."

Blake is silent, gazing at the curve of the beach and the thin closed-to-traffic street beyond it.

"Lover's Cove," she says. "What a name for a touristy marina with a museum and shops."

"Now who's being negative?"

"It was a joke."

A moment later, she says, "Remember, I did say when we were coming in that it looks like the Riviera. Even though I've never been to the Riviera."

"The way we imagine it, right?"

"And I like the name Lover's Cove. I do. I just meant—well, Lover's Cove. A marina and shops. You know?"

"You think it should be a line of heart-shaped beds surrounded by roses?"

He can make her laugh. It's one of the things she loves about him. "Yes. *Vibrating* beds."

"Oh. And surrounded by mirrors. Canopied by mirrors."

"Well, I wouldn't want to overdo."

Now *he* laughs. "The cove of honeymoons."

She waves this away. "Is, um, *honeymoon*, is that, like, a weird custom of these island people?"

"I don't know what else to do, Julia."

"Another little joke."

"I wish I had a tape of you earlier."

"Well." She draws in a breath and holds it a moment.

"That was classic."

It comes to her that she doesn't really like the way he uses the word *classic*. And he uses it a lot. She says, "I think I'm entitled to feel disappointment. Don't you feel it?"

The sun's obscured now by clouds and sea mist, far off. The boat, the last one, will arrive soon. They see it in the wide expanse of aquamarine and far blue water, cutting through the chop of breezy late afternoon on Emerald Bay. The water in that distance is a darker blue than you would believe can exist anywhere outside of a child's drawing, and there are the pearly twin sluices of foam where the bow is cutting through it.

"So your ex-father-in-law worked here."

"Odd-sounding phrase when the person's passed away," she says. "*Ex*-father-in-law."

"I'd like to ride the semi-sub. Looks like a cool trip."

"I think it was the only good memory he had."

"Poor man, and that was underwater."

"Well, he's gone now."

"How old was he?"

"Sixty-nine. I really liked him, you know. He treated me sweetly."

"Sixty-nine's a good long life. Maybe he thought he'd had enough."

"If that's a joke it's not funny. And *his* father and mother were still alive when it happened. Ninety-two and ninety-six."

Blake nods. "We should all."

"No," she says, smiling. "Not *all* of us."

Again, they're quiet.

Sitting here next to him, not touching, with an upset stomach and the beginning of a headache, watching the approaching boat, she thinks how the whole day has become fraught with unbidden surges of memory from the other marriage: everything she did wrong, back then; everything Will did to push her away. It's discomfiting. She has become aware that some part of her *wills* these thoughts, consciously entertains them, like a kind of half-conscious intellectual experiment, attempting to sort through the difficulties of those years as though, disappointment being general and so acute now, it's all part of some as-yet-undiscovered condition, a chronic something that has found a path through her experience, running toward some mysterious thing, surprising and awful: the island where Kenneth Broley was once young and happy, the stresses of being around Eunice, the man's suicide, her failed marriage, and this suddenly complicated week, all somehow linked.

How odd that a place, being only that, can carry so much power to confuse and trouble you.

It's true that she and Blake are in need of a change, even at this early stage. Their luck has been off. That's how they think of it and talk about it. He's an unrecorded songwriter, still waiting tables at the Hilton on City Drive in Orange and playing the clubs when he can. He's a fine singer and performer of his own songs. She teaches in the community college where they live, in Long Beach. They've been together almost three years, married for two, and have never even had a weekend to travel alone. They did without for months, saving every penny, for this, six days at Catalina.

"You can't see this mess with Charlotte as something I chose," he says now.

"I'm not doing that. Okay?"

The boat's engine becomes audible as it nears. It sounds like coughing.

Presently, she says, "You know, in her mind I'm a mistake you've made."

"Oh, stop that."

"Well. It's true—my being older. I mean she said it. Eleven years is a long time. You heard her."

"Eleven years *is* a long time. And she was talking about how long I've been waiting tables. That was not about our age difference. We're ten years—I mean *you're* ten years."

"It's one month shy of eleven, and you know the trouble with you, darling? You never see the underside of anything. She *was* talking about our age difference. She doesn't like me and you know it."

He leaves a pause. Then, in the tone of someone muttering to himself: "I think you've both just missed being the best of friends. You keep misfiring, that's all."

To their right, the semi-sub comes slowly into the cove, back from its last excursion of the day. Beyond that, there's a cabin cruiser from whose bow a girl shouts and jumps. Two young men and another woman stand at the gunnel and watch her flail in the water. She has something bright yellow in her hair and the water takes it. They all look to be having fun. The girl shrieks, laughing. Earlier today Julia went down to the beach and put her feet in the water, and it was cold, cold. She heard someone a few yards from her say that you'd expect it to be warmer off Southern California. She thought of Eunice then, too. And that was before she knew Charlotte was coming.

In less than an hour it will be dark.

"I thought yesterday was glorious," Blake says, as if to prove a point.

"It was. And we had a beautiful day and a lovely night. A lovely morning."

"Well, that's something, right?"

She looks at the buildings along the cove, the hotel where they have their room. The Hotel Macabe. The top of a forking lamp post conceals part of the façade. It looks like the wing of the letter *r* and it's blocking part of the letter *e*. "Take a look at the sign over the hotel from here."

He turns his head slightly.

"The way that big lamp pole—look at that. The top of it's blocking the sign—see? It looks like it says 'Hotel Macabre.'"

"I see the lamp pole."

She takes hold of his face. "Tip this way, just a little," and she lets go. "See?"

"Oh, okay. Sure. That's funny. If you want to read it that way. Hotel Macabre. Hey, we're staying at the Hotel Macabre. Wish you were here."

"The Hotel Macabre. Sounds like a fright flick."

He smiles. "Right."

A moment later, she says, "Everything looks different now."

"She kept the old man off me when we were kids, Julia. And now the least I—I mean she sounded terrible."

"It's fine, really. I'm over it. Okay? Maybe it'll actually be good to see her."

"*Maybe?*" he says. "*Actually?* That's like *suppose* and *nice,* isn't it?"

"Okay, okay. Stop it. I'm trying, God."

"We'll come back again and make it a real honeymoon. Things'll pick up."

She watches the girl in the water of the cove. They have money, surely, being able to afford a sailboat and all that equipment. How can they stand the cold water? One of the men has jumped in and bobs near the girl, spitting water in a high arc.

"I wish you liked her more," Blake says.

"I don't *know* her. I've only been with her four times. And one of those was our wedding."

"I know she can be rude," he says. "Always been that way. I think she may have some form of Asperger's."

"That's an excuse you hear these days for rudeness, and anyway, isn't there something they can do to diagnose that?"

"She'd have to be willing to take the tests, though. If there are any."

"Don't you think it would be cool if it was called the Hotel Macabre?"

"Cut it out," he says. Then: "She can't go back this time. He won't let her. You should've heard her. 'I'm fifty and fat and nobody wants me.' I never heard her cry like that. I mean it—never heard her so low."

"They looked happy when they came to LA and we went up to meet them. They seemed fine even when they were bickering, like they were that time in Ann Arbor."

"Longest three days of my life."

"But she was funny in LA. We weren't the slightest bit tense."

"I was."

"You didn't show it."

"I told you I never liked him."

After a pause, Julia says, "I still can't believe she just up and flew to Santa Ana without calling. And then she criticizes the fact that there's a statue of John Wayne in the airport. The airport's named after the guy."

"I shouldn't have said anything to you about that," Blake answers. "That's just—that's how she is."

"I thought you were laughing about it with me."

"Let's just forget about it."

"But to call from there—as if you'd be waiting for her."

"I said forget it. Please. You're turning everything into a negative. The hotel isn't the Macabre. It's the Ma*cabe,* for God's sake."

"That was a simple observation about the lamp post. Jesus. It was supposed to be funny."

A bad moment later, he says, "Tell me about Eunice."

She knows he's merely seeking to change the subject. But she goes on. Perhaps this is best: a way to get past the disquiet they both feel. "Well—what to say about Eunice without being negative."

"Yuck yuck," he says. "Tell me."

"Okay. Let's start by saying that Eunice had new and different ideas about relationships. She was so innovative about it that she didn't ever have to get a driver's license or write a check or work a job. She taught her lucky husband to be so happy taking her everywhere she had to go, and, oh, how inspiringly adept she was at letting him know where he was going off the track. He just adored being kept up on all the ways he could improve. Every single day of his life."

"Talk about macabre," Blake mutters, but he's smiling. He reaches over and takes her hand. "Maybe *she* has Asperger's."

"I'm sorry," Julia says. "I really was trying to be funny."

"It's too horrifying to be funny."

A few moments later she sighs again. "Everything seems spoiled now. We shouldn't've come here."

"I get it that you're disappointed. Okay?"

"But we're so sour now. It's supposed to be our honeymoon."

"Just keep concentrating on that, Eunice. It'll help you stay miserable."

She punches his shoulder, meaning it, but with a brittle smile. She moves slightly aside on the bench, away from him. "Point taken," she says. "Asshole."

The engines stop and the boat glides soundlessly to the landing. Men tie the moorings and open the ramp for egress. A crew member pulls back the small guardrail, and people begin filing out, carrying their bags. Charlotte's among the first. She searches the crowded dock for them.

Julia murmurs, "She's gained a lot of weight."

He's quiet.

"Christ. I really *am* sounding like Eunice. I'm sorry. Why did I even bring all that up?"

"You're really thinking about those folks a lot."

"It's Catalina. I told you. It's—it's being here where they spent so much time. Oh, God, Blake, I want to relax and be ourselves."

"You're the one picking at everything. The water's too cold, the hotel's macabre, Charlotte's ruining everything and she's rude and criticizing the freaking airport and she doesn't like you."

"Okay," Julia says, low. Two clipped, toneless notes. *Oh-kay.* Then: "I just *said* I sounded like Eunice. Please."

They stand and watch in silence as his sister comes up to them, carrying one bag over her shoulder and pulling another. Charlotte hugs Julia first, a peremptory little halfhearted squeeze, then turns to her younger brother.

"Oh, Blake. It's awful. It's just the worst." She smells like beer. Children run by them, shouting. Charlotte moves to the railing overlooking the water and the tied-up boats, her shoulders hunched. She looks like she might be sick. "Why don't people control their children."

"Here." Blake takes the bag from her shoulder. She just stands there, half leaning over the rail, as if searching for something in the water. Julia starts toward the walking path that leads to the hotel. The crowd moves in a kind of wave across the landing, some people already stopping to take pictures.

Charlotte turns finally and regards Blake. "You look overweight."

"I'm ten pounds lighter," he says. "You look *nice.*"

Julia hears the emphasis on the word and coughs into her hand.

"Let's get you checked in," he says.

They walk over to Julia, and the other woman's eyes trail down her body. "I like the yellow shorts. Good color on you."

"Thanks."

"I brought my pencils and drawing paper. I'm going to stay out of your way."

Julia's at a loss. Charlotte has never mentioned drawing or doing any kind of art. Her house is full of artificial flowers. There are books everywhere, of course, though she never talks about her own. Some Hollywood people wanted to make a movie out of *Mozart's Ghost.* There was option money for several years. But the interest died away.

"Let's have an early dinner," says Blake.

"I'm not hungry," his sister answers. "I'd like a beer."

He leads them toward the long pier and the little kiosk there, where they sell beer in paper cups. Two young men are serving it out of a big keg, along with sliders and fries, hot dogs, ice-cream cones, and other snack items.

Charlotte drinks while they stand there. Her demeanor's that of someone who has just arrived alone at the kiosk, looking around, observing the scene, the hills above the cove, the town, the crowds of people filing down to the long row of shops. After she drains the cup, she hands it to Blake, who throws it into the big trash bin near them, and then takes hold of her bags. "Let's go."

Julia walks a little behind them. No one says anything for a while. People are stopping to look at the views of the museum and the cove. Finally Blake says into the silence. "So you'll get a lawyer now?"

"Got one. Friend of the family. Catholic."

"He giving you a break on the cost?"

"Oh, Brian's gonna pay the cost. We'll make sure of that."

At the hotel she says to the young female clerk with the tattoo on her wrist that she wants a first-floor room. She stares at the tattoo. The clerk replies in a shaky but polite voice that unfortunately there are no vacancies on that floor. She's not much out of high school, and evidently she finds Charlotte intimidating. Quietly, but levelly, Blake's sister insists that she be accommodated.

"I'm so sorry, ma'am, but we just don't have a single one."

"Where're you from?" Charlotte asks.

"Alabama, ma'am."

"You don't have to 'ma'am' me. Just find a first-floor room for me. Not everybody's checked in, am I correct?"

"Ma'am, everybody *is* checked in. I have a nice second-floor room if you like."

"There's not one room you're saving for somebody?"

"Charlotte," Blake says, "come on."

The girl seems about to cry. Charlotte accedes to the second-floor room and signs the form, and when she puts the pen down she does so with a smack, the flat of her hand on the desk, so that the clerk jumps.

Julia leans toward her and says, low, "Don't worry."

Charlotte takes her bags from Blake and announces, as if to everyone in the lobby, "I'll be back down in a minute. Let's go to that Jack's Shack or whatever it is that I saw when we walked over here. The lobster place."

They watch her get on the elevator, and when the doors close, Julia thinks she can hear a sigh of relief.

"*Now* she's hungry," Blake says.

PERHAPS A HALF HOUR goes by. The young clerk greets returning guests and arranges the tour cards in the racks on the counter. Julia and her husband, sitting on a bench along the wall opposite the clerk, watch the elevator doors open and close, people getting on and off.

"Do you think she fell asleep?" he murmurs.

"What're we doing?" Julia says. "Can't you call her?"

It's full dark now out in the street. The lamps are on. People stroll by, families with children.

"I'm starving," she says. "This is ridiculous."

Blake goes up to the counter and asks the young woman to phone the room on the second floor. "There's no answer, sir." As she speaks, the elevator doors open to reveal Charlotte, in a bright yellow-and-blue blouse, too-tight red shorts, and flip-flops.

"Why didn't you go to your room?" she asks. "I wanted to give you some time together."

Julia laughs, and then stops herself.

They leave the hotel and walk in the teeming street away from the museum. Hired tour buses head in a line up the steep hill. The restaurant's on one of the side streets, and there's a line outside. They wait, talking little, because of the noise. A few feet away, street musicians are playing—bongos, guitars, a harmonica. Julia thinks she recognizes the song, and it causes an ache in her soul, beyond expression.

"Do you know that?" she says to Blake.

"Yeah," he answers. "Can't say what, though."

Inside, there's the clashing of voices and music. Television screens hang on the walls around the room, showing different sporting events. It's some kind of nostalgia loop—on one screen Michael Jordan lifts into an astonishing flight over two other players. On another, Jack Nicklaus bends over a putt. And directly across the room, a baseball game is in progress. The music comes from speakers in each corner. Their greeter's a willowy, tall brown man with long dreads, who wears a multicolored bandanna. He says, "A table's just opened up on the balcony outside facing the water."

"It's supposed to get a lot cooler," Charlotte says.

"Less noise," the man says, obviously not having heard her.

"Yes," Blake shouts. "Take us to it."

"Gonna be cold," says his sister.

They follow the tall young man out onto the balcony, which spans the front of the place above the street, with, to the right, a wide view of the bay beyond the low roofs of the cove with its dense forest of skinny boat masts. The moon shines over the water, not quite full, making a shimmering wide avenue of reflected light, running all the way to the beach. Children and others run back and forth in the sand, and several people are playing volleyball. The young man seats them at a table for four and puts menus down. Julia realizes that now, suddenly, she has no appetite at all. "I was so hungry," she gets out.

Blake has turned to Charlotte. "All right. Tell us."

Charlotte pauses, and then sits back in her chair. "I told you. You haven't told her?"

"I told her some of it."

"How much?"

"Okay, most of what you told me. Fill us in."

A waitress stops at the table with a notebook. She introduces herself as Paula and says she'll be their server. She has large round very pale eyes. Julia looks at her hands, which are slender, manicured, the nails long and silver.

"How old are *you*, Paula?" Charlotte wants to know.

Paula smiles. "I'm new. This is my first night, actually."

"Is everybody in this town underage?"

"Oh, I'm of age. I have two children. A boy and a girl."

"Ages?"

"Jona's three, and Lucy's eight months."

"I don't really care about the names."

"Do you-all need a few minutes?"

"Yes," Julia says.

The waitress moves off.

"I want the lobster," Charlotte says. "I don't need a few minutes."

Blake folds his menu. "Me, too."

Julia stares at the rows of choices.

"My darling wife has a history here," Blake says.

Charlotte doesn't look up. "Really. The restaurant?"

"My former father-in-law ran the semi-sub during the summer of 1966."

She keeps staring at the menu. "I know you're supposed to have white wine with fish."

The waitress returns. "What can I get you-all to drink?"

"Water," Julia says.

Charlotte orders a bottle of Chardonnay, and two glasses.

"I'm gonna have a beer," Blake tells her.

"Why be so contrary. Why embarrass me like that."

He shrugs. "I feel like a beer."

She turns to the waitress. "He never drinks beer."

"We have beer all the time," says Julia.

Charlotte gives her a disbelieving look. "Really."

"What difference does it make, ladies? I've taken a liking to cold beer."

"Okay, one glass."

When Paula returns with the water, beer, and wine, Charlotte says, "You're a little too deliberate. Very deliberate. Is it overbusy tonight?"

The young woman seems both puzzled and wary. "No, ma'am."

Charlotte tastes the wine and says, "No. Too sweet. Chardonnay is not supposed to be sweet."

"Yes, ma'am. Would you like something else then?"

"Bring me a dry Chardonnay."

The girl holds the bottle out a little and looks at the label. "This says 'dry white wine,' ma'am. I don't drink wine."

"Do you have a sommelier?"

"I don't know that drink, ma'am."

"Can you send someone to the table who's of age."

"Excuse me," Julia says. "She's talking about a wine steward, someone who orders and stocks your wine."

"That's right," says Charlotte with a thin smile.

"We don't have anything like that," Paula says. "I'm sorry. Do you want me to get the manager? I don't think he'll know anything, he's just the night per—"

Blake interrupts. "It's all right. We'll be fine. Maybe just bring us another bottle."

The girl leaves in a hurry, evidently wanting to get out of range before Charlotte can say anything else.

"Jesus Christ, Charlotte."

"She was getting ready to cry," Julia puts in. "Just like the hotel clerk."

"They're all too young for their jobs."

Blake says, "I wait tables, Charlotte. And if it was me, right now I'd be planning to spit in your food." He throws his napkin down and stands. "I have to use the restroom."

After he disappears around the wall, his sister sniffles and wipes her eyes, and then seems to slump in her chair. "I know you wish I hadn't come."

Julia waits a moment, and then says slowly, "This is between you and Blake."

"I'm not talking about this."

"Well, *I* certainly am."

"You know what he would do when he was unhappy with us?"

"You're talking about your father."

"There's a tendency in you to state the obvious, isn't there."

"I hadn't noticed. You have a tendency to be quite rude. I wonder if you've noticed that."

"It's obvious, isn't it?"

Now Julia throws her own napkin down. She folds her arms and looks out at the sparkle of the bay. But she can't refrain from saying, "Did you and Brian get a honeymoon?"

If Charlotte received the emotion behind the question, she doesn't show it. "A weekend in Denver. He got romantically drunk."

"This was supposed to be our honeymoon."

"I know that. I'm sorry. I said so, too. Didn't he tell you?"

Julia stares at her.

"Anyway, I was going to tell you how Daddy was in the evenings when he came home."

"He'd come home drunk?"

"You interrupt a lot. How can Blake stand that?"

"Because I fuck his eyes out in the nights."

Silence.

Julia sits there with her arms folded, one foot lightly tapping the floor, waiting for the other to speak.

"I was telling you something."

"Tell."

"I don't think you'd listen or care."

"Well, you'll never know unless you make the effort. Isn't that what they say?"

There's a long pause, during which Julia gazes through the window into the restaurant hoping to see Blake on his way back.

"Well, he was never drunk," Charlotte says. "Never touched a drop. No, Daddy was the storm-trooper type. Moral as the *idea* of morality, which of course means that he was very interested in morality in other people, particularly me. And Blake. But Blake was young. I know he says I shielded him, but do you know what that meant?"

"It's pretty clear."

Charlotte leans forward. "Really. Have you ever been beaten across the back with a stick? I mean a piece of wood, like a broomstick? He'd say, 'I'm gonna get the broom.' For any offense, including smiling when he didn't want you to smile."

Blake comes back to the table and stops. "Oh."

"Sit down," his sister tells him. There are tears in her voice. "You'll love this."

"Let's talk about something else, can't we?"

The waitress returns with another bottle of Chardonnay. She pours a taste, and Charlotte sips and nods. "It's fine, I suppose."

Julia looks at her husband, who's concentrating on the menu. "Are we ready to order?"

They all end up ordering the lobster. For a few tense moments they sit quietly, gazing at the lights ranged in the hills on the other side of the cove, while Charlotte sips the Chardonnay, and Blake drinks his beer. Julia wants to go back to the mainland and forget everything. Out in the water, there's the sound of the girl's shriek again, and the laughter, though it's too dark there to see clearly now. The moon has dipped behind a wall of clouds.

Two young men bring the dinners, and one of them pours more wine in Charlotte's glass. Anyone would say it's a festive occasion. Blake orders another beer, and Julia asks for one, too. They all begin to eat.

"I was telling her about Daddy-doo," Charlotte says, breaking one of the claws. She's gained control of her voice, her demeanor, and she speaks through her teeth. "I want to tell about Daddy."

"Oh, God," Blake says. "This is classic. At dinner, no less. Please. Can we do this later?"

"I was explaining. I was asked to explain."

Julia keeps silent.

"Let's talk about what you're gonna do now," Blake says. "Can't we? Are you gonna call Brian?"

"Why would I want to do that?"

"Isn't that the pattern?"

"I'm telling you something." Charlotte takes a long drink of her wine and pours more of it, filling the glass nearly to the top. She stares at the sunny color of it. "Daddy wanted to know what a child's reaction to being shot at might look like."

"Stop it, Charlotte."

"So—" She pauses, drinks, then shakes her head slightly, remembering. "He, um, chased me through the woods behind the house, shooting a pistol at me. Thwack into the trees just behind or to the side of me."

"Charlotte. That's your novel. Don't quote your novel at us."

"It's true," she insists. "It's absolutely true. You were a baby."

"But why go into it *now*? We should be talking about getting you through *this*. I spent the first part of this evening hearing about Julia's terrible mother-in-law and her suicide father-in-law. I don't want to hear *any* of it. I'm sorry for it all, really, but this is *my* honeymoon, too, and I'd like to try enjoying what's left of it."

"I was confiding in you," Julia says. "They—I never would've— they spent time here. So they came to mind. That's all it is, Blake."

"I didn't mean that the way it sounded."

"Let's just eat and call it a night."

"I was talking," Charlotte says.

"I just said I don't want to hear it," Blake tells her.

"You're right," says his sister. "I shouldn't've come."

"Oh, now don't start *that*."

She sits with tears running down her face, and yet Julia, gazing at her, receives the unwanted suspicion that there's something false about it all.

Charlotte sputters, "This is really it, this time, with Brian."

Blake says nothing.

"I have a headache," Julia manages. "I think I'll go back to the room."

"You know when we came though LA that time," Charlotte says, "and he had all those meetings he had to go to? Christian ministries?"

Blake nods.

"He was seeing a woman. Spending all that so-called meeting time with her."

"Why am I not surprised?"

"Really. Well, *I* was. And he's not seeing *her* now. That was over a long time ago. He's seeing someone completely else now."

Julia says, "I really do have this headache. Do you two mind?"

Charlotte appears not to have heard. "Do you understand what

I'm telling you?" she says to Blake. "He's been seeing these—other—these—these—he's been keeping relationships with other women the whole time we've been married."

"From the beginning?"

"That's what I'm telling you."

"Jesus Christ."

Julia stands.

"Hey, don't go yet," Blake says. "I thought we'd go down and sit on the pier. Just the—" He glances at Charlotte. "Just the two of us, in a little bit. Please, Julia."

"The woman has a headache," Charlotte says. "Let her go. Give her some room."

"You two need to talk." Julia reaches for her purse.

"Go down to the pier and wait?" says her husband. "Or stay up in the room and I'll come get you? Please?"

"Don't be absurd," says Charlotte, and then turns to Julia. "Go on to your room and get some sleep if you can."

Julia stares for a few seconds. "I'm going to the pier." It's an announcement, to both of them.

THE STREET IS NOT as crowded. The band's still playing. She walks down to the water, and along the sand to the pier. Light plays across the columns of the museum in the distance, and the paleness where the moon's behind the clouds shows on the surface of the bay. The moored boats move and bob gently. She goes up the little sand hill to the path and out onto the pier. It seems suddenly very important that she find the angle where the streetlamp gives you the hotel as the Macabre. For some reason she can't find it. She tries going farther along, past the kiosk and the little booths where the vendors are selling souvenirs. She comes along very slowly, one hand on the wooden rail, studying the big lit sign and the lamps along the street. It just isn't there. She sits down on what she thinks is the bench where she and Blake sat earlier. But either the bench has been moved, or it's the wrong one. Perhaps it's the next bench?

But a couple's sitting there necking, with food and drink containers next to them.

She stays where she is, not looking over, hearing the sighs and wanting to tell them for Christ's sake to remember where they are; and then, strangely, feeling the impulse to tell them about the optical illusion that makes for the Hotel Macabre. It's ridiculous. This day, with its disappointment and the revelations about Blake's father and his pistol, the thoughts about her other marriage, those people. Poor Kenneth Broley, pulling the plastic over his head. That gentle, worried, harried presence, with his quiet consideration of her and his dignity in the face of such constant hectoring. His kind smile, and her tender feelings for him.

The couple on the next bench moan into each other's mouths. She keeps her gaze fixed on the darkness and the water beyond the cove.

So Charlotte actually absorbed beatings to shield Blake from the casual brutality of their father. Julia has known this since the first days with him. But it's also true that the story about being shot at was described, with great harrowing detail, in *Mozart's Ghost*— except that in the book, it's a boy who's being chased. Julia feels oddly that she's been made privy to something her sister-in-law has taken pains to disguise. Though there's also an element of doubt in it, as though she's caught the other woman in a lie. Her memory of reading the passage is very clear because in fact that stopped her from finishing—it's the story of a little boy with great musical gifts, suffering at the hands of a brutal, aggressively atheist father who hates him because he can sing like his dead mother. The mother died having him. The boy believes in a faraway place called "the outermost world," which he keeps as a secret. In the nights, he's visited from there by a spirit, mysterious and frightening at first, but slowly revealed as that of his mother, who has prevailed upon the long-dead composer to help with the boy's musical training. Mozart appears to him and gives him piano lessons on a ghost piano.

People talked about the funny scenes with the boy trying to teach Mozart to speak 1990s teenager English, and they were moved by the depiction of the boy developing an inexplicably brilliant style. They believed Charlotte's portrayal of his triumphant entry into the music world, the prizes he wins and the money. And of course people liked it that, as the novel ends, all these victories placate the bitter old man. Julia knows these elements of the story because of the talk around it, but the scene of the man chasing the boy in the woods and shooting at him made her put the book down.

Thinking of Charlotte, the little girl running among trees, seeking protection in them, while the flash and crack of the pistol followed, she begins to cry. She's sad for everyone, and feels unkind, more like Eunice every day, hectoring Blake about his sister and being uncharitable toward her, with Asperger's or whatever it is, while carrying the terrible frights of a bad childhood. She wants to go home. It's her honeymoon and she's blue and low and she feels guilty and she wants to go home.

"Hey," the man on the bench with his girlfriend says. "Take it somewhere else."

Before she can stop herself, Julia, feeling a rush at her chest and along her arms, says, "Why don't *you* take *yours* somewhere else, asshole. Get a room."

Before they can respond, she gets up and walks over to the kiosk and orders a beer. She stands at the railing to drink it, and there again is the lamp post with its curved end like the wing of the letter *r*. The Hotel Macabre. She lifts her cup of beer and says, "Here's to the Hotel Macabre." Then she goes back past the couple, and on toward the beach, feeling strangely lighter, as if something has been lifted from her shoulders. And here's Blake coming toward her.

"I got her calmed down," he says. "She went to her room."

Julia walks up and puts her arms around his neck. "I'm sorry," she says. "For all of it."

"Nothing to be sorry for."

"Do you think it's—is she—did he really—I mean she wrote it in the novel—"

"You want to know if she's lying."

"No."

"Sure you do. So do I. And I don't know. She could be. But she did put herself between me and the son of a bitch. I know that because I was there for that."

"Let's go out to the very end of the pier and sit for a while. Just us. And then go back to the room and make love. Do you want a beer?"

"I had some of her wine."

"She's gonna live with us for a while, isn't she."

"I don't know. There's—there's really nowhere for her to go until she gets the separation finalized and some money from the bastard."

"Oh, Blake," Julia says, "what's gonna happen to us?"

She didn't mean it the way it sounded, but he straightens a little and seems to gather himself. "We're going to try to save money and come back here and have a real honeymoon," he says. "Right?"

I

They were both very old now, and at first neither of them expressed much interest in talking about the war. Robert Marson's medals—Purple Heart, Bronze Star, Legion of Merit, Silver Star, from the fighting above Naples—were somewhere in the attic of the old house on Union Avenue in Memphis, where he had lived since 1963, and he didn't want anybody crawling around up there looking for them. Eugene Schmidt's Close Combat badge, earned on the Eastern Front in late 1943, had been discarded long ago. They had both raised families, had lived their separate lives, their children were grown and mostly gone or dead. Their wives were dead. They did not like the prospect of traveling.

But here they were, two surviving soldiers from opposite sides, in Washington, D.C., on this soft springlike July 3, 2016. The *Washington Post* and NPR had contributed to bringing them together again as part of Independence Day, a small ceremony for the benefit of what Schmidt's grandson Hans called "the media," in a tone Marson characterized to his eldest son as being very much like that of somebody speaking about a condition or an era: the flu or the Great Depression.

The young man, Hans Schmidt, was the one responsible for it all.

His mother had come to America when she was pregnant with him, and he had been raised in the house of his grandmother's younger sister, Brigitte. He was studying communications and film at the University of Maryland and had been spending the spring as an intern at the *Post*. As part of his thesis project he had set up a reunion that he would film. When he mentioned this to an editor, and spoke about how his grandfather, deciding to surrender, had saved the life of a U.S. soldier near Monte Cassino seventy-two years ago, the editor looked up from his turkey sandwich and said, "Wait a minute. Tell me that again?"

The young man repeated it all.

"Your grandfather was a Nazi soldier?"

"He was a *German* soldier. He lives in Boston now. And the U.S. soldier he saved is also alive. In Memphis but originally he's from here. From D.C. They're both alive and well."

The editor, whose name was Will Smalley, stared for a second, then picked up his napkin and wiped his mouth. "And the one saved the other."

"Yeah. My grandfather. And the other one grew up here in D.C. They were even in touch for a while after the war. They became friendly."

Smalley, a unibrowed dark man with bulging eyes and a continual odor of bay rum about his person, leaned back in his chair, smiling. "This'll be quite a thing if you can bring it off."

"I've already got it set up."

"The Naz—sorry. The German lives in Boston now."

"He's my grandfather, and he was never a Nazi. His name is Eugene Schmidt. A Catholic. When he was a young man he was studying to be a librarian and wasn't interested in politics. He never had any kind of anti-Semitism, either. He was a kid, you know. He'll tell you about it. When he got a little older he thought it was a craziness that would go away. Then the talk and the speeches and the sewed-on stars. He went into the war like all the able-bodied men, and he fought in Russia first. Then he was in Italy, where he saved the life of Robert Marson. And yes, he lives with my mother and my grandmother's sister Brigitte now, in Boston."

"And you're gonna bring him and the American together again."

"Yes, sir. That's the plan."

Smalley grinned. "No waiting on this one, right?"

"In today's world, sir, they could outlive us both."

He looked out the window. "Yeah. Guess you got that right." On the desk at his elbow was the current issue of a news magazine, with the cover listing names of the dead in the latest mass shooting. "Aren't you a bit young to have a World War Two veteran for a grandfather?"

Hans Schmidt nodded, talking. "My grandmother and he met when he was in his fifties. He was fifty-nine when my mother was born. My grandmother was thirty-four. She saved *his* life, really. He was in bad shape, I guess. I grew up here, but my mother and great-aunt still speak German in the house."

"And how old is he now?"

"Ninety-five."

"Damn. And the U.S. soldier, Marson?"

"Ninety-nine."

"Jesus."

Hans Schmidt went on: "They actually kept in touch for a time after the war."

The editor grinned. "You told me about this because you knew what I'd do, didn't you?"

"What're you going to do?"

He opened his cell phone. "I know somebody at NPR. I bet we can defray some of your expenses, son."

Hans waited.

"How'd you come to this, anyway."

"I found a couple of old cards from my grandfather to him, addressed to a place here, in D.C.—well, Arlington. That's what gave me the idea. I mean at first I thought I'd see about talking to someone in his family. I located his eldest son, Patrick Marson, who lives here, in Arlington. And I found out the old man's alive and living in Memphis. So I got in touch with him. I just spoke to him again this week."

"And he can travel? *They* can travel?"

"My grandfather came over here from Ansbach about twelve years ago, after my grandmother passed away. He uses a wheelchair and a walker, but he can get around. Marson doesn't even need a cane. They've both been hesitant about the whole thing, but they're going to do it."

The editor held up one hand and spoke into his cell. "Kaye, I think I've got something for you-all."

I I

The word *friendship* describing the two men was inaccurate: they had written back and forth a few times just after the war, and had even met again once, in 1964, when Marson traveled to Naples after the two decades. Eugene Schmidt spoke a fairly rudimentary English—his mother had lived in Leeds for several years as a girl—so they could talk without much difficulty. They drank a bottle of Barolo together, and Schmidt had several snifters of grappa. Alcohol was a problem for Eugene Schmidt at the time, and there was tension as the evening wore on. They parted with frosty politeness, and for some span after that there were widely spaced postcards—birth announcements, holiday wishes, even a wedding invitation. But this had lapsed until Hans had gotten in touch with them.

The original incident had been reported in the *Post* just after it happened, in 1944. "Sgt. Robert Marson, 27, Unlikely Rescue."

A strong human-interest story even then: an American soldier, on recon patrol, wounded by a mortar round that killed the two men he was with. He saw them die and then got himself out of the ditch they had been in and walked a slow lurching mile in full sight of anyone on either side, bleeding, half blind, seeking some friendly ground, trying to go anywhere but where the mortar rounds were falling, too dazed and numb with shock to take cover. He had collapsed and was only half conscious when he saw the German soldier moving toward him, rifle in hand, all stealth. The American believed that this was his death—this that turned out to be his luckiest chance: a savior from the other side. Because the German, weary, sick of the war, and beginning to see that he did not even want his own country to win, put down his rifle, took the other's wrist, pulling him to his feet, and, with the arm held over his neck, got him out of the line of fire, to the American lines, and surrendered. Apparently neither man spoke during this. It was only when the German surrendered that Marson heard his voice, repeating as if it were a chant, in heavily accented English, "*I hef hed enough.*"

Marson had survived Palermo, Salerno, and Anzio, and the savage attrition around Monte Cassino, and the Liri and Rapido Valleys. He thought his prayers had failed at last, that it was God's will and this was his last wound.

In the years just after his return home, telling others the story, he spoke of the enormous sense of peace that came over him when, opening his eyes briefly out of the swoon, he saw the enemy coming near and understood that this would be his death. In the following ten or twelve years, whenever he had dreams about that day, even knowing the happy outcome, he still woke shaking, in a sweat.

It was all so long ago, now. And it was still, in its way, confusing.

His wife, Helen, had saved the clipping for their children: two daughters—the elder was gone, in a terrible car crash in 1974, when he was fifty-seven—and three sons. Helen was gone, too. Patrick, the eldest of his grown sons, was the only one who lived near enough to see once in a while. The other offspring were in Oregon and Kyoto, Japan. The remaining daughter, Noreen, taught English in an American school in Japan. The two younger sons ran a bike–and–Jet Ski–rental shop in Cannon Beach, Oregon, where they lived together in a kind of boathouse on the water.

He visited the boys once, on his ninetieth birthday. He took a first-class flight to Portland, where they met him. He wanted to show them that he could still get around on his own. And if *he* could do it, take the trouble to visit, so could they. But they stayed where they were. They did not get along with him well enough to visit. He had grown cantankerous. You tended to, over time. You had aches and trouble sleeping and memories that hurt, even when they were good memories—maybe especially when the memories were good. It was not for sissies, this life. He had said it many times. You did not get old being any kind of sissy. He had seen and been through very many awful things, and grief was the weather all the time, even as you were happy to see the sun rise in the morning.

He had talked about this some with Schmidt's grandson, and what a surprise that Schmidt was still living. All the years. He told the boy, "I have outgrown my own life." He meant it as a joke. He could joke. Helen was gone thirty-one years—thirty-one years this August. Barbara, the eldest child, forty-two years ago. The little girl in the picture he carried in the cigarette tin, in Italy. *Seventy years, seventy years.* And she only got to be thirty-one. There were her two children. His second daughter, Noreen, had five. They had, every one of them, gone off in all directions with time. Though Noreen had called to say she was flying home from Japan for a visit with her daughter Monica, in Atlantic City, and the two of them would make their way south to D.C. for the event.

"I don't know how much of an event it's gonna be," Marson said.

"Well, Monica wants to see whatever it'll be, and so do I."

"The fireworks on the Fourth of July don't upset me anymore," he surprised himself by telling her. "You know, I used to plug my ears with cotton around that holiday."

"No, I didn't know."

"Your mother kept all that stuff from you guys."

III

Patrick met him at Reagan National on the afternoon of the third. From the airport, he drove to Brookland—the old house, 1236 Kearney Street NE. It was a whim, he told his father. He wanted to see it. That was Patrick, with his obsessions about the past. Marson was tired from the journey but decided to endure it for him. He had not been there since 1963 and was sure it would be unrecognizable. And withal, he felt a thin, nostalgic curiosity about it, like a man courting some sort of dangerous thrill. Surprisingly, it was still there. It had been completely remodeled, of course, and looked brand-new, not much like its old self: the two floors and the gabled roof, the porch, the tall narrowness of it. The street was even more thickly overladen with trees and shrubbery, the lawns perfectly tended; it all looked very exclusive and expensive. "We used to play horseshoes in the side yard," Marson said almost to himself. "It was a working-class neighborhood."

"Every house has been redone. It's an exclusive neighborhood, now."

There was a white swing on the porch, big oak trees flanking the place, with its bright blue façade. A child's bike stood in a shaft of sun at the bottom of the porch steps. Everything seemed perfectly still. He looked at the street. "Right there," he said, pointing. "Your grandfather stood and watched me go off in a taxi to the train station and the war." He looked at the house again. "Your mother was pregnant with Barbara. She and your aunt Mary and your uncle Jack stood there, waving. From that porch. That very porch. It's amazing that it's still there. My God."

Patrick was silent.

"Your mother's old place?"

"Torn down a long time ago. I drove over there for a dance

recital of a friend of mine. There's a run-down apartment building there now."

Marson put the back of his hand to his lips and wiped across. For a moment he felt this street as it was then. *The Surround,* as he had thought of it. His place in the world. And it was gone, truly, someone else's now probably far longer than it was ever his. But he had grown up there. He said, "'S'a short trip through here."

His son sighed. "I remember you telling us that."

"Now you know."

They were quiet for a time. He was experiencing a heaviness in his chest, the signature of grief for him his whole life. "Nothing here anymore," he got out, then cleared his throat. "Well, we all have to make room for somebody else. That's what your mother used to say."

His son stared at him.

"Glad these folks have it, whoever they are."

"I remember the long backyard. And the horseshoe pit."

"You were ten."

"I remember it."

"Eight years later we were in Memphis."

"I hated it at first."

"I was forty-six and I knew then it was my last house."

"Maybe on Sunday I could drive you across the river, and you could see my new apartment."

"Maybe. I'm tired, Son."

Patrick drove him to the hotel, where Noreen and Monica would meet them the following morning. Patrick, at seventy-one, was unmarried and would stay in the hotel room with him. Since there probably wouldn't be time to visit the new apartment he'd just bought, a rooftop corner unit with a wraparound window overlooking the street, Patrick took the trouble to describe it. He was clearly excited about this visit, and Marson strove to be up for it all. Then Patrick began talking about all the publicity around his father and the old German. He had never lost the penchant for artless enthusiasms. TV! Radio! And, as was his nature, he voiced the obvious: that the human-interest element of the story was much stronger today because Marson and Eugene Schmidt had both survived so long.

Marson said, "It wasn't something we accomplished. Was it. It was just chance. Don't make it more than it is."

"I think it's amazing."

"Well, stop touting it like it's some kind of circus stunt."

"I'm not touting it."

"All right. But it's not like we deserve any awards."

"But you wouldn't be here," Patrick said. He had seen the original clipping, when he was sixteen years old, in 1961, and had forgotten it, really, until Hans Schmidt called. It had been such a wonderful surprise, finding out his father's rescuer was alive. "Think of it. You've both survived this long."

"Okay, okay," Marson said, thinking that it was merely odd, as it was odd to be within months of your hundredth birthday. "Sure. Surviving."

But there had already been phone interviews and articles about the concurrent personal histories, and some people even suggesting that Congress and the president might get involved. So, Marson thought, perhaps Patrick was right to be enthusiastic. It was true that the old German's grandson had created a small media storm.

They had dinner in the mezzanine restaurant. They each had lobster, and they drank a beer in honor of Marson's father, who used to brew his own. He had only lived to be seventy-three. Patrick had searched out the article about the rescue, paying an online archive service for the privilege. He read it aloud over coffee, and the old man let him, though he couldn't listen fully. It seemed like someone else's story. There was a blemish on his son's left wrist, some form of nevus or liver spot that he had not noticed before. The boy, his boy, an old man now, was seventy-one years old. How could it be that he could still feel about him that he was the boy he once was? The sight of the little blemish filled him with a sudden, reasonless sense of mournful shame, as if the imperfection were in some way ominous, and also a violation of the other's privacy. He looked away, and then took the last of the beer. His legs ached. He determined to be less short with him, yet there it was as he announced that he couldn't stay up all goddamn night talking; he had to get some sleep now.

I V

Hans Schmidt told his grandfather about the possibility of some further ceremony coming from the government. "Even the White House," he said. It was a bright morning, and out the window, past the canopy of the hotel entrance, you could see men in green uniforms unwinding red, white, and blue ribbons along Pennsylvania Avenue to funnel the crowds toward what would be the site of the fireworks on the mall. Sun shone through the diaphanous white curtains framing the window. The weather was cool, and there were breezes, and on the muted television a man in a blue suit was tracing a pattern of airflow from the north. Then there was a screenshot of the five-day forecast: temperature in the seventies today. A beautiful Fourth of July.

"The fireworks make so much smoke," Hans said. "You won't believe it. Or maybe you will. It must be the way things are in real battle."

Schmidt gazed out. The grass shimmered with sun. Under the canopy in front of the hotel an SUV had pulled up and two women climbed out. They appeared at first glance to be arguing. But one of them laughed, and he realized they were just animated. It had always seemed to him that people in this country had more quick force, more velocity, just moving through things. The older one was blond and held a cigarette in her hand the way a man would. She said something emphatic and then headed into the hotel.

"The whole city comes out for it," Hans said. "I was here last year. Wait till you see."

"Such expense," said Eugene Schmidt.

"Every year the same."

They were sitting side by side on an oversoft divan in their wide, white room on the first floor of the hotel. The divan had polished wooden claw-feet, like an old bathtub. On the walls were spare prints of sticklike figures in attitudes of striving, with faded blue-and-orange backgrounds, like some sort of dream dawn, repeated in two separate rows. It made the old man think of hunger. His wheelchair was parked next to the divan. Before them was a low table with a French press and two cups of coffee on it. They looked at the muted TV, a woman now, talking and smiling. There was a drawing of an exploding firecracker behind her. Such a pretty face, but he could not believe anything substantial might exist behind it. Something blank in the eyes. Well, it was a face on television, and he was wrong to make judgments. He shook his head slightly and turned his attention to his grandson's open, innocent face. They were both waiting for whatever this would be: Smalley and the NPR people would arrive soon. The reunion would be filmed in a small ceremony at two o'clock in the sunny yard in front of the hotel. Both Hans and his grandfather knew that Robert Marson and his son were four floors up.

"What iss this, a vedding?" Schmidt said. "Vee cannot see each ozer?"

"They're probably still sleeping. They got in late."

The old man leaned over and with surprising fluidity of motion, even to his grandson, poured more coffee into his cup. He brought the cup to his mouth and drank.

"Think of it," said Hans in German. "The president."

"Ziss president. A baby. So young. *Ein Schwarz*. In America."

"In my opinion he's the best in a very long time."

"I didn't sleep," Eugene said. "Can I have orange juice. I need energy."

Hans went to the desk against the wall, where there was a phone, and called room service. When he came back Eugene looked at him with an air of expectation.

"*Es wird in fünf Minuten hier sein, Großvater.*"

He sighed. "*Sprich Englisch.* Speak. English."

"It's on its way. Five minutes."

"I'm tired," the old man said. Then, in German: "He could die in his sleep. Should we have a translator?"

"I can do that, Grandfather," Hans answered, also in German.

"*Ich bin müde.* Sorry. *Englisch:* I'm tired. Let's please speak *Englisch.*"

"Do you want to sleep?"

"I can't sleep. Hef you talked to him yet?"

"Last night after you went to bed. They flew first class. His son. A nice man."

"*Wie ist sein Name?* Agh! Sorry. His name."

"Patrick. Very pleasant gentleman. Robert was a little out of breath."

"You—already you call him Robert. I never called him zat."

"He asked me to."

"A healthy man?"

"He was a little out of breath."

"Me too," Eugene said. "A little out of breath."

"We could order breakfast. More than this coffee and orange juice," said his grandson.

"No. *Ich bin müde.* I got very little sleep. My *Englisch* iss not vut it vas."

"It's very clear and good."

"*Mein mu*—my muzzer."

"I know."

"Girlhood time in Leeds."

"I know that. You've said that."

"The var ztill frightens. Zo big and terrible. I vas cowardly. I remember it like ziss morning."

"You were afraid."

"Everybody. I gave up. Others depended on me."

"You saved a man's life and he's here. You'll see him again, the man whose life you gave back to him. A beautiful thing."

"I vas a soldier. As a soldier it vas ze vrong sing."

"You did a good thing. Don't talk like that."

"Vell. Ziss iss how it feels zumtime now."

They waited.

"I vas a fool ven vee met in Naples. A chaser of vimmen. A drunk. Vee did not get along. I offended him and his vife."

"*Vor fünfzig Jahren.*"

"*Englisch. Englisch.* Please."

"Fifty years ago. And you hadn't seen each other in more than twenty years."

"You sink I don't know ziss? And you accuse *me* auf repeating sings." The old man smiled dryly at him, this strange boy, his grandson, from the daughter who left his house in Ansbach because she had gotten pregnant by an American navy man, she wouldn't say who. She never even told this navy man about his child. She went to America and broke her mother's heart. Her mother, who had been able to see her grandson so seldom, and became so sad. The woman he had left alone so many times, and she had been subjected to the rages that rode with him when he did come home after days of drinking and living in other rooms, paying hollow attention to other women, and one of them—was it really so? could it have been so?—had nearly starved to death on the streets of Berlin, fourteen years old at the beginning of the bombing, and four years later all she wanted to do was *ficken*. Her name was Elise.

No, wait. Elise was far ago, 1946. Far past.

Hans's mother had come from Em. Emma, the love of his life— young, thick-bodied, worried Emma, whose sister Brigitte used to hate him for his drinking and his infidelity. And Brigitte lived in America and took the pregnant girl into her house. Emma was never the same. None of the women in his life were ever really the same after they lived with him. He did nothing for them but take what they were willing to give. It seemed to him now that there were many. Elise had been the first adultery, and he went to the priest to confess it. *Vergib mir Vater, denn ich habe gesündigt.* I have sinned. But he went back to her and back to her. No one more wildly carnal. There were times, holding her after the erotic fits were expended, when she would talk about wanting to see through death into the future, that she could almost believe she would never die while it was all going on. But she did die, half starved and full of black-market heroin she had acquired with her body and its uses. And she had given him TB.

Nineteen forty-six. The whole world exacting reparations, as if the ordinary citizen were also a criminal. He was not a criminal, and like many other former soldiers he was working slave labor, as those people had in the camps. And he had been with Elise and caught the TB from her, and, oh yes, Elise was 1946, not this boy's grandmother, not that late wife, not Emma.

Poor Elise, from his twenties. And this journey to see the American was bringing everything back, a lot that he had forgotten and did not want to look upon anymore. Elise a little girl in a war who came of age while the bombs were falling and the streets were burning, and he had used her, as everyone used her. That first year of peace, he had gone through days asking for food, wandering hungry and wine-sick, a man who had wanted a family. And finally he was ill with the TB that Elise had picked up in some little corner of the wrecked city. He, Eugene Schmidt—who today would be honored for quitting, and for using the American to keep himself safe, and for getting too old to keep his own memory straight—he had spent days stealing and cheating and wanting to die or kill someone. And then the feverish days in a United States hospital near the Russian zone, and the other wife, the first, Melicent, yes, Melicent, whom he hardly knew, and who left him for some English soldier. Melicent, a girl, too, from a family with money, and her father became a Gauleiter, who died in a bomb raid on Essen in 1944. That was right. He had it now. The hero of her grown life, Melicent's father, and Eugene never understood her devotion to him, a stern, looming, dyspeptic official with a thin unsmiling mouth and a perpetual air of having just received news of some approaching catastrophe. Well, the catastrophe had indeed swept over everyone. But he would not have to talk about all this today. Would it be necessary to explain?

The second wife, mother of the boy's mother, Emma, yes, she was the one who gave him back to himself for a time.

Em had made him, for that small while, feel like the idealistic Catholic boy he had once been, who went to confession every week. He became the version of himself that he had been at twenty, for a few spare and beautiful months. No drinking. Going to church. Confession and communion. The boy he was before the war. He remembered now, though there were muddles. He called Emma "Elise" sometimes in those last years, especially when drunk. After he had started up again with it. He could be drunk and no one would see it. He knew how to carry it, like a kind of vivid energy, a good mood. He could still discern when to say or do certain things, could still walk straight. It was not an illusion. Emma would only know if she smelled it on him, and there was something about the way he slept, something in the breathing. She tried to understand; she was not a bad person. She went to Mass and communion every day of her life and she forgave and forgave and forgave. And her daughter Agnes going away was the end of her, really. He told her, "That was not me. Agnes can say it was me, but I was willing to go on and forgive and let her have it and accept the illegitimate child. She wanted to leave. She wanted out of my house." Emma sat looking out on the street from the second-floor window, her bedroom, where she slept apart, and her face was lined, looking older than it was. But suffering seemed natural to her. *Ich bin nicht dein christliches Jungen*. Not your Christian boy, he would say. I'm not your creation.

Or was that Melicent? He had said it outside a church, in sunlight, a Sunday morning, after a bottle of kirsch. No, that was another occasion. A baptism. What year?

Everything ran together. And sometimes it all seemed to rush at him when he was on the edge of sleep, all of life, a speeding blur, a hurrying.

He was in no hurry now, but Hans was anxious to keep him moving.

"I don't repeat zings so much," he told the boy. "I confuse zem. A little."

"I'm sorry," said his grandson. The boy had his mother's eyes, that strange shade of light brown. Agnes had always been a stranger to him.

"*Ich bin müde*," he muttered. "Tired. I'm tired." The phone rang. Hans went and answered it.

"Hello, are you up?" It was Smalley. Schmidt could hear it all the way across the room. He had a moment of absurd pride in his good hearing. At ninety-five.

"Yes," Hans said.

"Look, we've decided you should spend a little time before we film. The reunion doesn't have to be blind, does it? It's better if it's not."

"It's going to be, no matter what. Right?"

There was a pause.

"I'm going to film the first moments."

"I guess we can reenact the whole thing," Smalley said. "Like the raising of the flag on Iwo."

"Pardon?"

"Never mind. We should've planned this better, I think. We're only ten minutes away. We'll come and film the first minutes, and then the ceremony at two. The ceremony'll be the official version probably."

"Ceremony."

"People're coming from Congress, kid. Remember? You got the memo, right? Tennessee and Massachusetts. You know? Congressmen."

"Of course, of course. I know."

"Do you have a script or something?"

"I was going to write something after I film it."

There was another pause. "We'll be there in a little while. Call Marson and his son. I know he's got some other family coming."

"All right," Hans said.

The other was already gone. He touched the button and then asked the front desk to ring Robert Marson's room.

Patrick Marson said, "Shall we come to you?"

"That would be good, yes," said Hans.

He hung up and came back to the divan. "They're on their way."

His grandfather took a breath. "I heard." He coughed, remembering his bad lungs.

"You all right?"

"I hev nut seen him fifty years. *Ich kenne ihn nicht.* I don't know him. Vut vill vee zay? Does he even remember?"

"We've been through this," Hans said. "We've had this conversation."

"I tell him vee didn't die. But now vee *vill* die. And zoon, *ja?*"

Eugene Schmidt saw again the ruin of the cities, going home, the rubble-strewn roads and the broken sides of buildings in the sun of spring, the tumbledown farms, and he was not even wounded, had healed from the frostbite and the starvation. He went along a winding country road with birds singing in the blasted trees. The whole world shattered, with rows of graves and the soldiers of other countries everywhere. They were going to further reduce the country. Everywhere you looked there was destruction and murder, and the factories were coming down. It seemed that nobody had anyone to go home to. No one he knew.

Hans said, "Where is your orange juice?"

"What iss the use?"

"Not that again," Hans said. "Please leave that alone. That won't do anyone any good."

Eugene Schmidt grinned at him. "Zat vay madness lies. *Ja?*"

The young man did not respond.

"I am much older zan zee old *Englisch* king. Lear."

He nodded, without quite attending. He was looking at the door.

"My English. Thank Got *für* Mrs. Schmidt, who lived in Leeds."

V

Smalley and the NPR people arrived first. His friend Kaye and the two-man crew looked like they could not be long out of college. She had a sharp-featured, intelligent face, leanly muscular arms, and an athletic body. In her white blouse, black slacks, and wide red belt, she looked pleasantly suave and as if she were arriving at a party or soirée. Her cameraman had blond dreads tied in back, and the gray T-shirt he wore was already sweat stained. He was very tall and very round, with some kind of tattoo climbing his neck. For all his girth, his jeans looked two sizes too big and hung on him. He had the video camera in a canvas bag over his shoulder, and he set it on the chair just inside the door. His partner, who murmured, "I'm sound," toward Eugene Schmidt, was a pale, doughy little puffy-faced man with thick black down on the backs of his hands and fingers. His hair was cut close, so that you could see his scalp. Kaye ordered them around as if they were her children. She introduced herself to Hans and his grandfather, then turned back to the others: "Say your names, boys."

The big one smiled and nodded. "Stuart."

"Brent," said the puffy-faced one.

They all seemed to be trying not to look at the old man, whose gaze settled intensely on each of them in turn, and then seemed to retrace itself.

"This is my grandfather," Hans Schmidt said to them.

Smalley was in a blue pin-striped suit and therefore looked both out of place and as though he should be in charge. He stepped forward and shook hands. "It's quite an honor to meet you, sir."

"*Ich danke ihnen demütig.*"

"My grandfather thanks you, humbly," Hans said.

"*Ja,*" said the old man. "Zorry. Humble."

Then they all stood quite still, as if listening for something. The light changed slightly at the window.

"*Mein Englisch—*" Schmidt stopped, shook his head, the smallest side-to-side motion. "My *Englisch,* how you zay, not ze best."

"That's just fine." Smalley sat down next to him on the divan, hands folded between his slightly spread knees. "My father was in Vietnam. He was wounded there."

The old man nodded, staring at him, but said nothing.

"I almost went to Iraq."

There was another pause. Then Smalley hurried to explain. "I mean I thought of volunteering to go over there and report on it all."

"Oh, *Freiwillige,*" said Eugene Schmidt, smiling, trying a joke: "Zorry. Volunteer. Unheard in za army I served."

"No, sure." Smalley laughed nervously. "I guess not." He cleared his throat. "I understand you were a librarian?"

Schmidt looked at him. "I vas library ztudent."

"What was that like? You know, when the—uh—when Hitler came to power."

"I vas twelve years old."

"Oh."

"Vee did not sink of politics."

"No. But later—I mean, you must've been in the—uh—youth program?"

"I vas schoolboy."

There was a brief pause. Schmidt had another sip of coffee, which was cold now.

"And you fought in Russia," Smalley went on.

"*Ja*. Before."

"What was *that* like for you?"

Schmidt wrapped his skinny arms around himself. "Cold."

"I bet." It seemed clear from Smalley's tone that he was not terribly happy with the answers he was getting but felt chary of pressing. "I'm going to be asking you about some of that, if you don't mind. When we do my part of the interview."

"What could it matter now?" Schmidt asked him, smiling.

"People are gonna want to know what it was like." There was the slightest shrug of Smalley's shoulders.

Kaye had begun working on tying the drapes back for more light. The others were putting together the metal frame from which they would hang the extra lights they needed. She kept muttering orders at them. "We're going to need floods, and they're going to have to be higher."

"Yep," said Stuart.

They were all three working together. The one named Stuart looked through the camera at Eugene Schmidt.

"Might have to remove the glasses. The glare."

"Grandfather, can you take your glasses off?"

The old man removed them and put them on the table.

"Better," said Stuart.

"This must be so wonderful and strange for you," Smalley said. "To see this person you saved after all this time. So many years."

"*Ja*," Schmidt answered unsteadily, not returning his gaze, feeling nothing but a sudden welling up of avoidance. Years, yes. But always it's *now*. He wanted to say to the man that everything is *now*, everything only one vast *now*. And no one understood it. That even last night, half asleep in this hotel, waking to see his own coat draped over the end of the bed and thinking it to be his friend Marcus, about whom he had been dreaming, bending to take something—Marcus from forty-five years ago, and he'd had an argument with him, 1971, and only later, when they were no longer speaking, did he come up with what he should have said to him. A remark that would've settled him. And in the half dark of the July morning, Marcus, who had been dead thirty years, was present, enough for Eugene Schmidt to feel the chagrin all over again of not having had the nimbleness of mind to say it. What a triumph it would have been to say it.

This gathering seemed suddenly too early. It was all too early. Everything. He clasped his skeletal hands with their black patches between the bones and watched the others in the room. He had not been given time to acclimate himself. He saw his grandson talking to the woman, Kaye. Looking at her thin face, an insane thought came to him that she looked as though she possessed the brutal will to order young men to their deaths. Of course, that was preposterous. Probably a nice woman. Probably a nice Jewish woman, and he gazed at her, wanting to say plainly that the sickness was not with him and never had been. He was a boy studying library science who wept when they burned the books. He felt the need to ingratiate himself with her, soften what he might say because he did not like the severity of her features. And after all, who knew what he had ingested psychologically in that space of his life, that might still be with him? In the next instant he remembered again that it all *was* with him, all that he had seen and been. It was *present*. Contemporaneous, happening horrifically all at once. And this woman reminded him of someone. Feldwebel Myer. Sergeant Myer. With the chin like a steel wedge. He had not thought of Myer, or the shellfire in the cold, for such a very long time. Yet there it all was. There it was in its terrible *withness*. He could not believe it. And here were these people moving around in the bright room—with a weary, regretful old man nodding at them and pretending to listen—as if this for itself were important, were more than a punishing curiosity.

He shivered.

The knock at the door startled him. He watched his grandson go over to open it. Smalley was still sitting there next to him saying something about the present wars, repeating that he almost went to Iraq, as though it were necessary to emphasize the fact. It might have been an assignment he would have. His whole life, Smalley said, he wanted to be a newspaperman, and now here he was at the *Post*. He went on talking proudly of his work.

Schmidt kept nodding, having trouble concentrating for the tumult in his mind. The knock at the door had been room service, Hans announced. He held a tray with a bottle of orange juice and a glass on it. He set it down on the coffee table, then poured the glass full. In German, he said to his grandfather, "Five minutes, yes? More like half an hour."

Schmidt replied, also in German. "I'm so thirsty." He lifted the glass and took a long drink, then put it back on the tray.

Again, in German, he said, "Hans, for the love of God, please speak English."

Hans answered in English. "Yes, sir."

Smalley was discussing with Kaye how the filming would go. Everything was ready for the morning event, the initial meeting.

"I'm going to ask you both to talk about how this feels," Kaye said to Eugene Schmidt. "That's all right, isn't it?"

"If za oza von vishes. *Ja.*"

"I understand you kept in touch and got to be friends."

"*Ja.* Vell."

"I can't imagine what that must've been like. Both Catholic, too. Do you both still practice?"

"I don't know."

"Do *you?*"

"Zumtimes, *ja.*"

"Will you talk about all that sort of thing with him?"

Schmidt gazed at her. He had the inescapable feeling of being patronized. He said, "If he vishes."

"What do *you* wish for?" she asked.

He smiled, reaching for the orange juice again. But his hand shook, and he decided against it. "Peace," he said, keeping the smile.

"Oh, don't we all," she said. "Do you want some more of the juice?"

"Sank you, no."

She stood and moved toward the window, and he folded his hands again. In the same moment he experienced the contradictory sense that maintaining his dignity was necessary, and that this was impossible anyway in the circumstance. How do you maintain dignity when your hands look like the hands of a corpse found after centuries in the ground?

Again, there was the knock at the door. This time it was Robert Marson and his son and two women. Eugene recognized the women as the ones he had seen arriving in the SUV earlier. They came in first—he had only caught a glimpse of Marson, a skinny figure behind them. The two women looked very much alike, though the one with the blond hair was older. They were very serious, as if being led into a courtroom. The camera and the equipment were a source of great interest to the younger one. Patrick Marson introduced her as Monica. She had thickly made-up eyes, with lashes that looked fake and were too dark. There was a tattoo on her neck, too, and Schmidt looked over at Stuart, to see if he had noticed it. How curious, still to be interested, in spite of everything. He looked at the other woman, the one with the wild blond hair. He saw her round, smiling, wide-eyed face, and said, "I'm ninety-five years old."

She kept the smile. "I know, I'm Noreen."

He could not find Marson, looking at this woman and now her brother, Patrick, who loomed over him, reaching to shake hands. "What an honor it is to meet you, sir. And thank you for the life of my father. For *my* life."

Smalley said, "That's what we need to capture in the film. Kaye, are you all getting this?"

"Stuart?" she said in the tone of a command.

"Filming, but I need levels. Nobody's mic'd up. Jesus."

Schmidt nodded at him, feeling the air grow thin. The room was so crowded and he could not see Marson.

And then he could. Marson seemed smaller, his shoulders narrow, sloped, his eyes two horizontal tight lines, his mouth indrawn, clearly toothless. He had a beak of a nose. Schmidt did not remember the nose, and maybe age had heightened its prominence on the face. There wasn't a strand of hair on his head. When Marson was introduced to the young NPR lady who had the cruel green eyes, he had to bend his neck as if looking uphill, and he seemed suddenly shy. Brent had stepped close and was fumbling with the cloth of Schmidt's shirt, excusing himself, pinning a little wired mic to the collar. Then he went over to Marson and did the same. The wire from the mic went into a small cigarette-pack-sized battery or transmitter.

The others now stood back, and Hans bent down to say something Schmidt couldn't hear.

"Vas?"

"We're starting in a minute."

"Sound?" said Kaye. "We're all set, right?"

"Everything's ready to go," Brent the sound man said.

"Camera?"

"Got it," said Stuart. "Had it from the start."

Marson walked slowly over. Everyone grew very still and quiet.

V I

Marson's morning had begun with an old affliction—a recurring condition the doctors called corneal erosion. He had suffered with it intermittently for at least thirty years, and sometimes several years would go by without an attack. But it always returned. Perhaps this time it was the dehydrating ride in the jet from Memphis to Washington. But the truth was that neither he nor the doctors had ever really been able to discern a pattern or a cause. One doctor, not an ophthalmologist but a good general practitioner, attributed it to dryness, to having a fan blowing on you in the nights. But Marson never put a fan on, had always slept under blankets, even in the summer.

At any rate, in the predawn he woke from a busy dream of an airline cabin, two rows of seats crowded with weary passengers going off into the vanishing point, and immediately he felt the pain in his left eye. The condition did not endanger his sight or damage the tissue, but it was as if there were a small shard of glass under the lid. It hurt to move the eye, opening or closing it. Any slight motion of it, to either side, up or down, was excruciating. The only thing he could do was put some ointment in it and lie flat with eyes closed until the pain went away. Sometimes this took hours. His son snored in the next bed and made sudden gasping noises. Marson got up quietly and moved into the bathroom. The ointment was in his shaving kit.

Later, in bed again, he felt a pressure at the middle of his chest, a familiar and old sensation, having to do with the skein of muscle tissue on either side of his breastbone. He had strained it lifting his suitcase into the back of the car, in Memphis.

And still, of course, he thought of his heart. What else do you think about at this age in the nights, with your seventy-one-year-old son snoring in the bed next to you? The eye stung and watered; his chest hurt. He thought of Schmidt. Eugene Schmidt. He remembered the cold and the misery, the loneliness, even as you moved with others, even as you heard their voices, voices that you clung to though they drove you toward breaking down. Sounds grated on your nerves. Something singing amid the sprigs of pine where you walked, some small helplessly cheerful-sounding creature, and you wondered what could possibly live in this dead place, while you hoped to be able to kill it to stop its noise, and you went on, breathing gas and smoke and powder, and the memory-obliterating, sick-sweet, weighing-you-down stench of death.

"Bad," he murmured, lying there in the hotel bed. "God. Help." There was always the fear of breaking to pieces. He thought of the others, the dead, saw their faces colorless as cold water. This was what he had been afraid of, going into this situation where all of it could come rushing through the opening you made in memory. "Christ," he whispered. He should not have come here.

"Dad?" Patrick was awake.

"I shouldn't have done this," Marson said.

"What is it?"

"Go back to sleep, Son."

"You all right?"

"Fine. Christ. Go back to sleep."

"Maybe we should've found a way to see them last night."

Marson did not answer.

"But Schmidt had already gone to bed."

"Bet he didn't sleep," Marson said.

"I'm sorry. I'll shut up."

"Oh, I didn't mean anything by that."

A moment later, he said, "This trip's calling everything back. I bet it's doing the same to him. In my thoughts I'm back there. Christ. I'm twenty-seven again and expecting to die any second, even in the hours of doing nothing but waiting. Twenty-seven. And I don't want to go back. I never would've believed I had seventy-two years to go."

"Well, seventy-two and counting."

They were both quiet. Light was coming to the window, the one window.

"Twenty-seven," Patrick said. "Was anybody ever that young?"

"We both were," said Marson, "and only twenty-eight years between us. Think of that."

"God."

"Go on back to sleep," Marson said.

Soon he heard the snoring. He lay there quietly, experiencing the pain in his eye, seeing again things he had kept down in some part of himself. Seeing Helen's face, which had faded now so that it was closer to an idea than an image. How awful it was that a whole long lived life, with its pleasures and worries, its separate milestones, its incremental changes, and all the daily passages, could fall away under the weight of a single recollection. He was always trying to remember her face more clearly than he could.

Oh, girl.

The sting in his eye had begun to subside. The bed was uncomfortable. His back hurt. He drifted and saw himself get out of the bed and walk to the window to look out at the night streets, the avenues of his home city. But when he opened his eyes he was still in the bed and light was pouring into the room. The phone was ringing. He sat up with a start, feeling the hammering of his own heart, and realized that his son had gone in to take a shower. A phone ringing in the middle of the night. But this was morning. The phone kept jangling. Picking up the receiver, he held it to his ear without speaking.

"Hello?" Noreen's voice.

He breathed for a few seconds and said, "We just got up."

"Why don't you say 'hello.' You're supposed to say 'hello' when you answer the phone."

"Hello, Noreen," he said.

They made breakfast arrangements. She went on about plans for the evening, speaking with that rapid assurance that people had mistaken for rudeness all her life. And there was no one more softhearted or generous. Wherever she went, from her girlhood through a long marriage and life in five different cities including Kyoto—her husband, Mike, had worked for the airline industry— she created a wide community of friends, and she never let any of them go. In terms of sensibility and temperament she was exactly as she had been when she was twelve years old. With her children she was like a funny friend. But she was strong, too, and could be stubborn. Marson saw Helen in her, and he admired her while also finding her a bit exhausting. She rattled on about how she and Monica would attend the concert and fireworks on the mall.

"Have you seen Schmidt yet?" she asked.

"Later this morning."

"Any celebrities or news types?"

"We just got here ourselves, Noreen."

"What room are you in?"

VII

When Patrick was through with the shower, he helped Marson get into it and run water over himself. Marson had a stall at home. You walked into it and walked out of it. Here, you had to step into a bathtub. The women arrived as Patrick was helping him dry off. He got into the robe provided by the hotel and Patrick opened the door.

Noreen looked tired and vaguely aggravated, while her daughter was calm, perhaps even a bit drowsy. She told Patrick that she loved the ride down to D.C.

"Great company," Noreen said. "I might as well have been driving a hearse."

"The sleep I had in that bumpy SUV was spotty, especially with Mother driving."

"She was unconscious most of the way."

"Feigning sleep so as not to have to talk." Monica was forty, separated, childless, a psychologist with a healthy practice. Marson kissed her on the cheek and hugged Noreen.

"You haven't seen him yet?" Monica asked in a tone near reverence.

"No."

"It must be so strange to think about."

"The grandson seems nice," Patrick said. "An average American kid."

"NPR," Noreen said. "Congressmen. Maybe the president."

"No," said Marson.

They went together down to the mezzanine restaurant and sat talking quietly over breakfast. It struck Marson that they looked like a family at a reunion. And so it was, in its way. He turned to Monica and smiled, drawing her out of her lethargy.

"Tell me about your life."

"Life is good," she said, and smiled.

"How are your studies?" Marson asked, and realized that she was long past that. He shook his head and muttered, "Forgive me."

"Don't be silly. I'll never stop studying."

"You're very thoughtful," he said.

"You don't seem so grouchy."

"Monica!" Noreen exclaimed.

"What?" Marson's granddaughter turned to him and grinned. "You never minded frankness before, right, Granddad?"

He nodded. She looked so much like her father, who was blond and delicate featured.

"I remember," she went on, "Mom's story about how you'd walk into the middle of the living room while everyone was talking and being funny, and drinking, and you'd stretch real big and then yawn and say, 'Oh, God, I'm glad I'm home. I sure wish you all were.'"

They all laughed. They all remembered him. And he had been that person. He could remember that, too.

"I can't imagine coming face-to-face with the man who saved your life," Monica said. "I'll be awful happy to make his acquaintance."

"In a way, they saved each other," Patrick said.

"I don't think he sees it that way," Marson told him. "And as a matter of fact, neither do I." He got himself up, putting his arm out to fend off Patrick's. "I'm fine. Just have to use the restroom."

They all watched him start toward the entrance to the hall, and then turned to their own concerns, Patrick asking about whether or not there could be some expectation of the brothers showing up or any of the other grandchildren. Marson went straight, past the opening to the hall, to the balcony railing. From here, you could see all of the high-ceilinged lobby below and the doorway out onto the street. He put his hands on the smooth metal railing and leaned slightly, watching people move back and forth to the front desk. It was a busy place. The coffee he'd had seemed to have gone immediately to his heart, which was rushing as it always did with caffeine. Behind him, he could hear the women going on again, teasing about the sniping they had done at each other during their early morning drive down from New Jersey. He turned, looked at them, walked slowly back, and took his place at the table. Here they were, in life on earth. They walked the earth because of something a tired, scared, hungry German soldier had done on an impulse, something last ditch, not even thought out, borne of exhaustion. He himself felt suddenly exhausted. He wanted to go back up to the room and lie down. Noreen walked over and sat next to him. "What're you feeling about this event?"

"I didn't want to come," he told her. "And then I *did* want to."

She said, "I was something like fifteen when you and Mom went to Naples that time. I remember you were nervous about meeting the guy."

"I was always nervous about everything back then," he told her.

"I remember feeling scared, seeing my father so shaky."

"I don't think I was *shaky*."

Patrick said, "I just remember you and Mom being glad to fly to Italy."

"I saw things in Italy," Marson said, and felt suddenly a little sick to his stomach. The feeling astonished him, though he understood it as it took hold of him. He sipped the coffee and listened to them talk about Helen, and of Barbara's death.

"What is it," Monica said. "Forty years?"

"Forty-two," said Marson. "In September." He saw the long, dimly lit upstairs hallway of the house in Memphis, and himself walking it, toward the bedroom, where Helen sat on the edge of the bed, hands on her thighs, waiting to find out who had called at that hour of the morning.

"Oh, God, what is it?" she said, seeing him standing in the doorway.

Twenty-two minutes after three o'clock in the morning.

There was a reason you possessed all the things you gathered around you in the days. There was a reason for being too busy all the time, and falling into bed too tired to think.

He sat there having this thought. Ridiculous. Of course it was completely absurd. One hundred years of all that, and the going around and the coming back. His mind seemed to be faltering, folding in on itself. A man should keep to his daily routines and not dwell in the country of remembering. Where had he seen that? Who had said it?

"Forty-two years," Noreen said now. "Doesn't seem that long."

"I carried her picture in that little cigarette tin," Marson said. "A baby."

She reached over and put her hand on his shoulder. "Dad."

"That was more than seventy years ago, in Italy."

They were all quiet a moment.

He had seen so much of death. How many years since he had looked at the memory of John Deal and Tolly Miller. The two dead men whom he had crawled and then walked away from. All of that. The thing he would be talking about soon, with Eugene Schmidt. "Memory loss is sometimes a good thing," he said to Noreen.

"I know."

"The things you must be carrying around," Patrick said, as if paying some sort of tribute. "Next to you, I don't have any memories that qualify."

"What the hell does that mean?"

"Bad memories," Patrick said. "Trauma."

"I haven't thought about the war for long time. A very long time. It's always been there, though." He touched his finger to his breastbone. "Here, I mean."

He saw the two men, John Deal, whom everyone called Square because he gave everyone a square deal, and they had teased him about buying a used-car dealership, and Tolly Miller, who one day had picked up a miserable, rain-sodden stray cat and put it under his field jacket, thinking to get it warm and dry, and the cat went crazy, scratching to get out, caught between the folds of the jacket and Miller's body, Miller gyrating and turning and falling down and rolling in the muddy lane trying to get his jacket open so the cat could escape. Miller's body. And he, Robert Marson, almost one hundred years old, had lived all this time, and sold cars himself for thirty years, and kept customers and acquaintances and friends entertained with stories, like the funny memory of the cat and the friend wriggling in the mud, even as that very memory was woven, under the surface of his talk, behind his smile, into the moment, one day later, of the white flash and the thudding that none of them knew was an exploding mortar round. And he always saw it again, as he saw it now. Tolly Miller's headless body there in the ditch, soaked by the fountain of blood from his neck. He saw John Deal staring, sitting with his legs under him, his entire peritoneal sac in his cupped hands. Deal kept screaming from what had happened to Miller. Deal did not know what he was holding in his hands. Deal looked at Marson as Marson reached screaming for him, and then Deal looked down at himself, and quickly back at Marson, and said one thing: "Don't."

Always there. Always just behind the flow of living and being and dreaming and going on in time. Never very far away, and he wanted to say it out loud, as if addressing the two men, "I didn't mean to forget. I didn't mean to let it go."

"Dad?" Noreen said, staring, concerned.

His family was waiting for him to continue, and when he didn't, Patrick said, "You never really talked about it, Dad."

"No."

"Think you'll be talking about it today?"

Marson did not answer. But shrugged slightly after a pause.

"This must be hard for you."

"Oh, yes."

"Under the circumstances, I guess you'll have to talk about it, now."

"Do you think *he's* having the same onrush of memories?" Monica asked him.

Such a perceptive girl. Woman. "I don't know. The last time I saw him—" He left off.

"Mom came home that time pretty upset about things, as I recall," said Noreen.

"At me? You don't—"

"No, *for* you. You went to see this guy who saved your life, after twenty years, and it was a disappointment to you. She never liked to see you unhappy. You know that, Dad."

He was silent, squeezing the napkin under the table, watching them talk about Helen, and how it had been, growing up in his house, his and Helen's house. *Oh, Lord, let me get through this and I'll raise a big family,* he had prayed. It would be thirty-one years August 4.

It was all too much.

Helen, eleven years after Barbara, coming to him in that bedroom in Memphis and lifting her too-thin arm, pointing back to the bathroom, saying, "I just lost a lot of blood in there."

"Do you want me to call an ambulance?" he had said, sitting up in the bed.

"No." She climbed in next to him. "Just hold me a little while."

So he cradled her, breathed the slightly sour odor of her hair, which had thinned so much. "You know I love you," he said to her, patting the bony shoulder. She had lost so much weight, and the doctors could not find anything wrong. Eleven years of a broken heart. *And why had he lived so long? Why had he, Robert Marson, lived so very long?* That last night with her, he murmured, "You all right?"

"I'm dying," Helen said. Then, a moment later, reaching across him: "Hand me that pillow." And she was gone. And he knew it. He held her, crying softly, because she had wanted to go, sixty-seven years old, but she had been so tired, raising Barbara's children, so tired. And she had simply sighed away from him, lying there, and this was worse than any wound in the war, any terror or anguish he had ever suffered in the war. Barbara, the first, and Helen.

Patrick was talking to Noreen and Monica about the ceremony to come. "It's still kind of disorganized, really."

They were watching him, though. He held up one hand as if to reassure them. But it seemed aimless, he knew, not quite coming from conscious thought. He had been religious his whole life, and they had been, too. Through all the catastrophes, but in these last few years even that had atrophied some. It offered no solace. He looked into each of their faces and felt suddenly like a stranger; for a second, he did not know them.

"So he's ninety-five," Patrick said to Noreen. "And imagine. He's been living in Boston."

"I know all that," said Noreen. "We talked about it on the phone."

"I wonder if he's still a drunk," said Monica and her mother shushed her with a quick gesture.

So Helen had confided in Noreen about that last time, and now obviously Noreen had told Monica. The story had entered his family's lore, then. How could he have missed it?

"I'm sorry," said his psychologist granddaughter, who believed so much in talk.

"It's all right," he said to her.

During the long hours of that day in 1964 when the two men had met after two decades, he noticed alcohol on the other's breath first thing in the morning and thought it must be some sort of mouthwash. Almost immediately the German boasted with a rough nudge of his elbow in Marson's side that the lovely young woman who had accompanied him to Italy was *die Metze*, a paid escort. He went on to relate how his first wife had never liked sex and had come from society, how she had left him while he was in the hospital, suffering from TB, and this was why he wanted nothing more to do with *gesellschaft Frauen*, women of social standing, glancing with this last remark at Helen, as if she would certainly understand him. Then later, that evening after dinner—after endless talk and self-congratulation about being the American's savior (so much so that Marson began counting references to it, as if the man were trying to justify the whole thing to himself)—after the glasses of wine and the shots of grappa, Schmidt went on about what he drunkenly called his true first experience with love, someone named Elise, who had been in the bombing of Berlin as a girl and was only eighteen when he met her and loved to have sex, no matter with whom, boys and girls, he said, glancing at Helen's neckline more and more often as he spoke. Marson realized that the German had indeed been drunk all day, and when the time came to get up and leave, he came very close to striking him.

Even so, he had kept the connection for a few years, at Helen's insistence, because in fact Marson would not have survived that day were it not for the other soldier. If Schmidt hadn't decided to surrender, then certainly—there was no denying it—he would have killed Robert Marson.

That was true. That was the thing.

"His grandson, Hans, is a nice young man," Patrick said. "We've both talked to him."

"A nice young man," Marson told them, merely to be talking.

"How does the guy end up here?" Monica asked.

"His mother came to Boston when she was pregnant with him," said Patrick.

"No, I mean the old—the soldier."

Marson looked at his son. "I'm not sure."

"His wife died," Patrick said. "And his wife's sister agreed to take him in. She'd already taken in his daughter. The boy's mother."

"When did his wife—" Marson began.

"Years ago. Hans talked about it. The wife was only fifty-nine."

They were all quiet again. Marson saw himself holding Helen, saw the room they were in, and heard her cigarette-deepened voice utter his name. . . .

He looked at Noreen and sought for something to say to her. "You hear from your brothers?"

"Oh, you know. They're thrilled about it all. They've had something planned for months."

Marson nodded, holding on inside.

Other people wandered in and were seated. An empty buffet table stood along one wall, with a coffee machine set up on one end of it. Two men were there making coffee. The woman who had come in with them walked over. She went up to Marson. "Are you one of the two old soldiers?"

Marson stared at her, then nodded.

She smiled and pulled a chair over and sat down. She had reddish-brown hair knotted tightly on top of her head and eyebrows that had been shaved and then painted on in a different arc. You could see where they should have been on her face, and the difference was disconcerting. "We heard about it, of course. We're with the *City Journal*. I wondered if you'd want to talk to us."

The two men walked over with their coffee. They were both thin, with boylike faces. The tall one had brown teeth. He was the one smiling.

"I don't think I have time to talk just now," Marson said to them. "Have you been in touch with these other people? The ones from the *Post* and NPR?"

"Well, we all got a press release, you know."

The one with the brown teeth said, "Who you gonna vote for?"

After a pause, Marson said, "I don't ever share that, sonny."

The other man, who could not have been much beyond five feet tall, was florid faced, cheeks the color of a bruise, as if he were made up for some kind of stage role. He said, "The Republican candidate, I'll bet, right?"

Marson stood, and reached out for Patrick. "Isn't it time to go down to Schmidt's room?"

Patrick was signing for the breakfast. Noreen walked over and said, "Excuse me, please—this is a private breakfast with my father. But I will tell you he's a lifelong Democrat."

Monica, still sitting with arms folded, said, quietly and evenly, "And fuck the Republican candidates. You can quote *me.*"

Robert Marson was taken aback. But he smiled. "My granddaughter, gentlemen." Then he looked at the woman. "And lady."

"She's got quite a mouth on her, doesn't she," said the florid-faced man.

Monica said, "Oh, I do, don't I? And you're a little purple motherfucker."

The three people simply stood there as Marson and his daughter and son and granddaughter left the restaurant. As they got into the elevator to go down, Noreen said, "Monica, that's it, all right? None of that stuff with these people we're going to see."

"Sorry, Granddad," Monica said.

"No need," said Marson, remembering almost with embarrassment how he had felt when the men around him used that language during the war. "No worries," he said to her.

"But not again," said Noreen.

"I know the *City Journal* people, Mom. They have a big presence on Facebook. Jerks. Political trolls." She took hold of Marson's arm. "Believe me, Granddad. They're a bunch of smug assholes."

"Monica."

"I'm with her," Marson said, forcing a smile at Noreen. "Honor bright."

VIII

In the thronged white hotel room with the paintings of stick figures in something burning on the walls, Marson, feeling hemmed in, offered to shake hands with Eugene Schmidt, who was seated between his grandson and a man in a powder-blue suit. Shaking hands seemed the logical thing to do in the circumstance, with everyone staring at them, and the camera rolling. Schmidt lifted his bony hand and let it be taken. "Old fighter," Marson said to him, and evidently no one else heard it. Schmidt said, "Ja. Ve hef done ziss."

"Speak louder," Kaye said in a singsong tone, as if she didn't really mean it.

Hans stood and guided the American around to sit next to his grandfather, who now looked confused and frightened. Everyone else was ranged against the opposite wall, where the writing desk and the telephone were. Kaye made a signal to Stuart and Brent, who moved closer and to one side, and then she stepped over to sit across from the two old men. Marson and Schmidt were sunk so far down in the oversoft couch, it appeared that neither of them would be able to rise on his own.

She said, "Can we have an embrace?"

Marson reached over and put his thin arms around the other man, and noted that he smelled strongly of coffee.

Neither of them spoke.

For Marson, the experience was strangely separate from him. It was as though he were observing everything from a great distance. He knew there had been the fact of being carried, wounded, half conscious to safety, and he was also aware of the immense good fortune that had been granted him; yet remembering it now felt like some kind of intellectual exercise. He did not quite believe it anymore.

Schmidt felt that the moment was clouded, dark, fraught with his awareness of how badly he had offended the other man with his wife, in the previous meeting. He was also inwardly cowering with the recollection of deciding to abandon his post and to help the wounded soldier, who was nothing to him but a way to survive, and not die. In truth he had never felt any pride in the thing, for all his talk of pride, for all his talk of the vision he had claimed about the lessons of mercy and being a good Catholic. None of it was true. As, in his teens, it hadn't been true that he wanted to be a priest or even a librarian. He had once accepted his family's happiness for him about the fact that he was even thinking of the priesthood. Knowing that people around him were aware of it made him special when he was young, though it was not something to talk about in the street or at school. He was a dreamy irresponsible boy who wanted to find a way not to work. But he was also the library student, and he had wept when they burned the books. He had been filled with terror when people began disappearing. Now these people and his grandson with his open innocent expression, staring at him, the man who saved one life as his last act in the war. They were all smiling at him, and Robert Marson was smiling, too. Marson, who must know what was at the bottom of his act. *I hef hed enough.* There was something morbid about all of it now.

At this age, there should be some clarity of emotion, some purity of feeling.

He looked into Marson's narrow old eyes, saw the redness in the one on the right, the spot of blood there, and the lines and rucks and liver spots in the face, the patches of redness and dry skin on the bald pate, and murmured, "Forgive me."

Kaye came close. "What did you say, Mr. Schmidt?"

They were adjusting the little microphone on Marson's lapel, and Marson began suddenly to laugh. *Children,* he wanted to tell them. *Go live your lives.* But he kept nodding and laughing softly.

"Mr. Marson?" Kaye asked.

"I'm so glad to be alive," he said to her. Then he took Schmidt's hand and squeezed. "Look at my children and my granddaughter." Patrick, with tears in his eyes, his arm around Noreen's shoulder, brother with sister, and Monica standing close on the other side of her mother. None of whom would have been born. It was true. Nothing of the complications of things between Marson and his memory of Schmidt, or Schmidt and his troubles, whatever they were, meant anything next to that, and this was what Helen had known all along. They stood closer, Monica now also with her arm around her mother. A perfect picture. Hans Schmidt took the picture. Smalley, the journalist who felt wrong because he hadn't gone to Iraq, also took a picture with his phone.

Schmidt had patted his shoulder and now sat back, and Kaye the NPR reporter looked into the camera and began to talk about two men and a fateful encounter seventy-two years ago in the terrible late winter of 1944. Then she stopped. "Hold that. I want to start with Eugene, okay? We'll get his story first. Is that all right?"

Marson nodded. But it was Patrick and Stuart she was talking to.

"Let's just get it done," Smalley said.

"Then we'll ask what it was for Mr. Marson—you know, so we see what the—what Mr. Schmidt was thinking and what Mr. Marson thought was going to happen."

"All right," Smalley said.

"Is that okay with you?" she asked Patrick.

"Well, but there's the accent."

"I think it's charming."

Patrick shrugged.

Addressing Stuart again, she said, "Are we ready?"

"Ready," Stuart said. "Shite. We've been ready."

And finally she turned to Schmidt. "So, Mr. Schmidt, more than seventy years ago you were in a field near the Rapido Valley in Italy. Early March of 1944. The ongoing battle of Monte Cassino."

Schmidt kept nodding as she spoke.

"Can you tell us what happened to you?"

Schmidt straightened slightly, put his terribly emaciated hands on his knees, glanced at Marson and all the others, and then with his thickly German accent, began to speak.

A NOTE ABOUT THE AUTHOR

Richard Bausch is the author of twelve novels and eight other volumes of short stories. He is a recipient of the REA Award for Short Fiction, the PEN/Malamud Award, a National Endowment for the Arts Fellowship, a Guggenheim Fellowship, the Lila Wallace–Reader's Digest Award, and the Literature Award from the Academy of Arts and Letters. His work has been featured in numerous best-of collections, including *The O. Henry Prize Stories*, *Best American Short Stories*, and *New Stories from the South*. He is currently teaching in the writing program at Chapman University in Orange, California.

A NOTE ON THE TYPE

The text of this book was set in Ehrhardt, a typeface based on the specimens of "Dutch" types found at the Ehrhardt foundry in Leipzig. The original design of the face was the work of Nicholas Kis, a Hungarian punch cutter known to have worked in Amsterdam from 1680 to 1689. The modern version of Ehrhardt was cut by the Monotype Corporation of London in 1937.

Composed by North Market Street Graphics, Lancaster, Pennsylvania
Printed and bound by Berryville Graphics, Berryville, Virginia
Designed by Iris Weinstein